BUTTERFLY PINNED

PRAISE FOR *BUTTERFLY PINNED*

"A character-rich thrill ride." — *PUBLISHERS WEEKLY*

"An absorbing tale of dark psychological suspense." — *KIRKUS*

"BUTTERFLY PINNED is a beautifully written and haunting
psychological thriller that explores identity, power, and the
consequences of misplaced trust. Leslie Liautaud took me
on a gripping and heartbreaking journey, as Marin's
transformation kept me turning pages well into the night—
impossible to put down!"
— *PATRICIA HEATON, Emmy Award-winning actress*

"It was thrilling, unsettling, and impossible to put down.
BUTTERFLY PINNED is Euphoria meets GONE GIRL—
a psychological thriller that hooked me from the first page
and didn't let go until the final, satisfying twist."
— *KRISTIN CAVALLARI, New York Times bestselling
author of* Balancing In Heels

"Author Leslie Liautaud crafts a dark, real-world fairy tale
… Like its bewitching villainess, BUTTERFLY PINNED
casts a spell: the pages almost turned themselves."
— *CLARA SNEED, international bestselling author
of* Before We Turn to Dust

"A striking thriller and a profound exploration
of toxic love and trauma."
— *CHANTICLEER BOOK REVIEWS*

"An unflinching psychological portrait of the all-too-common
casual descent into traumatic relationships and events. This novel
doesn't just thrill—it illuminates what is possible for anyone who
has found themselves embroiled in a twisted reality through which
they struggle to see the truth of themselves."
— *CHRISTINE OWENELL, author of* Alchemy of Chaos

Butterfly Pinned

LESLIE
LIAUTAUD

For information, address:
Blue Handle Publishing
2067 Wolflin Ave. #963
Amarillo, TX 79109

For information about bulk, educational, and other special discounts, please contact Blue Handle Publishing.
www.BlueHandlePublishing.com

To book Leslie Liautaud for any event, contact Blue Handle Publishing.

Cover and interior design: Blue Handle Publishing
Cover art by Existence Creative, John G. Kraynak

Editing: Book Puma Author Services
BookPumaEdit.com

ISBN: 978-1-955058-26-1

*For Mom and Dad,
thank you.
For everything.*

"Here's what they don't tell you: When a caterpillar turns into a butterfly, the metamorphosis is gruesome. The creature self-destructs, disintegrates, and then morbidly digests itself. It rips its own cells apart, then uses those mutated bits to recreate its very being, like a phoenix rising from ashes."

If I'd known just how terrifying rebirth would be, I never would have stepped foot on that campus last fall.

The man stares at me, as if I haven't spoken a word. His gaze is intense, and I'm relieved when the intercom on his desk announces that Mrs. Ellison is in the front lobby. He excuses himself but stops at the door and turns back to me.

"You won't leave?"

I shake my head, and he disappears into the hallway.

I find I've been holding my breath, afraid of making any missteps or of saying too much. The voices outside the door grow fainter and finally disappear; they've gone elsewhere to finish their business. I don't mind waiting. I believe I'm somewhat safe in this room.

I stand, stretch my arms above my head, and do ten jumping jacks in short, quick succession, trying to shake off my nervous energy. My knees protest. The scabs that covered them fell off many months ago, but the damage to the tissue and cartilage will stay with me indefinitely.

A quick glance into the empty hallway tells me I've been allowed a brief moment to peruse.

The man's desk is custom-built in dark mahogany, matching the paneled walls. A framed law degree hangs front and center, assumedly to assuage any concerns that the man is not qualified. Built-in shelves flank the frame on all sides, as if the space had been designed around the certificate. Crystal awards and engraved plaques line the shelves, showcasing the man's many career milestones and achievements. I spy a "World's Greatest Dad" mug among his treasures and give a cynical chuckle.

I turn to the floor-to-ceiling windows behind the desk. The city of Chicago sprawls in front of me as far as I can see. The sun is out, belying the February chill that turns midday commuters into walking cocoons, wrapped in overcoats and bundled in layers of scarves. This city once represented a new life and endless possibilities—but now, it's lost all sheen to me.

I walk behind the desk and open the man's laptop on the off chance it's not password-protected. No such luck.

Various framed photos sit next to the computer, along with a yellow notepad and pen. One photo is of the man and his beautiful wife, triumphantly holding ski poles in the air.

The mountains rise behind them and they wear ski goggles and puffy, brightly colored jackets. Judging by their lack of wrinkles, the picture is from years ago.

Three photos are of groups of people—extended family, friends, and coworkers, from what I can gather. Beers are held up in cheers with arms slung around each other, loved ones flock around an elderly woman clutching a cupcake and bouquet of flowers, and four men pause mid-handshake while holding a plaque between them. Despite the dark rumors that must still swirl around him, the man is popular.

A small photo toward the back of his desk catches my eye. It's partially hidden behind a stack of manila folders, but I immediately recognize who it is. My breath catches as I pick it up. Her platinum blonde hair is longer, just past her shoulders, and her head is thrown back in laughter. Her cheeks are flushed, healthy. She's beautiful. Behind her is a blurred scene of Mediterranean-style homes.

Glancing at the door again, I slip the photo out of the frame and slide it into my back pocket, then toss the frame into the trash and cover it with discarded papers. I never knew her to look like this, but it's how I want to remember her.

I know I don't have much time left before the man comes back, so I open the drawers of his desk. I've made the step to come talk to him. He was overly eager to meet me, and he doesn't seem to be trying to hide anything. I don't know what I'm looking for, don't have a clue what I expect to discover, but I find myself back with the familiar, desperate urge to know more, to make sure I didn't overlook some key writing on the wall. I want to trust what I've been told, but I've learned that everyone has their own version of the truth—and it isn't always truthful.

I rifle through the top-center drawer, finding only a handful of identical pens and a bundle of Post-its. My hand searches the back of the drawer, and I pull out a stack of business cards bound by a rubber band. The top card reads Dr. Joan Kraft, St. Luke's Hospital, Psychiatric Care.

My heart begins to race. I palm the card as I close the top drawer and quickly move on to the next. The other drawers hold nothing of interest: A bottle of men's health vitamins, a clean tie in a box, a box of tissues. I begin to wonder why he needs desk drawers at all, since his laptop makes personal file folders obsolete. Stepping away, I spy a small safe under his desk, screwed into the floor. I had bent down to reach under the desk and give the safe handle a tug when I hear footsteps.

As the door opens, I jump to my feet and spin around to face the windows.

"Quite a view, isn't it?" His voice is calm and friendly.

I take a deep, silent breath and try to match his tone. "It must be nice to see the river every day." I turn to him and smile casually.

He returns to his chair behind the desk and settles in as I move back to my original seat. I glance at his face to see if he notices anything out of place.

He doesn't.

The man leans forward, placing his elbows on the desk, and closes his eyes as he laces his fingers together. He takes a moment, then looks at me. His expression shifts and his face changes, as if an entirely different being has taken over. One mask exchanged for another. I've seen this metamorphosis before, and it always gives me chills.

"I—" His face is serious. "I'd like to hear the story again."

"I've told you everything I know."

"I know you have, but this is a serious matter."

I bristle. "You don't think I know this is serious?"

The lawyer doesn't back down. "I need to know every detail. I want to make sure every stone is turned and thoroughly examined."

"I've told you everything." I haven't.

Of course he knows. He would know better than anyone, and I'm being naïve, thinking I can dodge the truth. My mind is racing like a trapped mouse trying to find an escape, but there is none. I stare at the ground, praying for some miracle to whisk me away from this room. Finally, I rub my hand over my face, flinching at the scar running across my cheek. He blinks at this, possibly remembering there is more than one victim involved.

"Haven't I done enough for you already?"

The man considers this for a moment and softens as he sits back in his chair. It swivels slightly, and I think of the safe under his desk. I wonder if it's filled with envelopes of cash, ready to be distributed at a moment's notice. He taps one finger on the desk as he regards me before speaking.

"I—I know this has been extremely difficult for you. It's been devastating for the family, as well, as I'm sure you can imagine."

Her family, I think. I crack, tears springing to my eyes.

He continues. "What I'm trying to do is to make sure we haven't overlooked anything important. When so many large details and events are involved, it's easy to dismiss something small as irrelevant. However, I've found, in my line of work, that the small details are the most important ones. I know it's hard to understand, but I'm trying to protect you—along with everyone else involved."

He hands me a box of tissues, which I gratefully accept with a nod.

"I'm not here to ask you to paint yourself into a corner. I'm

here to be your partner and am asking, after everything that has happened, if you can find the strength to be mine."

I'm crumpling a damp tissue in my hand, shredding it bit by bit. This is my life now. This room and this man are my truth. I will never again be an innocent. I will never again be able to trust blindly or be free of the memories that I carry in my heart. I may one day find happiness, I may find love, but it will be far into the future. It will take painful work to get there. It will take an immense amount of healing.

Maybe this moment is an opportunity to take a step in that direction.

I decide to tell him the whole story again, from the very beginning. This time, I won't hold back. I haven't forgotten anything. There are no small details to me. There is nothing I deem irrelevant.

I know who did this to me.

I know the girl who tried to destroy me.

She was once my best friend.

2

As I shoved the last of my faded jeans into a rickety dresser, my roommate came tumbling in, followed by a handful of girls, all with similar long, swirling hair. They held the plumpness, in both flesh and enthusiasm, that only young women are capable of producing. With flushed cheeks and exuberant confidence, their glow reminded me of the brochures for the university: A sanctuary filled with promise.

"Oh my God, you're here! Hi! I'm Cassie!" the bubbly blonde squealed, applying a swipe of lip balm.

"Hi." I put forth a practiced smile, but it paled in contrast to the natural collective confidence of the group. "Marin."

The girls crowded the doorway and waved, shouting over each other.

"We're going to stop in my room and grab the cooler bag!"

"I'm getting my sweatshirt!"

"See ya, Cass!"

Cassie laughed, exposing a perfect set of brilliant white teeth. "Okay! Be there in a few!" She turned back to the room. "It's so nice to meet you, Marin! I've totally been wondering about you. Like, what would you look like? What stuff do you like to do? What music do you like? Oh my God, this is going to be a great year, isn't it? Are you pledging a sorority? I'm Tri Sig, but I can't move into the house until next year. My mom was one, and so—legacy, ha!" She waved her fingers and winked. "How about you? What classes do you have? Oh, maybe we have one together!"

She rattled off rapid-fire questions and comments, while all I could muster was a dumbfounded stare. I didn't know how to respond. I didn't know how to be the kind of girl that Cassie apparently was. Instantly, it became clear that the transition into my new life would not be as seamless as I'd hoped; I realized I'd always just followed the lead of others. No one had ever asked me my opinion—in truth, I'd never needed it. My opinion had been whatever I'd been told it was.

In the deafening silence that followed, I observed the slight dimming of Cassie's sparkle—just enough for her body language to say, *This is my roommate? Bummer.*

Cassie smiled politely, grabbing a tube of sunscreen from her desk. "Do you need help with anything? Moving in the rest of your stuff or setting up?"

I shook my head and smiled as best I could. Anxious

tears formed low in my throat. "No, I think I've got it."

Cassie nodded slowly and moved toward the door. "Um, a few of my friends—those girls who were just here—we're heading over to campus. Frisk Field. There's a football game going on, Delta Chi vs. Alpha Phi. The frats have this competition before classes start every year and—" She paused, then added, "Anyway, would you like to go?"

With all my heart, I did. I had planned to make this my year of change, the year to break out and discover a new life, experience a new journey. Find any sense of self. I had put everything on the line for the opportunity, but the day—the entire past year—ignited a battle between my heart and mind, and my mind, seized with apprehension, was not ready to join my heart.

"I think I'll pass, but thanks." As Cassie walked out the door, I summoned everything I had to add, "Next time?"

With her self-assured smile, Cassie nodded. "For sure."

Two weeks later, cold rain pelted my face and penetrated my clothes. Cursing the weather, I began to run; then, realizing speed was futile, I settled for a glum shuffle across campus toward the library. In front of me, a notebook fell from an elderly professor's tote bag. I scooped it out of a puddle and handed it to her.

"Small kindnesses." She smiled at me. "Thank you." I nodded, blinking the rain out of my eyes, and moved on.

The university's new library wing was massive, its structure reminding me of a space station in a futuristic sci-fi movie, with its stilt-like legs and angular edifice. The arched windows and elaborate wood-paneled ceilings had the effect of a warm, weighted blanket. Once through the immense mahogany doors, I stood for a moment, allowing excess water to drip from my fingertips, willing myself not to shake like a dog after a bath. I fumbled with my umbrella as other students hurried past me through the entrance, finally leaving it with the others piled by the door. Rainwater collected around them, creating a small pond in the entryway through which I slid precariously.

The library was unusually packed. Arms overflowing, students bustled from rows of bookshelves to their laptops at long communal worktables. The first papers of the term were due soon, and most professors insisted the students rely on published books for research and citation, not just a quick Wiki search on the web. The ancient wooden tables were cluttered, overrun with mountains of reference books and scientific journals.

I scanned the room for an empty seat like a kindergartener on the first day of school, trying to find someone to sit with in the lunchroom. I paced back and forth along the vast center aisles, occasionally bumping people on the head or back with my bag, mumbling embarrassed apologies and quickly moving on, wishing for a miraculous invisibility shield to consume me.

Finally, I spied a small side table in the back corner, only half-occupied, and slid my backpack into the chair. A girl sat opposite me with her head down in a book. Her hair reminded me of an era gone by, a satin, platinum blonde that fell just below her ears, with pin-curl waves running throughout. The tiny table was obviously designed only for one, and I felt intrusive in the intimate space. I seemed doomed to intrude no matter where I was.

"Do you mind if I sit here?" I whispered to the head

bowed over the library table.

The girl slowly raised her head, fixing her eyes on me. Taken aback, I inhaled sharply. The girl's skin was flawless porcelain, her makeup so perfectly applied she seemed to wear none. What captivated me most were her eyes. Ice blue. Ethereal. At once piercing and frightening.

I shifted from one foot to the other in the uncomfortable silence as I eyed the chair again.

The blonde didn't say a word, but with an almost imperceptible shrug of one shoulder, her gaze dropped back to her book.

Glancing down, I smoothed my wrinkled clothes, embarrassed, all-too-aware of how disheveled and utterly bedraggled I must appear. My hair hung in wet, stringy clumps, and I hadn't opened my makeup bag in days. At best, I resembled a drowned rat in a frayed sweatshirt and jeans.

Quietly, I lowered myself into the chair, flipping open my laptop and notebook while stealing glances at the girl—no, the woman—seated across from me. She had an air of elegance and sophistication that could only come from predetermined birthright.

Pretending to pick something off the floor, I took inventory. The girl wore tailored, high-waisted polka dot pants and brown leather heels. Sitting up straight again, I noticed she wore a slim, expensive-looking gold watch, and a single gold ring set with an opal and a cluster of small diamonds.

I cleared my throat. "You must have come in early. Before the rain hit. I feel like I got stuck in a hurricane." I laughed nervously at the lame excuse for my unruly appearance.

The blonde looked up again and, to my horror, did not smile. In fact, she showed no emotion. I couldn't read her face at all. Uncomfortable, I started talking again.

"We don't get wind like this where I'm from. I'm not from here—Chicago, I mean. Or anywhere in Illinois. I'm from Kearney—that's in Missouri. It's small—Kearney, I mean, not Missouri—you probably haven't heard of it. You'd think we'd have the same kind of weather, both being in the Midwest, but not really. I mean, like the rain. Well, we get rain, yes, but it just feels kind of different. I'm Marin. That's my name."

I was blabbering. Crashing and burning. The longer the girl stared, her face blank, the more rattled I became.

Just as I began to explain the variety of farm animals raised in Missouri, what they ate, and which ones I'd had experience with, a miraculous, tiny grin appeared at the corner of the girl's mouth.

"Marin." She paused, as if considering whether the name held weight. She looked down at her book again. "I'm Bette."

I smiled, relieved. "Hi, Bette."

I pulled out my laptop and arranged my books and pens around me. While determined to concentrate on the schoolwork, I couldn't stop stealing glances at her. Not once, though, did Bette look up or return a glance, and it drove me mad, like I was trying to cajole an aloof cat into offering a speck of affection.

I picked at my cuticle as I stared at the laptop, then at Bette, then back to the laptop. A tiny trickle of blood appeared around my nailbed. I excused myself and retreated to the restroom.

In the sanctuary of the musty bathroom, I washed off my bloody nail and regarded myself in the mirror. Long, chocolate-brown hair. Light hazel-green eyes. Fair skin, thin nose, unremarkable lips. I hadn't considered myself conventionally beautiful nor conventionally ugly. Appearance had never been a focal point of my life, the repercussions of having a mother who favored correcting grammar over clipping in ribboned hair barrettes.

Reaching into my backpack, I felt around until my fingers found the small pouch containing a few drugstore staples. A beauty tip I'd read once said to always be prepared to refresh, but the reality was, I rarely wore makeup at all, and my "beauty kit" had never been touched.

I applied a swipe of mascara and ran tinted balm over my lips. My clothes were still subpar—a worn-thin sweater and stained jeans—but at least, I reasoned as I pulled my hair back into a tight, sleek ponytail, I could pass as civilized. I tilted my head and re-examined myself: Halfway presentable.

Sliding back into my seat, I cleared my throat. "I like your watch." Its thin band was gold with diamonds on its face. She didn't respond, but instead glanced at my wrist.

"It's my brother's," I explained, blushing at the bulky, mannish watch and worn leather band. "He left it behind when he went away to college. I guess I missed him and found this piece of him lying around, so . . ." I trailed off.

Bette's eyes flickered to mine, and she straightened her back.

"His name's Ty. He's six years older." Discovering the small opening of Bette's attention, my speech gained momentum. "He passed the entrance exams at

Columbia to study law, then decided he wanted to help the human condition instead of fight it, so he transferred to Penn and now he's in med school. Superman, right? And crazy handsome. We always joke around that the stork dropped him off by mistake."

Bette glanced at her watch. "I'm late." Without another word, she gathered up her belongings and walked out.

I swallowed hard, choking on a laugh, feeling foolish and alone. *What am I doing here?* As a junior moving in with underclassmen, I'd had hopes of becoming friends with all the housemates, if for no other reason than I would be older and, therefore, cool. I'd vividly dreamt of what a new start would mean and how it would change my life. But there I was in a strange city, a new school, and had barely dipped a toe in the water.

My stomach soured with toxic rejection. I looked down at my laptop, the cursor blinking mid-sentence on a paper about electromagnetic waves. Numbers made sense. Equations. Percentages. They fell into neat lines. Black and white. They didn't have emotions, judgements, or the power to expel and extinguish friendships. Numbers didn't have feelings, and they weren't purposefully cold.

You can be a victim and drown in self-pity. Or, you can move. That had been the advice my brother once doled out when he found me mid-anxiety attack before a middle school presentation. But I was learning the hard way that I could move in every sense of the word and still drown. Giving up on my paper, I retreated to my room and crawled under the covers, allowing the waves to take me under.

A turn in the manic Midwestern weather arrived the next

day. The sun came up blazing, drying the sidewalks and lawns, its warmth pulling students from the shadows of their rooms and hideaways. Pick-up games of soccer filled Frisk Field. Ever the glutton for punishment, as soon as the last class let out, I went to join Cassie and her friends on a large blanket to watch the activities.

The late afternoon sky turned pink as the sun sank toward the horizon. Cassie stood, brushed grass from her thighs, and turned to her boyfriend, Chad. "Ready?" And, as if their moves had been choreographed, everyone stood and motioned to move off the blanket. I looked from one face to another, confused, while a couple girls gathered up the empty bags of chips and drinks they had just shared.

I turned to Cassie. "Where's everyone going?"

Cassie's eyes popped with feigned innocence, a look which had become familiar. "We all got tickets to a concert at Metro. Didn't you get one?"

"No." I tugged at my hoodie string. "You never said anything about it."

Cassie shifted her weight. "That's strange. I'm sure I told you. Bummer!"

I realized all eyes were on me, waiting for a reaction. *Don't give them the satisfaction.* Swallowing the lump in my throat as best I could, I began to reply, "It's okay," but as soon as I opened my mouth, I knew I'd cry. Instead, lips sealed and nodding my head, I quickly headed back to the house before I completely shattered.

The next morning, I woke still wearing my clothes from the previous day, curled under thick covers. Wadded tissues were scattered all around my pillow. Looking across the room to a perfectly made bed, it was evident

Cassie had never come home. I could sense the puffiness in my eyes and hiccupped as another wave of homesick tears came over me. I thought of my mother and of Ty. My bedroom and its familiar smell, the worn furniture, the water stains on the nightstand.

The move had been a mistake.

But I also thought of my dad. Of the conversation I would have to have with him if I decided to leave school. Why did I drop out? Did I think money grew on trees? Did I think going away would be easy? I thought of how he and Mom would fight about it and about the way he would look at my mother—and, worse, the way she would look at me. How she might cry. I thought of Ty and, again, paling in comparison to his accomplishments. And then I thought of running into Sarah.

I couldn't go home.

Inching out from under the comforter, I threw a sweatshirt carelessly over my flannel shirt and pulled on a pair of dirty jeans laying on the floor. I didn't bother to brush my hair, or teeth for that matter, before trudging out to class.

Listless, I couldn't concentrate on the day's lecture and ended up wandering aimlessly from the bookstore to the cafeteria, from the commons to the sports field, replaying a looping reel of my life's disappointments. The breakup of my parents' marriage and the resulting fallout with my father. The glorious rise in Sarah's shadow, being engulfed, then snuffed out in her eclipse. Connecting with Cassie and then being evicted from her circle as she inched forward, and I was left behind.

I couldn't go back to Kearney. I couldn't go to my room at the boarding house. So, eyes cast to the pavement, I headed toward the library.

An empty seat was waiting as it had been before, but this time Bette sat, hands folded in her lap, eyes directly on me as I sat down across from her. Drained and defeated, I couldn't summon the strength to meet her gaze.

"You don't look very good."

I was too low for the comment to sting. "Yeah."

"I saw you yesterday."

Something fiery awakened. She was watching *me*?

As if reading my mind, Bette continued, her voice soft and lilting. "I was passing through on the other side of the field. I saw you with your friends."

"They're not my friends."

"I see." Bette studied me. As before, the unsettling silence became a trap, backing me into an emotional corner. The dam burst, the pathetic story flooding out as I explained what had happened the day before the months before, and the years before. Bette said little, but her eyes bored in, prodding, pushing me deeper into explaining the experiences. She didn't just listen—she *heard*—and I found myself physically leaning into the magnetic pull of her calm gaze.

I talked for an hour, then another, the tales of woe morphing into more casual conversation about favorite movies and books, most embarrassing high school moments, and cherished childhood memories. Bette asked most of the questions that day, revealing little about herself, and I happily obliged with answers. Never had someone made me feel so comfortable in speaking, as if I'd known her my whole life. As if what I had to say mattered. And even though I walked away knowing little more about Bette than I had when we first met, I had made her laugh a few times, a soft, satiny sound, and that alone seemed to confirm that I was not a shadow after all.

3

Bette and I fell into an easy comfort with each other, and long library sessions became the most anticipated time of my day. I didn't care that I barely saw Cassie or my suitemates. The few others I'd met since moving in seemed suddenly inconsequential. The separation didn't seem to have a real impact on any of their lives, either. They had their couplings, and I had a new best friend. Surprisingly, at times, curiosity seemed to get the better of my roommate.

"Where are you going?" she asked, leveling her gaze at me. We'd been working silently in our room before I started to load my backpack.

"Library."

"Why not just study here?"

"I'm meeting someone."

Cassie swiveled around. "And who is it you keep meeting? That *girl*?" When I didn't reply, an edge crept into her voice. "Chad says he knows her."

I continued to pack my bag.

"He says you should watch out. Something's off with her." She paused, visibly agitated. "He says she's bad news. They went to the same high school, you know. Like, she acts so stuck up but really, she's just whacked in the head. Plus, she's, like, a total slut. Guys, girls, you name it. And he says it's all for show. Like she just wants the attention." Needling for a reaction, she added, "Hello? Did you hear me?"

I looked her squarely in the eye and slung the backpack over my shoulders. "Yeah, I heard you." With Cassie's mouth agape, I walked out the door. A satisfied smile formed as I marched down the hall. I had found my own voice—tiny, at best, but still a voice. And in my experience, a voice meant strength.

Bette buried her head in a copy of Pablo Neruda's *Twenty Love Poems and a Song of Despair* while I trudged through Homer. My math prowess had served me well for a scholarship while attending the community college, with concepts like sines, cosines, and Fourier series falling into place with little effort. But I was finding it increasingly hard just to stay afloat in my new required courses. Bette glanced dismissively at me whenever I complained about math majors being required to take courses in classic literature.

Without even lifting her head, Bette whispered, "Listen to this one:

'A bough of fruit falls from the sun on your dark garment.
The great roots of night

grow suddenly from your soul,
and the things that hide in you come out again
so that a blue and palled people,
your newly born, takes nourishment.'"

Head still down, she stared at the page, silent in repose. I had no idea what the poem meant, but the way Bette spoke it, the way the words lifted and lilted like music made it beautiful to listen to.

"That's—" I didn't know how to express the effect it had without sounding childish.

Bette didn't answer for me or help in any way. She simply looked at me, her face impassive, waiting, while I blushed and shifted in my seat.

Mercifully, Bette eventually smiled softly and prodded, "How did it make you feel?"

When I couldn't answer, Bette closed her eyes slowly, prompting me to do the same. In a breathy whisper she asked again, "Now, tell me, how did it make you *feel?*"

With eyes closed and the library a million miles away from my mind, the words poured out. "Understood, but scared at the same time. Like he knows there's something lurking inside me, in my heart, that I've kept hidden. And it's a relief that he sees it, that he knows it's there. But at the same time, it's scary because I can't hide anymore. My secret is out." I took a deep breath, eyes slowly opening, and waited for Bette to respond.

She said nothing. Instead, she stared, silent, and placed her book face down on the table.

Her intense energy threw me off-kilter. I couldn't tell if the silence was disappointment, frustration, or simple shock at my stupidity. Swallowing hard, I wrung my hands under the table and asked sheepishly, "Was that wrong?"

Bette inhaled, breaking her gaze. "It's poetry. There is no right or wrong, only what moves you."

When Bette first revealed she was a poetry major, I had thought her choice was frivolous. A way to get a degree without doing any real work, an easy path to collecting a trust fund check. But in that moment, hearing Bette whisper that excerpt, I changed my mind. Those few lines of carefully chosen verse made my heart beat faster. I yearned, but had no idea what for.

"I didn't know that's how it worked," I said, gesturing to the book.

Bette smiled. "That's why you should try new things. You never know what will hit you here." Her hand fluttered to her heart and then pointed to my abstract algebra textbook. "Something tells me math doesn't move you the same way."

I laughed, relieved that Bette's smile had returned and recited haughtily, *"The only true wisdom is in knowing you know nothing."* My brother, Ty, had gone through a phase one summer where he constantly quoted Greek philosophers. He was that type of person. And while he spouted at least a hundred quotes from dozens of philosophers, the Socrates line was the only one I ever remembered.

Bette's eyes sparkled. "That's it. I know what you should major in."

I snorted. "I have a major. But I'll be honest—considering how spectacularly I'm destroying my grade in classic literature, I'm not even sure I'll be coming back next semester."

"Nonsense." She waved off the comment. "You absolutely are coming back, and you're not going to be some dull number cruncher. I can't bear to hear you utter 'I'm a math major' again. If I do, I'll scream. We are much more radiant than that. You"—she paused again, authority dripping in her voice—"are going to be a philosophy major. Much better."

I hadn't learned yet that Bette didn't make suggestions; she commanded things to happen.

"I don't know anything about philosophy. I mean, what would I even do with that degree?"

"What does anyone do with any degree? Honestly, do you know anyone who works in the field they studied?" Bette sighed, exasperated.

"My mom has a teaching degree, and she teaches."

Bette groaned. "And do you want to be a teacher, Marin? Is that what you want to do with your life? Be a math teacher?"

"No." Even if I had wanted to be a teacher, I wouldn't have admitted it right then. While I didn't know what was wrong, exactly, with a teaching degree, something in Bette's tone made me feel small and backward for even bringing it up and embarrassed for my mother.

"My scholarship is for math. I can't lose that."

"So, double major. What's the big deal?"

I swallowed hard and picked at my cuticle.

"Good, then it's settled." With a triumphant look, Bette swiveled my laptop around and began to type. "Yes. Here we go. They're offering some of the 201 classes next semester. You can preregister now." She clicked more keys. "Presto, you've declared your double major." With dramatic flourish, she hit one last key.

"All you have to do now is sign the form at the registrar's office." Bette smiled with the pride of a big sister.

"There's no way I can pay for a whole new set of classes. I can barely afford—"

Bette waved off my feeble protests and took my hand. My body electrified at her touch, and for a moment, all that existed was the warmth of her skin against mine. "You are on the cusp of greatness. You know that, don't you? You already possess it. You just need a little help finding the path that will free it all."

Caught up in Bette's adoration, I couldn't think clearly. I could barely breathe. Bette wasn't taking the spotlight for herself or selfishly basking in the sunlight; she was giving it all to me. An unexpected wave of affection washed over me. I reasoned that I'd found a way to get into the university in the first place, so there had to be a way to make this new possibility work.

The next day at the library, I slapped the printout of my new second semester schedule on the table with pride. "I did it." Bette didn't even look at the paper but, instead, smiled broadly. "I knew you would. It's perfect for you." She reached into her glossy leather satchel and pulled out a wrapped package. She placed a pale pink rectangle, tied with a chocolate brown silk ribbon, squarely on top of my class list.

"For you."

I cautiously peeled away the wrapping paper, folding it carefully, and rolled up the ribbon—precious artifacts I wanted to preserve. Under the paper was a worn book covered in oatmeal-colored linen. I turned it over in my hands.

"The Great Philosophers." I slowly sat the book down,

unable to think of anything to say.

Bette nodded her head toward the thin book. "Open it to a page."

"Which page?"

"Any page. Just open it wherever the binding is broken. Let it fall open naturally."

My hands fell to the sides as the pages separated easily. The smell of well-handled paper wafted up, the way it had when my mother had read bedtime stories from heavy volumes she kept on the tall living room bookshelf. Back when things were still peaceful, before the house had become silent and cold and she'd put away those books for good.

"Read what it says," Bette gently pressed.

"What?"

"Read what's on the page."

I began to quietly scan the page.

"Out loud." Bette grew serious again and leaned forward.

I flushed.

"Don't be embarrassed. This is what your life will be like from now on. This was a choice you made. Embrace your choice. Embrace yourself."

Bette's blue eyes locked with mine and the rush returned. It had been my choice. This moment was my doing. I had voluntarily leapt from the high dive, headfirst.

I swallowed hard. "I mean, it's just one sentence." Bette nodded for me to continue. "I just didn't want you to think I picked a whole page or something." I was losing confidence, beginning to babble, and so I shook my hands out at my sides, hard, physically releasing the fear, and read.

"*Be as you wish to seem.* Socrates. That's who said it." I looked up and silence fell between us. I prayed Bette wouldn't burst out laughing, mocking.

Bette's eyes floated to the ceiling, a tic I would come to know well, and a smile drifted across her mouth, then vanished.

I waited, the crush of vulnerability bearing down. I used to think I knew what it meant to be vulnerable. To be scared, to be alone, to build up walls and be closed off with no one around. But I had been wrong. To be vulnerable was to stand completely naked in front of someone, splayed open with no protection, no armor, desperately hoping that the other person will envelop you in her arms.

When Bette turned her head back, her eyes were strangely sad. "Appropriate, isn't it?"

I had no idea what she meant but nodded anyway.

Bette sat in a trance-like state, lost in her own thoughts while I shifted uncomfortably in my seat. Suddenly, like a light switch flipped on, Bette snapped back to the conversation and smiled brightly. "I'd like you to meet some people."

Unlike the popular off-campus blocks by the boarding house, filled with bars, grimy music venues, and Vietnamese nail parlors, this new neighborhood, like Bette, seemed to belong in another universe. The asphalt ended, and a brick road began. Rows of brownstones lined the street, their first floors housing small, expensive boutiques and a few lawyers' offices with gold plaques announcing names followed by *Esquire*. Potted flowers lined front walks, and thick trees, just beginning to turn shades of yellow and red, formed a multicolored canopy that hovered protectively overhead.

Walking at a clipped pace, Bette abruptly veered left, descending a set of basement stairs. An entry door stood at the bottom, painted a shocking, glossy red, its hardware made of worn brass and intricately crafted. The small metal sign read *Les Mots*. I hesitated at the top stair, but Bette nodded to follow.

The café was blindingly dim after the clear, bright light of day, every shadow accentuated by the deeper pitch black behind it. When my eyes adjusted, I leaned back against the door, taking in the room with wonder.

We had entered 1920s Paris. I gazed upon one large room, the ceiling low and made of embossed, weathered, copper tiles. Exposed brick wrapped the walls from the ground up. Blood-red velvet couches and tufted leather chairs created intimate seating pods, while framed black-and-white photos, art deco sconces, and heavy bronze statues of lanky women filled the spaces between. Vibrant Persian rugs lay end-to-end, and lamps with tasseled shades, staged in various nooks and crannies, washed the room in muted shades of red and gold.

The smell of strong coffee and buttery pastries permeated the air. A young waiter in black slacks and a white button-down delivered a teapot and single delicate porcelain cup and saucer to an older man sitting alone in a corner. His legs crossed gracefully while he hovered over a book. The customers looked noticeably alike in their dark clothes and mod eyeglasses.

I stayed glued just inside the doorway, but Bette breezed across the room to a cluster of oversized chairs, dropping delicately into one. I tugged at my sweatshirt hem, pulling it down where it had bunched up over my jeans, and quickly grabbed my hair into one hand, twisting it into submission. As I stepped forward, my sneaker snagged the corner of a rug, causing me to stumble. Flustered, my face reddening, I scurried into the chair next to Bette.

Two young men sat languidly on a dark green chaise across the coffee table. They studied me in silence, and I glanced to Bette for some clue as to their identities. Bette sat perfectly still, hands clasped in her lap; she smiled slightly, as if she were patiently waiting for the boys to finish an important task before moving forward.

The boy on the right lifted a slender finger to his pale pink bow tie, tapped it twice, and then pressed his lips together in a thin smile. All at once, his eyes bulged and he threw his hands in the air. "We can't believe you're here!" He placed his hand on the other boy's knee. "Can we?" No response came from the other boy—just a steely, dark gaze.

The two were complete opposites. Night and day. One looked like he had stepped off a yacht in Martha's Vineyard, everything about him fair, polished, and well-bred. The other's chiseled European features and brooding eyes gave him an intimidating, urban edginess.

Bette lifted her hand and nodded to the waiter. Immediately, a tea service was set in front of us. As a novice, I relied on Bette's cues to properly prepare my own cup of tea. She guided me wordlessly: A gentle splash of milk, a slow trickle of honey.

"Ozzie, Harry, this is Marin." Bette looked like a horse owner showing off her new prized filly. Ozzie smiled brightly and began to clap. I cleared my throat and smiled back, completely puzzled. Bette continued, "She's a philosophy major." That wasn't exactly true yet—I wouldn't start any philosophy classes until next semester—but I wasn't about to argue.

Ozzie yelped with joy, but I caught Harry mid-eye roll.

"Please, tell us about yourself. Every. Last. Detail." Ozzie's eyes glistened as he leaned forward, chin resting on his hands. He made the conversation easy, asking questions and prompting me with smiles and laughter. Ozzie told stories of his childhood adventures with Bette, growing up as neighbors, as close as a brother and sister, and Bette filled in the blanks with a nostalgic wistfulness. They seamlessly finished each other's sentences as they reminisced about summers at Bette's lake home in Michigan, winter vacations skiing in Vail, and boating in the Mediterranean.

I held my breath, drawn in and awestruck that people my own age had led such exciting lives. None of it seemed real.

Lost in their world, I was an invisible specter alongside them as they ran through the dense ten-acre wood separating their homes, drank champagne out of abandoned glasses at their parents' numerous dinner parties, and raised an orphaned baby squirrel, Miss Suzy, kept hidden in Ozzie's basement.

"It was all going smooth as silk," Ozzie said conspiratorially, "until that little rascal escaped and made her way into the wall. She went straight up, which happened to be where our receiving room is." I had to pause, thinking I'd never actually met someone with an honest-to-goodness receiving room. "Well, Grandmother Cecelia was there—"

"Oh, Marin, you would adore her." Bette interjected, sighing.

Ozzie rolled his eyes dramatically, dismissing Bette with a wave of his hand. "Grandmother kept hearing this scratching and scampering, up the wall, down the wall—it was driving her mad! Of course, each time the scurrying started, she'd ask if I'd heard the noise. And each time, I'd bat my eyes innocently and say no."

"She became convinced there was a ghost."

"And she wouldn't come back to the house after that." Ozzie looked thoughtfully at the ceiling. "Miss Suzy might have been the best thing that ever happened to us."

"Oh, Grandma Cecelia was a delight, and you know it!"

"You never had to spend a month with her at The Point."

I leaned forward. "What's The Point?"

A dreamy smile crossed Ozzie's face. "It's this beautiful spread in the Adirondacks. It once belonged to the Rockefellers. There was a tiny shack in the woods there, and we would go for picnic lunches of the most divine fried chicken I've ever had."

I then learned all about Ozzie. He was studying at a nearby culinary school and was a self-proclaimed "attention hound." With genuine fondness in his voice, he told me about his blue-blood family and how his father, grandfather, and great-grandfather had all worked in newspaper publishing. He described to me their lack of shock when he finally told his parents he was gay.

"They originally treated it as a passing phase. Like I had just told them I was dying my hair blue or was going to run off to join the circus with Bette."

"He actually did dye his hair blue once." Bette chimed in.

I noticed that Bette shared very little about herself, opting instead to only discuss moments that included Ozzie. The realization was fleeting, though, as my attention was quickly diverted by the story of Bette and Ozzie's attempt to write and film their own movie, only to be derailed when Ozzie's mother refused to allow them to shoot a real gun in the house. They'd been twelve years old.

Ozzie somberly finished with, "We had to stop. To use a cap gun would have compromised the integrity of the film."

The only damper to the afternoon was Harry, a dour and dark cloud who slumped lazily in the corner of the couch. I caught him intermittently glancing between Bette and Ozzie, his expression scathing. Only Ozzie could make him smile, as he took it upon himself to give me a favorable sketch of his silent boyfriend Harry.

"He's going to be such a brilliant architect. His sketches are gothic and dynamic and profound. Now, if only I could get him to stop dressing as severe as his buildings," Ozzie continued as Harry smirked. "I'm always trying to sneak a green tie or fuchsia handkerchief into his jacket. Just brighten it up a bit. I mean, it doesn't have to look like a funeral every day!"

Harry abruptly sat forward. "We have to go."

Ozzie's bottom lip jutted out. Harry smiled and clipped Ozzie's chin softly with his knuckle. "Gotta meet my parents for drinks."

Ozzie perked up. "Let's all go!"

Harry didn't acknowledge Bette when she shrugged a shoulder. "A martini sounds divine."

"I should probably get back. I've got . . . um—" I stammered. My college social life hadn't matured much past vodka and Red Bull, and the thought of proper cocktails with the parents of a boy who had an obvious deep disdain for me wasn't very appealing.

Harry was already walking to the door.

Bette didn't say a word. She just sat, looking at me. Waiting.

Ozzie clapped his hands together, pleading. "What? What do you have to do? Please come with us. Please, please, *please*?" He was cartoonish and over the top in every gesture and word.

Bette reached over and gently intertwined her fingers with mine, and my nerve endings came alive at her touch. "Harry's parents are wonderful. Trust me."

Ozzie hopped up and down in place like a five-year-old at Christmas, and I was defenseless to do anything but give in, riding the wave of their enthusiasm.

I laughed. "Okay, I'll go!"

Ozzie jumped into the air with a squeal and ran to the door.

Harry had already ordered an Uber and was waiting with Ozzie in the back seat of a big black SUV. I stopped outside the car, panicked.

"Where are we going?"

Bette stopped at the car door. "Downtown. The Four Seasons."

There was no graceful way to back out. I had to be honest with Bette. "I can't afford to ride all the way downtown. And back," I whispered, not wanting the others to hear.

Bette considered this. "We're splitting it four ways."

I shook my head, sinking with embarrassment and turned to go. "I'm sorry."

"Wait." Bette regarded me for a moment, then stepped close, her mouth brushing my ear. "I'll take care of you."

With Bette's breath on my skin, I stepped into the SUV and my new life.

The entrance to the Four Seasons was plain and unassuming and could have fronted for a large department store—but then we stepped inside. For the second time that day, my senses were overwhelmed. Heavily carved wooden tables and chairs filled the lobby, and the walls were covered with paintings depicting chaotic scenes of hunting dogs and horses. Giant urns and vases filled with elaborate arrangements of fresh flowers rested on every available surface, their fragrances wafting lightly in the air.

As with Les Mots, a specific species seemed to inhabit the hotel. Highbrow. Sharp cheek-boned, ash-blonde swans swathed in cream and camel glided past international businessmen in pinstriped suits who checked in while they scrolled through emails and whispered intensely into cell phones.

These people seemed to think nothing of the surroundings or their place in the world. A group of women chatted in the lobby. There was a flippant, careless air about them as they lightly touched each other's arms, heads tossed back in laughter. A certainty. Untouchable. Like Bette and Ozzie, they were cut from a cloth I'd never even known existed.

My father was a businessman in the dictionary

definition of the word, but he would have checked in wearing khaki polyester trousers and a turquoise golf shirt, asking where the free breakfast buffet would be served.

Harry paused just outside the entrance to the bar. His comment was directed to Bette, but it hit me hard and square in the chest.

"You sure she's dressed appropriately? Do you want to take her over to Saks and maybe pick up something more suitable?" His tone made it clear this wasn't an actual suggestion, but rather a dig. She didn't respond, her face remaining still and serene, as if Harry wasn't even standing in front of her. With a last glance at me, he turned and walked into the bar.

I looked down at my old sweatshirt and sneakers, more self-conscious than ever. I appreciated that Bette took the high road, but shriveled at the thought of being an embarrassment to her. I didn't understand then why Harry was being so spiteful—and wouldn't fully for quite some time.

Ozzie waved to a beautiful couple sitting at a low corner table. Though they were both dressed in dark denim and leather, they looked right at home, the perfect rock-and-roll accessories to the opulent interior. Ozzie ran to them, kissing both on their cheeks, and waved us over.

Harry wrapped his arms first around his dad, then his mom, holding them both tightly. His genuine and public display of affection toward them caught me off-guard, considering his mood since the moment we'd met.

Bette approached with hands outstretched. I noticed Harry's parents stiffen slightly, but still, politely, each kissed her cheek.

"Oh!" Ozzie beamed. "This is Marin!"

"Hello, Marin. So nice to meet you. I'm Khristos."

"And I'm Alexandria. It is truly a pleasure." They each had a soft accent I couldn't place, which added to their exotic allure. They hugged me warmly as we settled into buttery leather chairs and crewel-embroidered couches.

"You took a cab? Taking one home, I assume?" Alexandria asked with an arched eyebrow.

"Uber, Mom." Harry winked. I saw a tender side of Harry that evening, one that I wouldn't see again for quite some time.

A tall waiter in a crisp white shirt and black vest appeared to take orders.

"Wonderful!" Khristos exclaimed. "What would you all like to drink?"

Ozzie clapped his hands together. "Gin gimlet!"

"I'll have a dirty martini."

"A Manhattan, please."

"Oh, that sounds good, I'll have the same."

"Make that three."

Then, in the following silence, each of them turned to me expectantly for my order. I looked at the ground and picked at my nail.

Bette leaned in, placing her hand on mine to stop my nervous tic, and offered gently, "You don't have to have anything. But if you do, I'd recommend a Cosmopolitan." I raised my eyes, questioning. Bette touched my arm, "But you also can have a soda with lime," she added with a whisper, "and no one will know the difference."

The waiter stood patiently with a cordial smile. "Miss?"

"Cosmopolitan. Please."

I looked at Bette, and the corners of her mouth turned up as our eyes met, as if sharing a secret. When the order arrived, I marveled at the sweet, citrusy concoction, and gave Bette a quick nod over the rim in appreciation. Gingerly setting the martini glass on the low coffee table in front of me, I took in the tableau around me, smiling in the knowledge that Cassie was no doubt in a dirty college bar or frat house, chugging beer out of a keg.

The mood was light and amiable as Alexandria told the story of how she and Khristos had introduced Harry and Ozzie to each other. Ozzie and his parents had attended an opening for a new hotel designed by Harry's parents' architectural firm.

"The moment I met Ozzie, I knew he needed to meet Harry." She smiled fondly at the two boys, obviously proud of her matchmaking skills. "They're complete opposites. Ozzie is all enthusiasm and light and glittery brightness. Harry is pragmatic, somber, logical, introverted. You need yin and yang to work. Magnets need to be opposite to attract, no?" She smiled at me, and I smiled back, nodding, as the first sips of my drink wormed through my body, warming it inch by inch.

Bette took a sip and tipped her glass to Alexandria. "That's why you and Khristos work. One is consumed by color, the other by a ruler."

Khristos went on to explain that, while he and Alexandria were equal owners of their architectural firm, they oversaw separate divisions. Khristos was the technical lead of the firm, while Alexandria was the artistic lead.

Alexandria leaned in. "We're lucky. Our magnets, our yin and yang."

The night became a hazy blur, as if swimming through a cloud, as the drinks continued to arrive. The conversation and company enveloped me even as we said our goodbyes, giving fond hugs and kisses on cheeks, along with promises to meet again, then sliding into a black SUV that appeared magically right outside the hotel door.

My head rested on Bette's shoulder, her head leaned against mine, a smile on my lips. A thought of Bette calling me radiant flickered in my mind, *If Sarah could see me now, she would know what she had lost.* I closed my eyes and drifted off to sleep.

I should have found Bette's confidence in her powers of persuasion somewhat odd. The way her chest puffed with pride should have given me pause. I didn't realize I was hiding in Bette's shadow of an idea; instead, I believed I was rising up to meet her. There was no way to understand the price I would pay for the journey ahead.

4

I woke the next morning to a well-deserved headache and the troubling realization that I had only five minutes to get to class. Normally, I would have left my hair in its rats' nest, but instead cinched it tightly in a sleek bun. Pulling on a pair of jeans, I reached for a flannel shirt wadded on the floor. One day before, it would have sufficed, but instead I threw it back to the floor, deciding it had neared the end of its non-washed lifespan. I rummaged through the bottom dresser drawer and chose a black boatneck sweater. Finishing it off with a swipe of mascara, I proudly examined the image in the mirror: No longer a street urchin, but a chic, urban woman. My head still ached, but I found I was racing to class with a skip in my step.

During the morning's lecture, my mind drifted.

Midterms were imminent and, while I had been borderline competent in my classes at the start of the semester, I found it increasingly harder to concentrate.

The new classes Bette had picked for me wouldn't start until after holiday break, but I wanted to get a jump on them, surprised by how much I'd taken to the philosophy book Bette had given me. A part of me wondered why I had never been interested in this kind of reading before. I should have been concentrating on multivariable calculus, but the voracious appetite I had for anything Bette put in front of me seemed to skew all priorities. I would not have admitted it if questioned, but the appetite had been for Bette's attention, not for the actual subject.

Later that week, as we sat at our opposite desks, Cassie removed her earbuds and turned in her chair, tapping me on the shoulder.

"We're all going to the game tomorrow night. Want to come with us?"

I barely pulled my eyes away from the page. "I already have plans, but thanks."

"What are you doing?"

"Going out. With Bette."

"You're with her every day."

I turned to face her, draping an arm over the back of the chair. "Yeah, I guess I am."

Cassie pursed her lips in an exaggerated pout. "We never go out anymore. Come with us."

She was right. We hadn't spent more than a few casual moments together since the night I had been uninvited, by omission, to the concert at the Metro. And I suddenly realized that I really didn't care. The days at the library with Bette had taken over my every waking thought while I dreamily went over and over our many conversations. Bette had obliterated any need for Cassie or her friends. They had been completely replaced by a glamorous new companion, and Cassie's attempts to rekindle the friendship made it clear that she didn't appreciate it.

I looked at Cassie, her hair in a messy beach-style top knot, her nails painted a bright blue with tiny fake diamonds, her side of the dorm room a tapestry of hot pink zebra print. She reminded me of the outdated shopping mall at home, and the thought of going to a football game seemed just as small and provincial. Boring. I felt sorry for Cassie.

And happy for myself.

In truth, I didn't want to miss a single evening with Bette. The time with her was what I looked forward to most in my day. And adding Ozzie and Harry into the mix only amplified my mood. Our nights shimmered like a dream, one that I wanted to continue, one I didn't want to give up, and one I didn't want to share.

I smiled sweetly at Cassie. "Rain check." But we both knew it was a false promise.

Later that night at Les Mots, Bette, Ozzie, and Harry were in a frenzy. A former high school classmate had sent out invitations to her first art exhibit. A student at the School of the Art Institute, Tessa Kempe was breaking tradition by showing her work early, in her junior year, instead of waiting until she was a senior.

"How did she pull it off?" Harry asked, seeming genuinely dumbfounded.

"Class project—and she's masking it as an independent

showing." Ozzie enunciated every word, as if suddenly revealing the secret ending of a spy movie. With dramatic flourish, he scooped up his martini glass and eyed us over the rim.

Bette sat stock still. "Bitch." I had never seen Bette show so much contempt for a person. It rattled me.

"Why's it so bad for her to show her work?" I asked.

Ozzie turned to me, a sparkle in his eyes, ready for a full-blown gossip session. "It's not so much her work. It's *her*. She's—"

"Oz." Bette cut him off, glaring. Ozzie inhaled sharply, a protest to the reprimand.

Harry motioned to the waiter for another round of drinks while Ozzie egged Bette on: "She's not even that talented."

Bette seemed lost in her own thoughts as she answered, speaking directly to the coffee table. "Not even remotely."

"Let's go to it!" Ozzie squealed. "At least we'll get free drinks."

Harry sat back, obviously bored and tired of the conversation. "There won't be drinks. It's a school function. They'll want to keep it on the up and up."

"It's not at the school. That's the thing. Her dad is sponsoring it. It's at some space in the South Loop. I hear she's going all out. And when Tessa Kempe goes all out, she goes all out. Believe me, there will be drinks. Want to go?"

Bette broke from her trance and turned to Ozzie with a malicious, "Oh, we're going."

Ozzie, reading Bette's secret thoughts, smiled devilishly to each of us in turn. "Oh my God, I love karma and the bitch that she is!"

Stepping out of the Uber in front of the Odessa Art Gallery, a small, grimy piece of real estate squeezed between a pawn shop and a local deli, Harry shook his head with distaste. "Who in the world would have an opening down here?"

"I know. Isn't it fabulous? More ammunition!" Ozzie swept onto the sidewalk, arms stretched wide.

Bette's eyes gleamed as she locked arms with him and sauntered into the gallery.

As Ozzie predicted, an acne-pocked waiter greeted us at the door with a tray of champagne. He had all the markings of a struggling art student: Brooding, arrogant, and seemingly resentful that he had to serve drinks to the gallery's patrons instead of mingling alongside them as they cooed over a display of his own genius work. Bette scooped up a delicate stem and scanned the room intently until she found her target, a pretty brunette holding court in the corner. The group followed as she made a beeline.

As soon as Tessa spotted Bette, she burst through the crowd and wrapped herself around Bette in a bear hug. "You came! I'm so glad. I didn't know if you got the invitation. Hello, Oz." She gave Ozzie the same warm treatment and held out her hand, introducing herself to Harry and me.

Harry smiled and observed a large painting. "Congratulations on the show."

Tessa gave an embarrassed laugh. "Thank you. I had to do a presentation for school and thought I'd just go for the real thing. It's a little unconventional, I know, but I couldn't stand the thought of unveiling my soul under the harsh fluorescents of a classroom. There's so much

I've done on my own, outside of class, that I wanted to present all the work together, side by side."

She swiveled to gaze tenderly at the paintings on the wall: Large abstracts, some with cascading waterfalls of color, others with simple strokes thoughtfully bleeding into one another. "I found myself while I made these. The work brought me some much-needed peace. Still does." Tessa paused, thinking. "I guess I just wanted to share it. Maybe someone else will be inspired to heal through paint, too." She smiled again. "At least, that's what I hope."

Harry, obviously disarmed by Tessa's candor, took a step backward to regard her pieces with softer eyes. I tried to do the same but wasn't quite sure what I should be looking for, so I smiled and nodded, which seemed to please Tessa enough.

We stood in a circle, in awkward silence, until a short, portly gentleman interrupted, voice booming. "How's the champagne? Seem to be going through it like water!" He smiled, his hands friendly on Bette's and Tessa's backs.

"Daddy, you remember Bette Winston? We went to high school together."

"We sure did. And middle school." Bette's eyes speared Tessa with an iciness that matched the brittle tone of her voice.

Mr. Kempe wrinkled his face in thought. Tessa prodded, "Daddy, the Winstons. Eleanor and Thomas? And Ozzie's parents, Theresa and Charles Arrington?"

"Of course, of course!" Mr. Kempe exclaimed. "How are your parents? My goodness, it's been a long time, hasn't it? You both look wonderful. Are you in school?"

Ozzie jumped in. Instantly consumed with excitement to be talking about himself, he forgot the contempt he was supposed to display. "Yes! I'm in the culinary program at Kendall."

Mr. Kempe's eyes widened with approval. "Well, well, isn't that impressive!" His charm was impossible to ignore; his welcoming smile and thoughtful words were disarming as he asked question after question. I found it harder and harder to understand why we were expected to hate Tessa, as I was quickly falling under her spell, as well as her father's. There was even a flash of envy as I wondered what it would be like to have my own father beam with pride.

Moving to the appetizer table, Ozzie skeptically sniffed a small bite of green paste while I popped a miniature quiche into my mouth. "What's the deal with Bette and Tessa? She seems totally nice."

Ozzie shrugged, giving a quick glance behind him. "Between you and me, she's not that bad. But when we were in middle school, *Bette* was." Ozzie paused, caught himself and rephrased. "She was having a hard time—and everyone knew it. Tessa had planned this big crazy party. I mean, it was all anybody could talk about for weeks. She had hired a DJ and a caterer and, supposedly, some of her older brother's friends promised to bring alcohol and pot.

"The day before the party, Bette gets chicken pox. Chicken pox! I mean, come on. Who gets the pox when they're fourteen years old? Obviously, she couldn't go to the party. So, mean girls being mean girls, Tessa took the opportunity to become Queen Bee Main Bitch." He popped a cherry tomato in his mouth. "She got a bunch of people together at the party to get on different landlines. They called Bette at home. Of course, she thought people were calling to be nice and check on her. To say they were bummed she wasn't there, right? Except everyone started making these shitty comments about her. Like, 'Hey guys, look at me! What am I? A blobfish? A warthog? Nope, it's just ol' Bette!' Then everyone starts laughing and joking around about how she looks like a fist-walking orangutan when she dances. Or how she wore the same weird style of pants every day. They said she was a psycho and should be locked up. Crazy things that weren't even true."

Ozzie leaned in close, whispering, "Someone started a rumor that she'd given blowjobs to, like, twenty guys in one night. It was dumb stuff, you know? But it ripped Bette to pieces. And when she finally was able to go back to school, she was finished socially. A total pariah. A nonperson. It's brutal in junior high, you know?"

Ozzie's eyes dropped. I saw then how deeply he loved Bette, why he was so vigorously supporting her cruel behavior today. "The worst part was that Bette was already in a bad state. What Tessa did—it pushed her over the edge. It was unforgiveable."

"What do you mean Bette was in a 'bad state?'"

Ozzie poked at his piece of quiche, ignoring the question.

I switched tactics. "So, this goes back to eighth grade? She waited all this time for retribution?"

"Oh, honey, Bette is a coiled rattlesnake. She'll wait until you think she's surely out of your life, or you've simply forgotten she was ever angry with you. And right at that moment, she'll strike." Ozzie shrugged his shoulders again.

I shivered.

We returned to the group, which had grown with the arrival of some professors and art friends of Tessa's. They laughed, shared stories, and complimented Tessa on her work. As the party became more jovial, Bette grew more and more agitated until, unexpectedly, she grabbed my hand and snapped at Tessa. "So, anyway, we have another party to get to. Thanks for the drinks."

Tessa followed as Bette quickly ushered us to the door. "Thank you for coming. It really meant a lot to me."

Bette spun around. "I didn't think you'd have many people show up. I was just trying to be nice and save you from the inevitable embarrassment. It's obvious from this showing, I was right. But don't feel down about your lack of talent." She took a long look around the room and then back at Tessa. "Really. I'm sure countless dentists' offices and home goods stores will be knocking down your door for these priceless works of finger-paint art. And if they don't, you can just suck off a dozen guys or so, and eventually one will hang your work out of pity."

My jaw dropped, nausea immediately overtaking me, but I didn't dare say a word. Tessa's lip quivered as her night, which should have been filled with promise and pride, was shattered.

I waited silently at the curb with Bette while Ozzie ordered a ride on his phone. Bette stood, her spine straight, her chin in the air, and her back to the glass door where Tessa stared out at us, tears falling. The only one who looked back at her with remorse was Harry. Harry, who had been the constant negative, with his cynical voice, his callous off-putting air, his better-than-thou carriage, looked back.

What did it mean when the coldest friend had the most empathy? Maybe empathy was what made him cold. Self-protection from what he knew was spinning out of control.

No one heard from Bette for several days after that. She didn't reply to texts, and when I called, her phone went straight to voicemail. I tried Ozzie, who offered only chatty commentary on his day trips with Harry and the unsatisfying revelation that Bette had a long history of going off the grid without notice. Not to worry, he said, she'd show up eventually.

Taking advantage of the downtime, I finally returned one of my mother's many calls. The exchange was tedious, and I held my tongue as my mother talked about running into Marjory Ingram at the grocery store and the broken upstairs toilet that had cost a fortune to fix and the strangeness of the weather that fall. I wasn't just disinterested; I was embarrassed for her. I hated the smallness of my mother's life, the sameness, that her colors were brown, taupe, and beige while mine were suddenly those of rubies, sapphires, and emeralds. She was content in her little life, but I had seen too much to ever go back.

Mother asked the typical questions, and I bit my tongue as I obliged with lies: *Are you making friends?* (I didn't tell her about Bette and the boys and instead kept it to lame stories of Frisbee on the field and makeovers by Cassie.) *What are you doing on weekends?* (Pizza at a local joint, frat parties, no mention of martinis at the Four Seasons.) *How are classes going?* (Great! The biggest lie.) I couldn't hang up with her fast enough.

The short time period Bette disappeared was the first time since we'd met that I devoted any real attention to my studies. Even with so many hours spent at the library together, my growing fixation with Bette had taken over every minute of the day and, coupled with the increasing frequency of late nights out, I had gradually just stopped doing homework. Without keeping up with the reading, I had little understanding of my professors' lectures. I'd overcome so many obstacles to gain my scholarship. I'd taken on back-to-back part-time jobs to pay for my schooling and endured the wrath of my father's indifference. Even more difficult, I had convinced myself that I deserved to try. Yet, despite it all, the only thing I could focus on was Bette.

I could have easily asked for help or attended group study sessions, but my new routine was to go back to my house immediately after class and to try to reach her. When I couldn't, I would head straight to the library, where I would sit at our table, books closed, waiting for her to appear. I sat, wondering where she was, if she was okay, and how I could help her when she returned. I obsessed over the possibility that I had done something to anger Bette, or worse, to embarrass her. I scrutinized every conversation we'd had the last day I saw her.

Even gone, Bette was all-consuming.

Finally, my phone buzzed with a text: *Meet me at Les Mots? Xo, B.*

I ran the entire way.

A half-block from the café, my phone buzzed again. Panting, I read the text from Ozzie: *Stick with our sweet pea today. She needs you. Love you, doll face!!!*

Bette had two frothed coffees waiting.

"Where have you been?" I gasped.

"I ordered you a drink." Bette seemed far off, averting her gaze.

Taking a deep breath, I calmed myself. "Two drinks. No Ozzie? Harry?"

"No. They went to Wisconsin for the weekend. Ozzie's parents have a cottage in Lake Geneva."

"That sounds nice." I kept my voice even as I studied Bette's mechanical movements.

Bette reached into her purse and pulled out a slender orange Hermes box tied with brown ribbon. "I saw this. It reminded me of you."

I opened the box and pulled out a small silk scarf, a rich blue covered with abstract horses in reds and greens, flecked with sharp gold. I kissed it softly and smiled at Bette. "It's absolutely beautiful. I don't know what to say." Frivolous gifts had never been a part of my life. I had grown up in a home of necessities. There had never been financial room for more.

Flattered, I tied the scarf around my ponytail and glanced at Bette, all emotions fallen away, save concern. I wanted to scoop Bette up in my arms and push away her pain. I ached to see her serene smile, to hear her melodic and airy voice.

Bette stared at me, her eyes heavy and melancholy. "You look very pretty." She leaned back, sinking into the couch.

I nestled in next to her, our shoulders touching, and whispered, "You seem sad."

Bette took my hand, then turned and pressed her body into mine. Instinctually, I kissed her forehead. We sat in silence, nestled together, until the waiter came over to ask if we wanted another drink, even though the originals sat untouched. When I shook my head, he moved to the next table, but not before turning to glance quizzically over his shoulder.

Finally, with her chin hooked on my shoulder, Bette asked, "Will you stay with me tonight?" Ozzie's earlier text flashed through my mind: *She needs you.* With an overwhelming want to take care of Bette, my heart swelled. I didn't wonder how we'd come to such a desperately close place in such a short amount of time, or how it came to be that I was seemingly Bette's only anchor. Instead, I was blinded by the position of savior, washed over with Bette's vulnerability. Unable to see clearly, the illusion of my power had rendered me powerless.

Bette quietly suggested we go to her apartment. Wrapped up in all the excitement of having new friends, I realized I'd never even asked where they lived. We walked out to the street and Bette hailed a cab, surprising me. I'd falsely assumed everyone lived within walking distance of school.

Twenty minutes later, the cab pulled up to a gothic stone house a block from Lake Michigan in the Gold Coast neighborhood. Bette trudged up the steps, opened the door, and entered. I stood frozen on the sidewalk until the cab driver shouted at me in broken English, "Another ride? Someplace else?"

I stared at the house until a fluttering curtain caught my eye as Bette drifted past and answered, "No. We're home."

Bette's apartment occupied the bottom floor of an

impossibly large house, complete with its own three bedrooms, living room, dining room, parlor, and kitchen. It was a replica of Les Mots, every design detail mimicking the café: Art deco sconces, Persian rugs, velvet curtains. Everything whispered lush, intimate, and opulent. Old money.

I couldn't fathom how a college student could live in such a stately home. I could barely afford my own crumbling room in the communal house.

While Bette filled a teapot and set it on the stove to boil, I continued to explore the rooms with awe. Peering through the doorway, I watched Bette floating from counter to counter in slow motion. Silently, she opened several bottles of prescription pills, measured out quantities, and tossed them back dry.

When Bette emerged from the kitchen with two mugs, I followed her lead and sat on the plush gold couch. Bette handed me a small blue pill. I hesitated, rolling the pill over in my hand. Bette spoke without looking at me.

"It's just Xanax. Don't worry, it won't kill you or anything."

Aspirin was the strongest drug I'd taken up until that point. Ignoring a small voice in my head that warned to put the pill in my mouth would open Pandora's box, I listened to the louder voice shouting to feed the need for Bette's approval. I took the pill with a sip of tea, which scalded my throat as it went down. "Hot," I croaked, giggling at myself, hoping Bette would laugh with me. Instead, I remained invisible.

Bette did not drink her tea but simply stared impassively out the window. The falling sun cast a dark glow over the room, increasing the melancholy feel of the afternoon.

Bette sighed heavily. "Bed?"

I glanced at the gilt gold mantle clock above the fireplace. *4:36 pm.*

"Okay." Afraid of accelerating the strange situation, I didn't know what else to say.

I followed Bette to a large bedroom filled with elegant antique furniture. Centered in the antique laden room, her bed stood like a celestial shrine, bedding piled high and soft, luminous as a cumulus cloud. Bette flicked her hand toward a silk chemise draped over the back of a vanity chair, then went into the bathroom, closing the door behind her.

Gingerly, I touched the slip and looked back toward the door. I half-expected Bette to jump out and say it all had been a practical joke. But it wasn't a joke, and a dark knot of worry began to form in the pit of my stomach. Something was terribly wrong, but I pushed aside the needling sixth sense and rationalized that, as a good friend, I needed to be strong for Bette. She was obviously in some sort of pain and had come to me for help.

I undressed, put on the nightgown, and slipped into the bed. Pulling the thick, downy covers and velvety cotton sheets over myself, I relaxed deep into the pillowed mattress that seemed to wrap around me like a nest. A womb. I didn't *need* Xanax, so I incorrectly concluded the pill would have a minimal effect or none at all. Instead, I drifted into a languid trance, my brain numbed and limbs heavy with drowsiness.

Assuming she would sleep in another bedroom, I paused with wonder as Bette emerged from the bathroom wearing only lace underwear and slowly slid in next to me. I didn't panic as I would have an hour earlier, ashamed in my own skin and confused as to how to act in the unexpected situation. The little blue pill had removed all defenses, and Bette's warm body under the covers seemed the most natural thing in the world. I welcomed it.

Bette stared at the ceiling and sighed. Her eyes were moist as she whispered, "Thank you for staying with me."

I turned my body to her and she curled into my embrace.

"Of course."

"Don't leave, okay?"

"I'm too relaxed to get up."

"No. I mean ever. Don't leave me. Ever. Please."

I found her hand under the covers and took it in my own, threading our fingers together. "I won't leave you."

Bette inhaled deeply and moved closer, placing her head on my chest. Her body grew softer, and all angles of elbows and knees faded away. I held myself still in that moment, taking her in: The heady scent of her gardenia perfume, her chest rising and falling as she drifted to sleep. I breathed her in, allowing myself to fall into rhythm with her.

I watched the colors in the room change as bits of sunlight angled in through gaps between the drapery panels and thought of home. The lights in my own bedroom never cast such subtle variations in color. My room was stark, either shockingly bright with brash overhead lights or completely black, nothing in between.

Nothing at home was gentle. No magic, no mystical shadowy hues lived there. The house I grew up in reflected only our shared lives, its staleness, and my family's unhappiness, which seemed trapped inside. But in Bette's beautifully appointed bedroom, with its impressive furniture and rich fabrics, I felt welcomed and safe. I could be anything there, with Bette's hand folded in mine.

I fought the sleep that pulled at my eyelids, wanting to languish in our bedroom tapestry. But in the end, sleep won, and I allowed the dreams to wash over, then swallow me whole.

I wasn't awake and I wasn't asleep. I floated in darkness, lightly suspended, and couldn't pull myself fully from the tangled web of slumber.

Lips brushed my collarbone. My neck. Across my lips.

A dream, I thought, smiling, while being lulled back into unconsciousness for what felt like a hundred years.

When I finally woke, I stretched, cat-like, diagonally across the bed. Except for the hum of the day sounding outside the windows, it was silent. The clock read *11:00 a.m.* Startled by the late hour, I flung off the heavy covers and rushed from the room, still a bit hazy and confused.

The sight in the kitchen stopped me in my tracks. The entire scape recalled an impressionist painting. Bette lounged in a silk chemise and robe similar to the one I wore, her legs gracefully resting on a chair, a steaming cup of coffee in her hand. Her hair, slightly disheveled, was nevertheless brilliant, a glowing white halo caught by the sun streaming through the large window directly behind her.

I smiled sheepishly. "I'm sorry I slept so long."

A bright smile covered Bette's face. Something had changed. A wall was gone, the heavy weight lifted, and the soft layer just beneath her skin dared to show itself.

Warmth.

"I hope you slept well. Are you hungry? Here, let me pour you some coffee. Cream and two sugars, correct?"

The table held a magnificent spread of flaky croissants and dense bagels, delicate slices of smoked salmon and spicy hot sausages.

My mouth watered. "Did you already go out this morning?"

Bette handed over the coffee. "First, it's hardly morning. Second, no. The delicatessen down the street delivers." She smiled again over her dainty mug. "I looked in on you. Just to make sure you were okay. You were an angel sleeping."

Embarrassed, I flapped imaginary wings and sat, tearing off a piece of croissant. "Hey, yesterday—are you okay?"

Bette waved off the question, fixing her eyes out the window. The small tug of worry was finding its way back into my mind. Her disappearance, the Xanax, the dream of her lips grazing my body . . . In the sober light of day, the whole scenario seemed suddenly more complex and confusing. I ate slowly, quietly, until Bette's eyes finally fell on me.

"Do you like the apartment?"

I nearly choked. "Are you kidding? It's amazing. Beyond amazing! How did you get it?"

Bette regarded the ceiling, the walls, the floor. "A friend is letting me stay here."

"That's it? She just lets you stay here? Nice friend to have."

"He."

"Oh."

"It's not like that. He's just someone I know, and he's not in town very often. He knew I was looking for a place. The arrangement just worked out well for us both."

"I'd say." I shoved another piece of pastry in my mouth. A spark of something foreign jolted me. Jealousy.

Bette looked pleased and leaned in. "Stay here with me today? There's an art show tonight. Would you go with me? Please?"

"I'd really like to, but I need to go to class." I looked up at the clock. "Whatever classes I have left, anyway. You're not going to school, I take it?" Bette only rolled her eyes. "Okay, then, how about I come back after I'm done, and we can go together?"

Bette sat back, satisfied. "Wonderful."

"Are Oz and Harry going?"

She stood and began to clear the food, her delicate hands whispering past mine as she reached across my shoulder. "No. This isn't really their thing."

Timidly, I moved to Bette. "Are you going to be all right today?"

She brushed a stray hair from my face and kissed my cheek. "I will be. Because of you."

Her affection continued to ripple through as I got dressed.

Bette yelled from the kitchen, "Oz and I have a tradition of going to my parents' cabin in Michigan for Thanksgiving break. Harry started coming a few years ago as well. Would you like to join us?"

I grabbed my backpack and met her in the entryway. "I think I have to go home. To my mom's."

Bette wrinkled her nose. "You don't think you could miss?"

"It's tough for her, especially if my brother doesn't come home."

"Well, if you change your mind, it's a lovely little place in the middle of nowhere. There's a beautiful lake during the day and a cozy fireplace at night. Oz does all the cooking and orders us around like his little minions. But the food is delicious." Bette grinned, nudging me. "And, really, no one I know goes home for Thanksgiving anyway."

I groaned. "It's just still complicated with my parents, and I'm the last one to leave home, and—"

Bette cut me off with a playful sweep out the door. "Say no more—I understand. And I'll see you tonight. Check your pockets."

She winked and was back inside before I could say goodbye.

Bette had hidden a small envelope of cash in my coat pocket while I slept. That kindness would become her signature departing gesture, making sure I had enough money to get home. When I eventually pressed Bette to stop, she told me that I gave her so much, she was glad to have at least one thing she could do in return.

Climbing into the sticky back seat of a taxi, stale heat blasting from the vents as it headed toward school, I pulled out my cell phone. Real life had become so grand, so exciting since I'd met Bette that I found myself less attached to my phone. The outside world disinterested me. There was rarely a need to check it except for messages from Bette as to when to meet up. I didn't need to escape online anymore. Bette said social media was plebian and fake. I agreed. Her real world was just too good to miss a moment.

But, according to my phone, I had actually missed a lot. Calls from both my mother and Ty, along with a myriad of texts. Biting my nails, I listened to Ty's voicemail first.

"Hey, Marin. You okay? Seriously, give Mom a call. She's past the worry stage and on to the 'Oh my God, she's dead in a gutter!' stage. Anyway, I told her I'd try to get hold of you . . . and there, I just did it. Hope you're hungover as hell and doing the walk of shame. Love you. Call Mom."

I cringed. The phone calls had started a few days before, and by the time I finally checked, their frequency had grown dramatically. I took a deep breath and dialed. Mother instantly picked up.

"There you are! I'm so glad to hear from you. Are you all right?"

"Yeah. Hey, I'm sorry . . ."

"Marin Elizabeth, I have been worried sick. Do you know how many times I tried to call—"

I cut her off with a lie. "My phone died, Mom. I'm really sorry. Then I couldn't find my charger and I've been really busy with school. Honest. Everything is fine. I'm sorry."

The line went quiet.

"Mom?"

Mother's voice cracked. "I understand. I know school is so busy for you with classes and friends and parties. And goodness, my phone dies all the time. I never remember to plug the thing in." She paused, breathed out audibly, and laughed. "I'm just so relived you're safe."

"Yeah, I'm fine." I stared out the window as the Lake Michigan shore flew past, thoughts drifting to the feel of Bette's skin on my fingers.

"Listen, while I've got you on the phone, do you know what day you're coming back for break? Aunt Irene is hosting Thanksgiving this year. I don't think Ty will be able to make it, but Aunt Shirley and Uncle Dave are coming to town the Tuesday before, so I thought we could have dinner with them when they get in. Charlene is coming in with her new husband and I haven't even met him yet, so we should invite them as well." She prattled on for ten minutes listing various cousins and friends of family that would be stopping by the house and ticked off a myriad of to-do items we would tackle in preparation.

I couldn't breathe. I rolled down the window hoping to save myself from the suffocating guilt. It didn't work. My anxiety rose, crushing my lungs. The cabbie shot me a dirty look, so I rolled the window back up as Mother continued the litany of relatives' ailments and necessary accommodations. I closed my eyes and lowered my head between my legs, but that only brought my nose closer to the putrid smell of the car's upholstery.

"I guess if you come in on Wednesday, we'll have time to do all the shopping and make anything we can ahead of time. Uncle Louie wants Agnes to do the turkey and ham, so at least that's taken care of. But you know how it is—if we don't make other side dishes we'll end up with turkey and twenty desserts. Everyone loves making desserts—"

I couldn't do it. Couldn't do the Jell-O mold and the deviled eggs and Uncle Brian's racist jokes and my bedroom with the peeling window varnish and the bed without a proper headboard. I couldn't do my mother's neediness or my father's apathy.

"Mom, I don't think, um—I'm not coming home for Thanksgiving."

Her silence dropped heavily, like a cement block falling through space. Its weight was tangible and as real as the separation from the ties of my old life.

I was ready for the passive-aggressive attacks to begin— Mother's default behavior when she deemed herself slighted, unappreciated, or neglected. I knew I'd hit all three of those nerves when I said I wasn't coming home and was expecting her full fury, disguised as flippant indifference. But I reeled when the punch finally came, shocked at how low she stooped.

Mother cleared her throat, *"If you change your mind,* please let me know because Cousin Sophie might stop in on Wednesday afternoon and I don't want to give up your bed that night *if you decide to spend the holiday with your family."* I was about to cut the guilt trip short, "delete and ignore" in my mind, when the stealth-like blow was dealt.

"Oh, I almost forgot. There was a beautiful write-up about Sarah in *The Gazette.* It seems she made Stanford's soccer *and* crew teams this year. And she's never even rowed before. Can you imagine? She made the team at *Stanford!* The article was so nice. It talked about her scholarship and plans to study in Europe for a semester. Did you know she was going to study abroad? Anyway, I emailed you the article. She'll be coming home for break."

Poison swirled in my stomach, a bitter mix of resentment and animosity. My mother hadn't stayed with the typical method of slowly adding jabs and jabs until I gave in to her wants. This time she had gone for the jugular, as Sarah was the one topic that put me immediately back into the darkest, most uncertain period of my life. Two years had passed, yet just a mention of Sarah could splay me open anew in an instant.

Of course, Sarah is succeeding at Stanford, I thought bitterly. Sarah epitomized the ideal student: Intelligent, talented, disciplined. She had been a star soccer player in high school, senior class president, drama club VP, school newspaper editor, National Honor Society member, and class valedictorian. She'd volunteered at the local women's shelter, spent her Saturday mornings serving meals at a soup kitchen and her Wednesday evenings leading bingo tournaments at the nursing home. Sarah had inherited her generosity from her parents, our neighbors, who'd treated me like their own daughter for most of my high school years while my own parents battled through their divorce, going so far as to allow me to live with their family for weeks on end.

Sarah had taken me under her wing, and I happily became her shadow. I volunteered where she volunteered, had signed up for the sports she had played, and even had visions of attending college with her. I followed her like a puppy, and she relished having a smitten lackey. When the dust of the divorce eventually settled, I was squarely replanted into my own home with my mother. The contrast was jarring. Money was tight and my mother was depressed. It quickly became clear that my fantastical dreams were much too far out of reach. It wasn't until Sarah received her Stanford acceptance letter, and I did not, that I realized those dreams had been mine alone. When she left for college, she didn't even tell me goodbye.

"Well, Sarah always was the superstar." I said through clenched teeth. "I gotta go." My hands shaking, I quickly ended the call. I didn't want to give my mother the satisfaction of hearing me cry.

5

Bette took my hand, amused at my brows furrowed with worry as I looked out the town car window. Our previous excursions, though widespread and varied, had one thing in common: They had all been upscale. Either lunch at RL on Chicago Avenue or meeting new friends at The Drake. We would peruse ancient artifacts at the Field Museum or pop into perfume boutiques in Lincoln Park.

But on the way to that evening's art exhibit, I wasn't sure what to make of the neighborhood we were rolling through—if it could technically be called a neighborhood at all. Train tracks and dilapidated storage facilities spread out on both sides of the crumbling road, along with scatterings abandoned houses, shattered windows, collapsed porches, and dirt front yards.

Spray-paint tags covered every inch of available real estate.

The car pulled up to the back of an ominous, rusted warehouse. There wasn't a soul in sight.

Rickety steps led to a loading dock covered with several inches of moldy trash. I clutched Bette's hand as my eyes darted across the landscape.

"Be straight with me." I leaned back in the seat. "Are you planning to kill me and dump my body here?"

The yellow pill Bette had placed on my tongue before leaving her house had left me jittery and hyper-aware. I had considered the beautiful dreamlike state the blue pill had put me in and reasoned that it had done no harm. What was the worst that could happen, taking a different one? Bette had taken one herself, after all. So I had happily accepted the yellow pill from Bette's palm and washed it down with my cocktail.

Bette pressed her lips to my cheek, took a dainty crystal tumbler from the cup holder, sipped, then held it to my lips. As I drank, a small rivulet of vodka dribbled down my chin. Bette wiped it away, whispering into my ear, "You have to admit, it would be a lovely way to die. Like this. Together. Forever suspended in this moment."

A chill crept down my back. But as fast as the instinct to flee came, it evaporated, replaced with a need for her affirmation. The magnetic carrot Bette dangled in front of me worked its magic. I squeezed her hand, an agreement that we were, indeed, suspended in the moment together. Taking her hand from mine, she quickly checked her phone, leaving me once again with myself.

Bette had an otherworldly way of placing me on the

edge of a cliff, scared to move for fear of falling, yet simultaneously wanting to see what would happen if I let go. She lingered at my ear, breathing softly, "Ready?"

We stopped at the bottom of the steps, the large building looming over us. A tinge of anxiety crept back in. "So, an exhibit is going on? In there? Seriously?"

Bette turned and her languid smile vanished. "Why wouldn't there be? Do you think I'm lying?"

"No. No! It's just that—I mean—I was kidding, but not really kidding. It looks like a set for a chainsaw slasher film."

Bette took my arm. "I want you to open yourself up. There are two ways to live. You can either stay trapped in the holdings of convention: A life of obligation and premeditation, a small world set by rules of civility, of routine and order. Or, you can free yourself. You can soar into unknown territory with joy and exaltation. A life filled with your senses on fire, your soul awake with expectation."

Bette turned her head toward the warehouse and closed her eyes. "With a free mind, I can expect the unexpected and be unafraid of what that could bring."

With her face in profile, I stared at her. The high cheekbones, the halo of curls, the healthy plump of her lips. Her slight smile, radiating confidence and certainty. In contrast, I was, by nature, a shrunken person, one who hid behind corners, fearful of the next unknown turn, fearful of the next blow, the next bombshell.

The move, the new school, was to have been a turning point but, if I were to be completely honest with myself, that had been a lie. Somewhere down deep I'd known it wasn't a chance for change; it was a way to escape. An extra layer of protection added by the physical distance from home. There couldn't have been any real intention of change because I'd had no idea there was any other way to live. Years and circumstances had slowly and methodically taught me that life was an ambush, not a roller coaster ride. But there, in that moment, Bette pulled the curtains back. I had two choices, two ways I could live my life.

Expecting the unexpected, unafraid, I walked past Bette and up the stairs.

Once inside, Bette checked her phone again, then took the lead navigating us through dark, damp corridors and around dangerously sharp, ragged, rusted corners. Water dripped down the walls and shadows jumped from sparse, naked bulbs lighting our path. Discarded cigarette butts, condoms, and needles littered every corner. I grabbed the edge of Bette's blouse, closing the distance between us as my resolve to be unafraid faltered.

Graffiti, some faded and old, some bright and fresh, speckled the ceilings and walls with various gang symbols, cartoonish images, and threatening messages. True fear crept in as Bette led me further into the building, and I didn't see another soul until, suddenly, Bette opened an unmarked door. I had wondered if we were aimlessly wandering, but Bette knew exactly where she was going.

The room was dimly lit by dark red lightbulbs, casting a ghoulish filter over the trash and debris cluttering the floor. A peculiar texture coated every surface, suggesting time, weather, and neglect had taken their toll. On the far side of the room, a door led to another room with people circulating in silence and past that, another door and another dimly lit room.

An eerie, oppressive silence seemed to hold everyone suspended. Attendees sat on the floor and leaned against walls, dressed in torn lace camisoles and dirty, ragged jeans. Black boots and tattered cardigans. Girls with shaved heads and tattoos up to their jawbones. Boys with splotchy, unkempt beards, metal pegs in their ears, and T-shirts stained brown. The hodgepodge semicircle they formed created a makeshift space for the performer.

She stood naked, lit by a harsh, unfiltered light in the corner. Her auburn hair, streaked with greens and blues, was piled high on her head, twisted into a messy bun. I shifted from one foot to the other, uncomfortable with the woman's unabashed rawness. She was inches away from the crowd, in their faces, practically skimming their hands with her thighs, looking every single person square in the eye as she passed them. Where Bette held the woman's gaze, I quickly looked away, embarrassed.

Moving back to the center of her "stage," the woman picked up a green seltzer bottle, breathed in with a flourish, and tipped the bottle over her head.

I gasped.

Red liquid, thick and congealed, came pouring out, covering the girl's head, face, and body. She put the bottle to her mouth and drank.

"Is that *blood*?" I whispered, gagging slightly.

Bette didn't answer. She was glued to the performance.

With slow, sensual strokes, the girl began to rub the liquid over her body. Streaks ran down her arms, over her breasts, round and round her stomach. A young urchin of a man, leaning against the doorframe, lifted a bottle of beer to his lips as if watching Sunday night football.

Two girls sitting cross-legged on the floor, rings in their noses, dreadlocks, nodded in approval as the performer moved on to covering her thighs and buttocks.

Bette reached down and accepted two used cups from a man sitting on the floor and thanked him as he poured what I assumed was vodka into them out of a dirty bottle. I wrinkled my nose as Bette pressed the cup and another pill into my hand. "I don't think I want it," I quietly protested, already swaying, the mix of alcohol, drugs, and visual stimulation taking its toll.

"Take it." Bette's tone was serious as her focus returned to the girl. I reluctantly placed the pill in my mouth and took a large swallow of the cheap vodka, cringing as it burned my throat. The energy in the room had changed, and I grew increasingly anxious as the performance continued. People shifted where they sat and leaned in, ready for more.

Mixed with dread and curiosity, I stepped closer to Bette. The girl ran her hand in between her thighs, her fingers thrusting in and out as her head rolled back. Filled with a mixture of shame and Protestant prudence, I buried my head into Bette's shoulder.

Immediately, Bette gripped my chin and cheeks in one hand, her knife-like fingernails digging in, and forced my eyes back to the girl. "Watch."

Maybe it was the vodka, maybe it was the pill, maybe it was the fierceness of Bette—whatever the reason, my modesty began to dissolve. The veil of fear fell, and I leaned in for a closer look. We were voyeurs, watching an intimate act. I was simultaneously flushed with embarrassment and charged by the eroticism. It was a peep show for one that twenty-five people were watching together. I was sure there was a deeper meaning behind the show but grappled with the basics of simply trying to watch without judgement. I realized my chest was rising and falling rhythmically with the performer's, matching her growing intensity.

The girl climaxed with a low moan, settled herself, and reached for a mop. Slowly and methodically, she began to clean up the "blood." A couple of people clapped with their palms, barely audible, but most of the crowd either turned away, taking a small break, waiting for the next performer or silently, morosely, made their way into the next room.

When I turned to Bette, the room spun. I began to sit, sliding down the dirty wall behind me, but Bette pulled me back to my feet.

"Don't. You won't be able to get back up, and there's more to see," Bette said sharply. I quickly obeyed, trying to right myself, stumbling.

I didn't understand the change in Bette's mood All her sweetness and softness had been replaced with fire. She reminded me of a snarling animal, ready for attack. I held Bette's arm tightly for balance. Panicked butterflies swarmed in my stomach, the same as when my parents would yell and fight, a blanket of worry that my world was going to crash down, and I had been responsible somehow.

With the up light turned off, the room returned to its initial eerie red, a shade lighter than pitch black. I squeezed Bette's arm as she moved across the room. We paused just long enough to see a graffiti artist working on a large wall mural. A man in a black trench coat moved past us, his hand running across my backside as he passed. I yelped but said no more when Bette turned, glaring at me. I took a drink of the ragged vodka, then another, forcing myself to swallow in a misguided attempt to calm my nerves and hold it together.

We walked from room to room: A group of men and women with blank white masks in various stages of sex, a gray-haired woman in a long Indian-print robe with a loud, booming voice reciting poetry, a man and woman sitting at a table staring at each other, two women and a man performing a modern dance piece to no music, and on and on. Never settling in, only stopping long enough to glance, we took in each tableau. Bette, it was obvious, was on a mission.

With each bizarre performance, a chunk of my confidence slipped away. I didn't understand any of it. I was scared.

After what appeared to be the last room, a line of people lingered at the exit on the left. Bette turned right. She led me down three flights of rusted metal stairs, only passing one other person along the way. The man shot us a quick look and kept moving. My heel caught on a tread, and I slipped, sliding down three steps, nearly crashing into Bette. She didn't slow down or look back.

Hitting the lower level, I followed her through more corridors, grabbing her hand so I didn't lose my way in the dark. The echo of our steps in the hollow hallway were the only sounds I could detect, and when we came to a stop in front of a closed door, it took all my willpower not to turn back.

"Bette," I whimpered, "I don't like this."

"Shh."

I rubbed my face hard. The cocktail of vodka and

pills was peaking, giving everything a sharp, disjointed sensibility. Bette finally turned, a sinister glint in her eye I had never seen before. Adrenaline rushed through me as I scanned the nightmarish scene. The large space was concrete, and the only door was the one we'd come in. No windows.

Unlike the rest of the building, this room was clean. It had been manicured. Someone had taken special care with the details. It looked like a gothic scene straight out of Dracula. Large tapestries of deep red velvet hung from the ceiling, some against the walls, some used as dividers. The lighting came from myriad candelabras set up in clusters around the room, the flames throwing off glowing images like playful dancing demons.

Gigantic ten-by-ten digital screens wrapped the room with various gruesome images. I shuddered as I watched a 35mm video of a young girl, beautiful, with long chestnut hair and creamy taut skin, eyes that were brown and bloodshot. Walking with Bette from screen to screen, my nausea increased with every video shown on loop: A girl, close to our age, throwing back shots, laughing as she dribbled pink liquid down her chin; a close-up of her snorting white powder, her hair falling around her face; licking a man's face, her leg thrown around his waist; her breast being manhandled; the girl tied to a chair, a hand slapping her across the face as she cried; a syringe shoved into her arm as she wept; the girl, unconscious, naked; a man on top of her, the bed squeaking in rhythm.

She wore the same tattered, sequined top in each film.

A voice inside me screamed to flee. A warning of danger crawled up my spine: *Run.* I tugged at Bette's sleeve, croaking out, "What the fuck is this?"

Bette turned to me, her face, bland, serene. "It's Scott's take on beauty. How we all strive for it and then abuse it, whether you're the one with the beauty or the one seeking out the beautiful. It's very powerful, isn't it?"

I glanced again at the films. "Are they . . . are those real? They look real. Please tell me that's not real." My voice cracked with panic.

Gentle Bette appeared again as she put her arms around me. "This is art. There's no real or not real. Try to step back and see the message that he's putting out there."

I tried but couldn't shake the feeling that I was committing some crime just by watching the movies, as if I was there, abusing the girl myself. Was it real? If not, the girl was an incredible actress. But the world was filled with incredible actresses, wasn't it? Was it so hard to believe that this was just another elaborate performance piece? Like the girl with the bottle of blood?

"There's Scott—come on."

The artist was mammoth in stature, and as he turned at Bette's greeting, I saw that his demeanor matched. He loomed over us, menacing and hulking, with steely, oppressive eyes. Cold. At one time, he had been quite muscular, and though he had lost the chiseled look of a body builder, the size of his forearms and chest would still make a man think twice before fighting him.

I took a step away. His large hands were the ones in the video slapping the girl. It was his body that had been crushing the unconscious girl beneath him. There was no mistaking his size.

"Hello, Scott." Bette rose to her tiptoes and kissed the

giant on his cheek. "This is my friend, Marin. Marin, this is Scott. This exhibit is his."

I cast my eyes down, paralyzed as he took me in. "Hello, Scott. This is a really"—I paused before using Bette's words—"powerful piece." I shook his hand. It engulfed my own.

"Thank you. Have you enjoyed the other works?" His eyes bore in.

I cleared my throat. "The other exhibits? Yes. I mean, we only really watched the first room, the girl with the blood—I mean, the—" I was stammering, overstimulated and frightened. A salacious grin spread across his wide face.

"That was Agnes. If you're not familiar with this type of art, it can be a tad shocking. I believe her piece tonight was on a woman's place in the world. Creators of life, losing blood—as you mentioned. Being sexual creatures. Yet so often relegated to the mundane. Mopping up the mess she has made. Yet the mess is giving life."

Bette stared at Scott with breathless admiration.

I considered it, forgetting some of my anxiety. "I guess that actually makes sense."

"And this," he went on, gesturing around the room, "what does this mean?" He took a step closer to me and I felt my body tremble involuntarily. I looked to Bette for reassurance, but she only nodded, prodding me to speak. I opened my mouth, but nothing came out.

Scott leaned down and spoke softly in my ear. "'*What a strange illusion it is to suppose that beauty is goodness.*' Tolstoy said that. It's so true, isn't it? We grow up being taught that the fairy princess is always beautiful, with long flowing hair and sparkling doe eyes, while the wicked witch sports mangled hands and endless facial warts. As adults, we like to believe that we've evolved enough to never judge a book by its cover. But in the end, we all still gravitate to the fairy princess, bejeweled and regal, despite what truly goes on behind her castle walls."

His hot breath clung to my skin. "We've been conditioned to think that if a person is beautiful, then that person is worth more. But I wanted to challenge that. I believe you must test a person to see their true beauty. Experience them raw and vulnerable. That's my job as an artist, to break people open and show you their real value."

The hairs on my neck stood on end, while his cigarette-laden breath held me in place. He smiled again and stood his full height. "Please, don't let me keep you from seeing the rest of the exhibit."

With that, I turned and walked to the corner of the room, my nose in the concrete, trying to catch my breath. There was a terrifying quality about Scott, as if his essence alone embodied the grotesqueness of the evening.

Bette slid her arm around my waist and tugged. "We still have to see the last section of his work."

I wanted to tell Bette I was finished, that I wanted to leave. I wanted to tell her that we didn't belong there, that what we were witnessing wasn't art. I couldn't marry the horrifying scene with the ethereal Bette I knew. Worse, Bette's enthusiasm for it all made my stomach turn. But as clear as thoughts were racing through my mind, my tongue felt swollen, mushy, filling the entirety of my mouth. And so, unable to protest, I surrendered.

Bette walked me down another black hallway to a dead-end with one door. Inside was a continuation of Scott's video viewing scene. Again, red velvet and candles filled the small space surrounding the main attraction. Solitary, in the middle of the room, was the display. My eyes widened as we approached the large marble slab. Bette reached it first, her chest visibly expanding with each deep breath, her excitement palpable.

I froze.

On the large rectangular table was the girl from the videos. Or, at least, a mannequin depicting her. In the low, flickering light of the candelabras it was hard to tell. She wore the same torn, dirty party clothes, and her skin was blotchy, swollen, taut. Her long hair fanned out around her head. Her eyes were closed. I scanned her body, looking for some sign of plastic or acrylic. A *Made In China* stamp. A seam. Something fake. Paper-thin cuts ran up and down her legs. Her arms as well. Razor blades were strewn about the body like morbid party favors.

Bette placed her hand on the girl's forearm, a tender gesture, a look in her eye of empathy and longing. "Oh Alexa. Silly, beautiful, girl," she whispered.

"What is all this?" I stammered, stepping away.

Bette turned and smiled, satisfied. "We celebrate beauty, only to destroy it."

"Is she—? That's a doll, right? It's so real. Like, so real." My vision swam, and my heart raced. I couldn't catch my breath, and my stomach churned violently as bile rose quickly up my throat.

Bette glanced back at the girl. "The climax of his piece. Self-destruction."

Adrenaline and panic forced all the air from my lungs.

As I began to black out, frenzied thoughts swirled around me: Scott, the terrified girl in the video, the realness of the flesh on the bier. I prayed I'd wake in the morning, laughing that the night had been some terrible practical joke, and I had played the part of a gullible victim perfectly.

It would be some time before I realized how terribly wrong I was.

6

The car ride to Bette's family home occurred in almost complete silence. We hadn't spoken a word about the art show and, as each day passed, it felt increasingly taboo to bring up. The entire evening was an elephant in the room of my mind, and I used my fine-tuned skill of pushing its bulk so far inside myself that it was almost as if it hadn't happened, mentally packaging up the gruesome details and storing them all neatly away.

But images of the night continued to find cracks, escaping, demanding to be seen. Sitting on my hands, clutching the backs of my thighs, shaking in the aftermath, I forced them back down.

It was art. It wasn't real. It wasn't real.

I sat stock still next to Bette in a newly waxed black town car with an equally silent driver wearing a suit. We pulled into the entrance of a long, winding driveway. Ancient oak trees stood guard in a line along each side. The driver, who had not spoken a word to Bette or me since leaving my boarding house, navigated the curves with ease, obviously familiar with the varying forks in the road. Suddenly, the art exhibit was the furthest thing from my mind as I gazed, gobsmacked, at the manicured paradise.

The questions came in quick succession with my childlike wonder.

"Where does that go?" I asked when a small dirt pathway jutted out from the main drive.

"Gardener's shed."

"What's that?"

"Ski shed."

"That?"

"Stable."

"Oh! That's so cute! What's that?"

Bette eyed the small cottage, emotionless. "Playhouse."

When we finally neared the end of the drive, the trees parted to reveal acres of rolling hills and a grand stone home fronted by a circular drive, set amid glorious landscaping—manicured shrubberies, expertly mowed and edged grass, and a garden of heirloom rosebushes. A fountain, complete with angels and cherubs, sat in the middle of it all.

The car stopped directly in front of the massive front doors.

I was thunderstruck.

Bette stepped out of the car. "Come on."

"I just need to grab my bag."

She nodded toward the driver. "He'll get them."

I walked into the imposing entryway, feeling like a movie star on set. Or an alien on another planet. I couldn't even begin to fathom what it would be like to grow up in the splendor of that house. The two-story-height walls were covered in floor-to-ceiling wood panels, topped by intricately carved crown molding. A heavy wooden rail ran along the curved staircase and medieval tapestries hung between oversized oil paintings in gilt gold frames.

A soft voice sounded from a back hallway. "Bette? Is that you?"

"Here we go," Bette muttered. "Hi, Mom."

A slim woman with honey-blonde hair floated into the room. She moved just like Bette. And although mother and daughter were both dressed exquisitely, this woman embodied old-money perfection. She wore tasteful gray slacks, kitten heels, and a camel cardigan held closed around her waist with a thin alligator belt.

She approached, hugging Bette warmly, then leaned back and assessed her lovingly. "My beautiful girl."

Bette wore her best *I'm already bored with this* face. "Mom, this is Marin."

"Hello, dear. I'm so happy to meet you. Please call me Eleanor. Bette has nothing but wonderful things to say about you."

I beamed, flattered that Bette had been talking about me with her family. As Eleanor pulled me close, I caught a glimpse of her eyes. They were Bette's. Ice blue. But different. Soft, kind, welcoming. I immediately warmed to her.

"Please, girls, come into the conservatory. We'll have

lunch."

To Bette, I mouthed, *Conservatory?* to which Bette rolled her eyes.

I followed Bette and Eleanor down rich and winding corridors, passing a handsome library behind closed French doors. For a moment I paused, imagining how happy I would be in that room, surrounded only by books. We arrived at the conservatory, a room recalling the Garden of Eden, where the walls and ceiling were made of glass and covered in flowering vines that crept up, slithering, casting everything in a soft and earthy green tint.

A large table, covered in delicate lace cloth overflowed with platters of finger sandwiches, bowls of fruit, and small cakes. Plates and sterling silverware and thin-stemmed crystal glasses were already on the table. A bottle of white wine chilled in a silver bucket to the side.

I never wanted to leave. I wanted to walk the halls and sit in this fairy-tale setting for the rest of my life and couldn't understand why Bette seemed so put out to be home.

We spent the first half-hour with Eleanor as she asked us both about school, social events, and boys. Regarding our escapades, I realized Bette was as tight-lipped with her mother as I was with my own. However, I found Eleanor incredibly comfortable to talk to, moving easily from how Bette and I met, my planned double major, and about how life in Kearney compared to Chicago. Eleanor listened neutrally, with an inviting smile that never left her face.

Bette, however, grew more agitated as the minutes passed. She stared out at the lawn; she fingered the tablecloth's lace edging; she took short, anxious breaths. Only once did Eleanor risk a glance at her daughter with a nervous flutter. Finally, Bette excused herself, leaving me alone with her mother.

I assumed Eleanor's days were spent the way she looked—manicured, serene, and carefree—but learned that was not the case as we continued our comfortable conversation. She was not a lady who lunched. Instead, she ran several charities, all tied to children's welfare. Her favorite was an orphanage in Calcutta.

"Did you know that, for the girls, if they aren't adopted and educated, the overwhelming outcome will be that they are forced into prostitution? Terrible enough for sixteen- and seventeen-year-olds, but some of these girls are only five and six." There was genuine concern in her voice as she went on to talk about another passion project she established, a center in downtown Chicago for troubled teens. "They need love. They need hugs. For some, it's as simple as giving them shelter and food. Those teens are so grateful for the basics, they gladly attend the tutoring we provide. We have a high success rate of helping them get their GEDs and procure jobs and housing. However, the ones who break my heart are the teens who need real psychological help. They tend to flee when they have episodes, so medication is the key. But it's so hard to get the correct medication without trial and error. Unfortunately, sometimes all it takes is one error and they're gone."

She broke off, tears welling in her eyes.

"Marin, I presume?" I jumped at my name as a handsome gentleman came around the corner.

Eleanor rose from her seat and kissed the man on his

cheek. "There's someone I'd like you to meet."

Bette's father, Thomas, was the perfect Ken to Eleanor's Barbie. Tall and athletic, with sandy hair and a dazzling smile. Anywhere else, I would have found myself blushing under his gaze.

"Finally, we get to meet in person!" He gave me a warm embrace. "Eleanor has told me how close you and Bette have become. I'm hoping you two can stay over tonight. We'd love to get to know you better." His eyes were pleading.

Eleanor's smile was painted on her face, a frozen mask, as she fiddled with the dishes on the table, avoiding my eyes.

Pouring himself a glass of wine, Thomas said, "What do you say?"

"Well, I don't know. I'll ask Bette, but it sounds great to me."

"Brilliant!" Thomas exclaimed and took a sip from his drink, giving me a conspiratorial wink.

As if on cue, Bette entered carrying a large leather duffle. She dropped her bag upon seeing her father.

"I thought you were at work."

"Your mother called and said you were stopping by, so I thought I'd run home to see you."

Bette glared at Eleanor.

I cleared my throat, perplexed by the unspoken drama.

Thomas picked a grape off the fruit tray and popped it in his mouth. "Any chance you two might stay tonight?"

Bette redirected her frosty gaze from Eleanor to Thomas.

"No. We're heading over to pick up Oz, then going to the cabin."

Thomas visibly deflated. "Can you at least stay for dinner?"

"No."

The silence that followed was unbearable. I wanted to hug Bette and tell her that there was nothing to be distressed over. But even though I had been through plenty of my own parents' fights, this battle was different. The air was charged, a tsunami already flowing full force under their calm facades. I prayed for someone to yell, throw a dish, anything to break the silence.

At last, Thomas lowered his eyes and took another grape.

"I have something for you. Shall we go to the library?" His voice was serious, determined.

Thomas left the room, and I began to follow. Bette grabbed my hand, squeezing it hard. "Stay here," she whispered. "I'll be back in a minute. Then we'll get the hell out of here."

She bent and quickly kissed Eleanor on the forehead, cold and dry. "Thanks for lunch, Mom." She turned and left before Eleanor's outstretched arms could find her.

Eleanor's smile faltered, but she quickly composed herself and offered me another cup of tea.

"No, thank you. But could I use the bathroom?"

"Of course. Follow me." On the trek down another long hallway, I commented on a few large-scale contemporary art pieces. Paint flung and slashed across canvas. They were vicious and violent. Jarring.

"Wow. I really like these." I said, stopping in front of one of the pieces.

"Thank you. This one came from an especially dark place. It had to come out. The only way I can describe it is it's like a monster clawing at my insides."

Confused, I turned to her. "You painted these?"

"It's my outlet." Eleanor's smile had disappeared, and she slowly lifted her chin toward the painting, reverently, as if reliving the emotion of creating it.

I thought of Tessa, who had also needed to do the "work" to heal. But where Tessa's paintings had been fluid and serene, Eleanor's painting invoked violence.

It was unsettling that something so deeply disturbing could live in such a seemingly tranquil being, that she had to unleash something so savage in her for fear it would overtake her.

I excused myself, hurried to the bathroom, and locked the door. Something was off in the home. Fingers of tension had found me the same way they had Bette. Only, where Bette obviously knew why, I was left clueless. I knew nothing about Bette's family coming to their house, and realized I knew even less after the afternoon with them all.

Heading back to the conservatory, I purposefully averted my eyes from Eleanor's paintings. The wall opposite the paintings was covered with framed family photos. They hung clustered in groups of three and four and spanned generations. I became an observer of Bette's history, studying the pictures of her parents' wedding, of their parents' parents, of a long-ago family golden retriever, of Bette as a baby, then as a little girl with a crooked smile pointing to an Independence Day parade float. I took my time, ingesting their private world, my heart opening more with every captured moment.

I stopped abruptly, my attention drawn to one photograph. Two young girls, identical in every way, with their hair pulled into tight pigtails, wearing matching Easter dresses. My breath came quickly as I tried to decipher it, my eyes skipping around the photo, captivated, consuming the image.

I went back to a few of the first photos in the hall, trying to make sense of them. What I had assumed was one girl, Bette, was actually two. As the girls aged in the pictures, their differences became more noticeable. The wall showcased two completely different girls, one joyous and outgoing, one pensive and withdrawn. The only similarity was they shared the same face. The same eyes.

Eleanor found me and I pulled my face away from the frames. "I love these photos. There's so much life in them. You guys look really happy."

"We had some happy times."

"My folks split up." I was immediately embarrassed at myself for blurting out such a personal piece of information. "I'm sorry."

Eleanor gently placed her hand on my shoulder. "Why are you sorry?"

"I don't know. You've been so nice to do all this for us. I mean, the lunch alone—I've never experienced anything like that. I guess I just don't want to be a downer."

Eleanor smiled and led me to the picture of the twins. She glanced back over her shoulder and lowered her voice.

"These are my girls. This one is Bette. And this"—she gestured with a pause—"this is Olivia." My brow creased in confusion. Eleanor watched closely, then nodded. "She hasn't told you."

"No, Bette never mentioned a sibling." I was confused

why Bette would keep such a huge part of her life, a sister, from me, and the tone of Eleanor's voice made it clear there was a reason why.

Eleanor looked over her shoulder again and smiled kindly. "Let's go sit at the table. Where we can talk."

Back in front of the spread, she poured herself another cup of coffee and laced her fingers together under her chin.

"Olivia was Bette's twin sister." She smiled wistfully. "Oh, she was a wild child."

"Wilder than Bette?"

Eleanor chuckled. "Bette has always danced to her own drummer, but Olivia tried to keep up best she knew how. She was quieter. Sometimes that was good, sometimes it was worrisome. I think back now and wish I'd told her that it was perfectly okay just to be herself. There were few things Bette was afraid to try, and Olivia always hesitated a moment, considering what could go wrong. But overall, she was a typical teen, I suppose. Liked boys, her friends, parties. Or, Bette would talk her into liking it all, I should say. Sometimes, I think leading Olivia around was Bette's favorite activity."

She paused to sip her coffee, gathered herself and continued. "When the girls were fourteen, they went out one night. Nothing unusual. We were at the lake that summer, just like every summer. There's a beach about ten minutes from the cabin that the local kids liked to go to for nightly bonfires. They had so many friends. Lots of the kids from their school here used to go to that lake, too, so there was never a dull moment. The parents— well, we'd all tried to stop them at one point or another, but—I don't know. I've tried not to blame myself, and

I have to remember that it's more normal than not for teens to rebel. They ignore warnings and do dangerous things.

"Thomas and I were out of town, and we left the girls alone at the cabin. Olivia and Bette went to the beach." Eleanor paused, seeming to be reliving the moment. "From what we could piece together afterwards, from their friends who were there, Bette and Olivia decided to go swimming. They must have had too much to drink, or it was too dark. But either way, Olivia got disoriented. She drowned."

Eleanor looked out the window, quiet. I sat silent, still as a statue.

"Obviously, it was hard for us to process, no matter what the reason. But for Bette . . ." Eleanor spoke into her coffee, smiling sadly. "For Bette, the sun rose and set around Olivia. She fell apart. She insisted it was her fault, that she should have been able to do something to save Olivia. And I suppose in our own grief, at the time, Thomas and I needed someone to blame. She . . . Bette walked in on us once as Thomas was saying to me that our Olivia would still be alive if it weren't for her. My heart still breaks now even thinking of how painful it was for Bette to overhear that."

Eleanor covered her face with her hands and took a deep breath. "Then it was all she could focus on. That Thomas thought it was her fault Olivia died. Thomas tried to convince her otherwise, swearing to her up and down that she heard the comment out of context, but she tuned him out. He became the target of her rage and confusion and loss. Once she moved out for college, Thomas kept a thin thread of connection with her the only way he could, by giving her money, paying her bills. It's the only way she allows him to nurture her. Maybe one day she'll see how much he cares, how deeply he loves her, but that's such an uncertainty now."

Eleanor cast her eyes down. I thought of all the meals, drinks and cab rides Bette had paid for, not to mention the small rolls of cash she would sporadically hand over, and a bowling ball dropped in my stomach.

Eleanor shook her head slowly. "Bette was perfectly fine before. That's what makes it all so much worse. That she was fine before."

"What do you mean?" I asked.

Eleanor leveled her gaze. "How has Bette been? Her mood? Her behavior?"

I didn't know how to answer. Bette was the most remarkable person I'd ever met. She was eccentric and worldly. She was vivacious and adventurous and unpredictable. In my eyes, she was perfect. I loved her.

Eleanor continued, "Since Olivia's death, she's been different. Unstable. She'll be fine for a while, dramatic but safe."

I suddenly thought of the numerous unnamed pills Bette kept with her. Pills I'd been taking.

Eleanor's voice lowered and her speech quickened. "I need you to do something for me. I need you to watch her. If she becomes a danger—"

Suddenly she straightened and a mask of calm composure fell over her face as Bette walked into the room. "Hello, darling. We were just talking about what classes Marin will be taking next year."

Bette's voice was tight. "Let's go."

I thanked Eleanor and hurried after Bette.

Outside, a tired-looking Jeep Wagoneer sat in the drive with our bags already loaded. Bette threw in her duffle, slamming the door furiously. She stood, staring at the car, breathing hard.

I took a cautious step towards her. "Hey."

Bette turned, tears threatening. She grabbed my hand and quickly led me around the house and down an enormous rolling backyard. We moved silently along the property line toward the dense woods until we reached a small gap leading to a trail. Bette's steps quickened as we moved through the opening, pulling me along the path, ducking low to dodge branches and brush.

We came upon a lean-to built in the center of a clearing, sheltering a small down bed and fire pit. An image flashed in my mind of Bette and Oz as children, "camping" under the stars. But in the present moment it looked out of place, sad and abandoned, a physical representation of the Winston household spirit. Bette pulled me onto the bed, placing her head in my lap, and pulled a plaid woolen blanket over herself. I stroked her hair, bewildered in the curious setting, until Bette's chest began to heave.

"Are you okay?" I bent over, trying to see her features, but Bette pressed her face deeper into my lap, wetting my jeans with her tears.

"It's an impossible situation. It's them. It's him," she mumbled. In the midst of such obvious pain, I thought Bette would open up, let me in, tell me in her own words what had happened to her sister. But instead, she pulled a prescription bottle from her jacket and poured three small blue oblong pills into her hand. She put two in her mouth and gave one to me.

Bette's eyes dropped, defeated. "It's always him."

My heart pounded in my throat. "What just happened in there?"

Bette sighed and nestled herself back into my lap. "He gave me this." She dug into her jacket pocket and pulled out a white envelope. She dropped it in front of her like a rotting piece of garbage. I opened the envelope. Cash. Lots of cash.

"You take it. I don't want it." Bette's voice was distant, unfeeling.

"I can't take this."

"You might as well. It's where your cab money's been coming from. Keep using it for that. Or for whatever you want. I don't care." I looked down and saw her tears were drying. She gazed forward, into empty space. "He's paying me off."

"Why?"

"Just take the envelope. Please? I don't want to look at it."

I slid the envelope into my inside coat pocket. "Should we go?" I wanted to leave right then, to get away from the oppressive secrets held inside the beautiful house, inside the beautiful people who lived there.

"Can we stay for just a few more minutes? Tell me a story. Please?" Bette sounded like a child, pleading and inconsolable. I didn't tell her a story. I didn't want her to sleep. I wanted to ask why she had never talked about her sister, why she never talked about the accident and death. But I knew there was a reason, and as much as I wanted to know, I also knew pushing Bette too much would only push her away—and I couldn't risk that.

I held Bette tightly until her breathing calmed. Her

face looked ethereal, and I wondered how in the world this beautiful creature could be dangerous, as Eleanor warned. I kissed her cheek and looked toward the great manor of a home. From the outside, a little girl could fantasize about a beautiful queen and handsome king walking the halls in their palace while a fair princess gazed out the window. Suddenly, Scott's words about beauty not equaling goodness came to mind. I swiftly pushed the thought away.

The morning left me melancholy. I thought of my own home with similar distaste. How heartbreak and worry had seeped into the walls and the couch and hung in the air like secondhand smoke. A wave of compassion swept through me as I looked down at Bette's curls, splayed out on my lap. We were two girls bonded by dysfunction thrust upon us, both simply searching for some semblance of family.

Bette sighed and reluctantly stood, offering me her hand. As we made our way out of the woods, I looked back over my shoulder at the lean-to, wondering how many times Bette had fled there in the past, how many nightmares had been buried in those fallen leaves. Bette walked ahead, shoulders straight and unbothered. I checked my phone to find a list of notifications. All the texts were from Ozzie.

Sooooooo excited to see you, doll face!

When are you guys getting here??????

OMG. My family has morphed into the Mansons . . .

Seriously. When are you coming???

I'M BORED!!!!!!!!!!!!

Warning, Dalton

"We better get going. Ozzie's freaking out." I showed

Bette Ozzie's message rant. "Who's Dalton?"

"Oh God. Just the biggest menace to society." Bette slid behind the wheel, and the Wagoneer protested before rumbling to life.

I smiled reassuringly and squeezed Bette's hand while unanswered questions swirled in my mind. We drove just a mile before turning into another grand driveway. The house and grounds were as palatial as the Winstons' home, but this was a sprawling Colonial Revival, with a large, two-story main, flanked by side wings and porches resting under the eaves. By the time Bette pulled up, she was relaxed, and her self-confident smile had returned.

Ozzie burst through the main door, dragging a Louis Vuitton trunk across the front portico.

"Thank God you're here! Literally, I almost died."

"That makes two of us, love." Bette pecked him on the cheek and brushed past him into the house.

"Will you help me get this on the roof? Please?" Ozzie pleaded, beads of sweat clinging to his hairline.

"Don't do it!" A booming voice exploded from behind me. "If that princess insists on packing a month's worth of clothes, he should have to lift it himself." Thick-bodied and wearing a rugby jersey, a young man moved to Ozzie. "You might actually grow some muscles, fairy boy!"

I was mortified at the verbal attack until Ozzie turned to me, rolling his eyes. "Meet my Neanderthal brother, Dalton."

"Who are you?" he barked.

"Oh, I'm—"

"You look like the lead actress in the 1961 Oscar Best Picture winner. Go!"

"What?" I looked between Dalton and Ozzie for a clue. Dalton prodded, "Come on. Who won Best Picture in 1961? This is easy."

"I . . . I don't know—"

"Oh God. *West Side Story*! You look like Natalie Wood. I mean, if you wore makeup. And had better hair. Jesus, Oz, are all your friends so dumb?"

"Shut up, Dalton! Go get your bag, you brute."

Dalton snorted and shuffled back into the house.

"What was that all about?"

Ozzie waved it off. "It's his 'thing.' Movies, music, anything that falls under 'useless trivia' gets him off."

After several unsuccessful tries at manhandling the trunk onto the roof, Ozzie grunted as we shoved the large case into the back of the car. "Sorry about him My parents joke that the *real* Dalton was switched out in the hospital. I personally think the issue is a brain tumor but what're ya gonna do?" He pulled a handkerchief from his suit jacket and dabbed at the sweat running down his temple. "I've always said my parents don't give me a hard time about being gay because they're just so relieved I'm not another Dalton." He hooked his arm through mine. "Come on. You can meet my circus of monkeys."

Where Bette's home was eerily silent, a perfectly staged museum exhibit, Ozzie's home was school recess gone wild. Three young children raced around the large kitchen in a boisterous free-for-all, shrieking as Bette chased after them, threatening tickles. The counters were strewn with crumbs, newspapers, and coloring books. A TV blared from the living room, and plates from a half-eaten meal sat forgotten on the table.

"Mom, this is the magnificent Marin."

A plump woman wearing a sequined caftan grazed each of my cheeks with air kisses. "Hello, sweetheart. I'm Theresa. And this is Charles and Karen."

An equally plump man thrust his hand forward. "Call me Chuck! I'm Ozzie's dad."

"Hello. I'm Karen, Chuck's . . . Valerie! Get down off the table! *Now*! Sorry, I'm Chuck's wife."

My brow creased in obvious confusion. Ozzie grinned, "I'll explain our tangled web. Help me take the rest of my bags out to the car."

"The rest of your bags?" Chuck guffawed.

Theresa waved him off with a heavily jeweled hand. "Leave him alone. It takes work to look as fabulous as he does all the time."

"Thanks, Mom!" Ozzie shouted over his shoulder. There was a loud crash, breaking glass, followed by silence, then hysterical laughter. I heard Karen shouting at kids from the other room.

"So basically," Ozzie began as we climbed a large, carpeted staircase, "my mom and dad got divorced when Dalton and I were younger. Mom moved to Palm Beach, thank God. Have you ever been? It's a-ma-zing! Then a few years ago, Dad met Karen, they got married and started popping out these beautiful little monsters. I love them to death. To! Death!"

"So, your mom and Karen get along?"

"Oh my God, yes. They're like the best partners in crime when they're together. They totally gang up on my dad when he gets too patriarchal, and Karen is always asking my mom for advice on how to raise the hellions. I think it's fun for my mom. She gets to be a grandma without actually having to grow old herself and use the title."

I couldn't fathom my mother and Helen even being present in the same room, let alone acting like accomplices who swapped toilet-training techniques and sipped strawberry daiquiris on the back porch. The atmosphere of Ozzie's home was bright, jolly, as lighthearted and animated as Ozzie himself. If a person absorbs the environment in which she lives, I wondered what I was sponging up and withered at the thought.

Following Ozzie down the stairs with two enormous suitcases, we paused at the conversation booming in the kitchen.

"No. No way are you coming with us." Harry had arrived and was already agitated.

"Hell yeah, I am!" Dalton sneered.

"Hello, sweetie-poo! I've missed you so much." Theresa's spirited voice matched her vibrant clothing.

"Hi, Theresa. I've missed you, too. You look beautiful." Theresa squeezed Harry, her billowing gown engulfing him. Harry picked right up again. "Dalton, why don't you go hang out with your own friends? There's only room for the four of us in the car, anyway."

Dalton sat atop the kitchen counter, shelling peanuts and carelessly scattering the remains around him. Chuck gently smacked the back of his head.

Ozzie lightly pinched Harry's arm. "He's only coming for the afternoon, then going to Aggie's. She's not getting in until tonight, so I said he could catch a ride with us." Ozzie turned to me. "Her parents' cabin is down the lake a bit from Bette's."

Harry sighed heavily and sank into a chair. "Defeated at Waterloo."

Theresa shrieked. "Isn't he the most beautiful thing? So brooding and dark."

Ozzie groaned. "Mom, stop hitting on my boyfriend."

Harry wiggled his eyebrows. "Think I have a shot?"

"Oh my God! I literally just threw up in my mouth." Ozzie gagged.

Bette reappeared, breathless and flushed, happier than I had ever seen her.

Karen grinned as she washed the dishes. "I hope you did your job."

Bette beamed. "Oh, don't worry. They're exhausted and will be sacked out by six o'clock tonight." She jumped behind me, wrapping her arms around my waist. "Who's ready to go?"

Our goodbye was the longest I had ever experienced, but filled with more love than all the interactions in my life combined. There were hugs and kisses for each, from each. "Stay safe," "I'll miss you," "Don't eat too much," and "Wear life jackets." In that moment with Ozzie's family, even if we headed straight home, I could honestly say it had already been the best Thanksgiving I'd ever had.

As soon as we got into the car, Dalton's frenzied persona shifted into overdrive, shouting into my ear as I sat sandwiched between him and Bette in the front bench seat.

"Hey, Oz! You remember Billy Carter? That douche from McKinley? He went on that camping trip like six years ago? Do you remember him? Billy Carter?"

"Yes. Calm. Down." Ozzie sat in the back seat with Harry, his suitcases piled high on their laps, overtaking the space.

"So anyway, remember how he was such a moron, and he couldn't even name the top ten songs of 2008? And then he didn't know what movie had won Best Picture that year, either? Or anyone who was nominated? Even though, I have to admit, it really wasn't the best year, in my opinion. I mean, not everybody is as good as the Coen Brothers, okay? But he didn't even know—that was the point."

Harry pretended to hang himself. "I swear he was dropped on his head as a baby."

Ozzie reached over the front seat and tapped my shoulder. "I like to think of him as an idiot savant."

Dalton continued as if no one had said a word. "So, I was at the Ice House Mall the other day and I ran into him. He totally pretended like he didn't see me, but I knew he did. What a douche, right? I mean, that's a weird thing to do. So, I go up to him—"

Harry shook his head. "Nope. Just a plain idiot." Bette and I dissolved, giggling.

"—and I say, 'Hey, it's Billy Farter!'" Dalton slapped his knee, laughing at his own hilarity.

Harry whispered loudly, "Yeah, *so* weird he was trying to avoid you."

Dalton went on. "And so, he starts to walk away, but I go after him and ask, 'What was the Best Motion Picture of 2013?' And the dude couldn't even tell me! What a dumbass, right?" Dalton whipped around in his seat toward me. "Who won Best Picture in 2013?"

I froze, afraid the horrible tirade would next be aimed at me. Mercifully, he belted out, "*Argo*! Jesus, and that was like almost yesterday, even."

Bette whispered in my ear, "Those are his gifts. Lists

and calling people dumbass."

"A real class act," I whispered back.

Bette took my hand, laughing, as we watched Dalton dance in his seat and head bang to the heavy metal from the radio station he insisted on. I glanced in the rearview mirror to catch Ozzie shaking his head goodheartedly, a loving smile on his face. He reached over the seat and gently ruffled Dalton's hair.

We drove that way for three hours, Bette behind the wheel and Dalton playing Trivial Pursuit with himself. Harry navigated tyrannically from the back seat, causing Bette to threaten to pull over on the overpass and force him to drive if he didn't leave her alone. We turned onto side streets, then country roads, where condos gave way to picket fences and fields bare from harvest. The scenic palette morphed from cement grays and asphalt charcoals to the rich browns of dirt and yellows of dormant crops.

Dalton threw his meaty arm around my shoulders, rocking both Bette and me heartily. We sang songs from the radio at the top of our lungs, rolled the windows down until the chilled late November air made our fingers freeze, and, when we couldn't stand the biting cold any longer, rolled them back up and huddled together, laughing. Giving in to Dalton's whims, we argued over celebrity quotes, over who was the most notoriously inebriated writer, the most overrated visual artist, and the most underrated stage actor. That day, we drove without a care in the world.

7

Pulling into the Michigan beach town was like returning to 1955. As we crawled down Main Street, Bette and Ozzie regaled us with tales of summering on the lake, trips to town for sweets from the locally owned ice cream and candy shops, live music in the park, the Fourth of July celebration, parade, and fireworks over the harbor at dusk. More than once, Dalton stuck his head out the window, shouting greetings, and then profanities, to acquaintances and shoppers.

Ozzie wiggled his way up toward Bette. "We need to make a grocery stop."

"Babe, there's no room left back here," Harry protested. "None."

I glanced back to find him drowning under a hulking designer duffle.

Dalton brayed and tried to grab Ozzie into a backward headlock. "You guys are not letting this dumbass cook for you, are you? Oh man, that's rich! I'll alert the emergency room. Get the stomach pump ready!'"

As if addressing a toddler, Bette maintained an even tone. "Dalton, stop misbehaving. No one likes a bully."

"I didn't mean anything by it." He sulked and released Ozzie's head from his grip, lightly shoving him off. "Why don't you guys roast hot dogs and marshmallows? Make s'mores!"

"You are such a cretin," Ozzie rolled his eyes. "Hot dogs."

Harry moved the bag from his face so we could hear him. "Actually, that's not a bad idea." Ozzie shot a dirty glance in his direction. "I mean, just for tonight. We've been traveling all day—we'll need to open the cabin, get all our stuff unpacked."

Harry craned his neck toward Bette. "What's your vote?"

Bette shrugged her shoulders leisurely. "Ask Marin. I'll do whatever she wants."

"Well, maybe it's not a bad idea. I mean, just for tonight," I suggested gently.

Ozzie threw his hands in the air. "Fine! You win. Tonight, we eat like trailer park kings and queens. But tomorrow, I'm making up for it!" He threw himself backward with a flourish, sending bags hailing down on himself.

"All I know is that I'll be long gone by then. Saved by the hot dogs! And for the record, you're the one who said 'queens,' not me." Dalton rolled down his window again and began to howl at the setting sun.

The cabin sat in the center of several acres of forest on a large glassy lake. It was a simple log home, once well-maintained, but that was many years ago; what remained was a dusty shell of its former self. Still, it maintained a charm and undeniable coziness. The sunset had cast the cabin in deep pinks and purples, with the remaining autumn leaves, burgundy and burnt orange, creating a kaleidoscope canvas under our feet.

A key was hidden under a rock next to the porch swing, safely guarded by a network of spiderwebs. We carried bag after bag up to the creaking wooden porch while Bette shoved open the sticking door and flipped on the light, illuminating the small, chilly cabin. The tiny entryway opened into a living room with a mismatched couch and two well-worn, stuffed reading chairs. They flanked an oversized fireplace, complete with a bear-skin rug at the hearth. Plaid woolen blankets had been placed over the chairs and sofa, along with stacks of books on every side table.

A pass-through cut into the back wall of the living room framed the small, dated kitchen, with blistered yellow Formica countertops, unfashionable metal cabinets, and rusted sink handles. The oven and refrigerator were antiquated, the residue of years of cooking fumes coating the appliances with a greasy film.

Worn and threadbare, the cabin was nonetheless cozy.

Bette pointed to one of the two bedrooms at the back of the cabin. "We'll stay in there." I carried her bag to the tiny room, obviously once a small girl's room. But upon closer look, I realized it had been a room for two. The large bed was made up of two twins pushed together, their white wrought-iron headboards still attached. The bedding, a twisted mess of sheets, blankets, comforters, and duvets, was thrown together to cover both mattresses.

A child-sized bureau sat against one wall, hand-painted with delicate yellow roses. As I pulled out a top drawer, I noticed the tiniest personalization. *Bettina* had been scratched into the soft wood by young hands, inexperienced at writing. Looking at the drawer directly below it, my brow furrowed. It was also personalized: *Olivia*.

Bette came in and thumped her suitcase on the floor. I jumped, laughing at myself. "I was going to go ahead and unpack."

Bette unzipped her bag. "Good thinking. You take that one." She pointed to the *Olivia* drawer. I tried to hide the trembling in my hands as my fingers slid over the engraved name, suddenly remembering that the cabin, the bedroom I stood in, was the last place Olivia had been before her death.

Bette grabbed her toiletry kit and slid into a corner alcove, her back to me. There came the unmistakable sound of a pill bottle rattling, and I feared she was having the same thoughts of Olivia as I was. Fortunately, Bette seemed unaffected as she turned back to the room and hung the last of her clothes in the closet, leaving the room with a small air kiss.

We reconvened in the living room; Dalton had already lit a fire, and the cabin was slowly growing toasty. The fireplace generated a penetrating heat, one that warmed us from the inside out as we cuddled up to the blaze, basking in the pleasure of the thaw.

"Dalton and I are going to go to the store to get the

hot dogs." Ozzie wrapped a crocheted scarf round and round his neck.

Harry grabbed his heavy jacket. "Marin, you and I can get the bonfire going."

"I'll go find extra kindling." Bette's movements were slow and mechanical. Precise.

My friends had traded their light fall jackets for heavy winter coats. I hadn't anticipated the weather change, never having spent time on a lake during cold weather, and was immediately an outsider again. But I refused to acknowledge my mistake, especially in front of Dalton, whom I feared would use it against me, so I slipped on my thin jacket.

Dalton and Ozzie left, arguing whether Oscar Mayer all-beef hot dogs or gourmet duck-liver dogs would be most suitable for the evening meal. Harry followed them. "I'm going to get started. I'll meet you out there. Just head down toward the lake."

Wordlessly, Bette entered the room and placed her down coat over my shoulders.

"That's okay. Really, I'm fine." I started to give it back, but Bette held up her hand.

"Wear it. I want to wear my mom's old fur anyway." The sight of Bette donning a floor-length mink coat to stay warm in the mildewing cabin sent me into spasms of laughter. "I'm just trying to class up the joint," she joked, looking smug as she fanned the coat out over her shoulders like a New York fashion editor.

"Is it weird I find it totally normal for your mom to keep a fur coat out here? Like, it's just an old throwaway extra?" I pretended Bette's down coat was a fur and mimicked her model twirl.

The moment the bitter cold air hit my lungs I was grateful for Bette's generosity, wrapping the coat tightly around myself and nuzzling my nose deep into the down collar as we walked arm in arm down to the lake. As Harry warmed his hands over the small bonfire he'd started, the light danced against the sharp angles of his face. He was concentrating, his eyes fixed and squinting, looking like a comic book's handsome villain.

Bette nodded approval at Harry's fire. "I better go find some more kindling. It's so damp, I'm afraid it'll snuff itself out." She turned and disappeared into the woods.

I looked after her. "Maybe I should go help?"

Harry snorted dismissively.

Irritation simmered low in my gut. Not wanting Bette to hear, I whispered, "What is your problem with Bette? Did you guys have an argument or something?"

He shook his head disdainfully. "It is what it is."

"'It is what it is?' What does that even mean?"

Harry snapped. "What is it with you? With your weird codependency? You guys basically just met."

Harry's question caught me off-guard, my thoughts suspended midair as I ingested his words. The truth was, he was right. I had known Bette for barely three months, but could scarcely remember life without her.

Harry continued, gaining momentum. He cocked his head, peering straight into me. "You don't hover over her, but you're deeply invested. You're drawn to her, and she's drawn to you—you two run side by side. Parallel lines on a parallel path. Not mothering but, still, a type of love."

I straightened my shoulders.

He raised an eyebrow. "Or are you in love with her?"

He paused, then bellowed, laughing. "Oh my God." He shook his head, amazed by what he obviously saw as a preposterous notion. "Oh, that's fantastic."

"Don't be stupid. I'm not in love with her." The words came out with a tremble, much weaker than I had intended. I couldn't even convince myself with such a timid response. My skin prickled with embarrassment.

I stared at the growing fire, thankful the rising heat masked my burning face. Harry emitted a long sigh, his features softening the same way they had at the gallery, his armor visibly falling. I was humiliated this time, though, to be the recipient of his sympathy. Or maybe it was pity.

Harry poked the fire with a stick. "I understand why, you know."

"I'm not in love with her," I said with more force.

Harry held up his hand in surrender. "All right, I believe you. I didn't mean to piss you off. I'm just saying I understand why her pull is so strong. Ozzie's hooked, too." He looked up at me and waited for me to look him in the eye, making sure I heard his message. "But no matter what label you give it, it's not what you think it is." He paused. "She doesn't feel the same."

When I didn't respond, he added, "She doesn't feel the same about you. As you do about her."

"Why are you so hateful?"

Harry continued to jab the stick into the fire, causing small explosions of sparks to dance in the air. "I'm not hateful. I've just seen this happen so many times before. I know her. I know what she does. And it's not right. It's not healthy, especially for the one who ends up with the short end of the stick."

His brow furrowed while his eyes concentrated on the fire. "And I know what you're going to say. That I don't know her like you do. That she lets you see a part of her that no one else is allowed. That there's so much more to her than what I see. She's inspiring, she has foresight, she follows a path no one else dares to go." He looked at me for a moment and, sensing he had struck a nerve, plowed on. "She's free, she's borderless, she's dazzling."

Harry threw his stick in the fire. "The problem isn't that she won't reciprocate those compliments. And it's not that she doesn't think you're all those things. It's just that her brain doesn't process it the same."

I had no idea what Harry was trying to tell me, or why he felt the need to make me doubt my friendship with Bette. I had finally found a soulmate, of sorts, a real best friend, and my far-flung dreams of happiness were finally coming true. Yet, here was Harry trying to create small fissures in it all. Tears threatened at the corners of my eyes as Harry rolled over two large logs, their ends cut flat to act as stools, and gently sat me down next to him.

"She creates her world. It doesn't just happen naturally. It's not organic. She forces it. She stages her life for public view. A life of glamour and sensuality. And yes, it's fascinating and beautiful, but it's also not real. It's like she cherry-picks the elements she wants and then fabricates a diorama around herself. Her home, her clothes, her voice, her friends. She chooses all of them very carefully. One thing fits perfectly with another. Marin, you can see that, right? She lines them up, then she sews them all together the way she wants them to be. And there it is: Her flawless, but false, world."

Harry turned to the fire. For the first time since I

had met him, he looked genuinely sad. There was no vitriol or animosity, just a heavy heart. Bette had broken something in him, or someone close to him, and I sensed his words were not intended to hurt anyone in retaliation. He was trying to save me, even if I wasn't ready to listen.

"Think of it this way: It's like you're a beautiful butterfly, Marin. She's captured you, and she has pinned you in her shadow box. She is a collector. She collects people and things and feelings and ideas. You're an object she keeps. So that she can gaze at you. You and Ozzie. Both butterflies."

Quietly, I responded, "She didn't choose me, though. I'm the one who started talking to her. I'm the one who kept seeking her out." I waited and, when Harry didn't protest, continued. "And she might have brought up a change in my major, but I was the one who made the decision. Just me."

Harry shook his head. "I know it feels like that. And Oz would say the same thing. But he never had any intention of being a chef until Bette talked him into it. And it's not like he's a prodigy. I mean, he's a decent cook, but I think the version of Ozzie with culinary talent is the only Ozzie who fit into Bette's world. Artists, lofty thinkers, creative types. A best friend, the math major, wouldn't fly so well in the art scene she's so obsessed with. The same goes for her own major. Poetry? Really? Have you ever read anything she's written?"

I gazed into the fire, realizing that I hadn't.

"I thought so. And you know why you never have? She doesn't want you to. Because it's crap. She can't write to save her life. But it sure sounds chic, doesn't it? To major in poetry." Harry blew out a frustrated breath. His hard exterior was returning. "I've been trying to get Ozzie to spend less time with her, but she has a magnetic force, and he keeps coming back." Harry threw another log on the fire, watching it catch and come to life. "He doesn't know it, but I'm going to move him away with me right after we graduate."

I couldn't picture Ozzie leaving his family and all the comforts of his world. "Where? How will you get him to go?"

"My parents have a small branch of their firm in London. They have a modest flat in a cool neighborhood that we can rent. He'll flip out, really. I won't have to sell him on it at all. His bags will be packed before I can even finish telling him about the little tea shop around the corner."

I bristled. "So please, tell me why Bette is horrible for planting ideas in other people's minds, but you're not?"

Exasperated, Harry snapped. "I'm helping Oz get out so that he can live his own authentic life. That's the difference. Bette's world is an escape from reality. A distraction, a disguise. Frankly, I don't think she could live one day with the actual truth."

I still didn't know what "truth" he was talking about. I sat silently, a lump forming in my throat.

Harry looked at me again with sorrowful eyes. "You're a good person, Marin. You deserve to be loved for who you are, not what someone makes you."

Headlights from the car rolled over the ridge as Ozzie and Dalton pulled up with the groceries. The driver's-side door flew open, and their voices tumbled out. "No, for the millionth fucking time, I do *not* know who *should* have won the Oscar in 1974!"

"Come on, man! Think! I know you got this."

"For the love of God, I beg you to stop talking."

"Just give me one more guess. But a good one!"

"You are such a moron!"

"Hey! I'm not the moron! At least I know who—"

"Looks like the boys are back." Bette's silky voice came from the dark, startling both Harry and me, making us teeter on the log stools. Her arms were full of sticks and branches. "I think this should do it."

She dropped the kindling into a pile opposite Harry. Her mouth broke into a wide smile that sent shivers through me. "I'll make drinks." She held Harry's steely gaze.

Blood drained from my face. Had Bette heard the conversation with Harry? His scathing assessment of her and of our friendship? Had she heard how little I had protested? There was a sinister sparkle in Bette's eyes that told me not to press for an answer.

Dalton's cackle broke the silence. "We got your favorite, Harry—wieners!"

Harry rolled his eyes, and Bette chastised Dalton for the rude comment. Like a magic wand had waved over their heads, the tension disappeared, and we all settled in, picking out roasting sticks and doubling up on the overturned logs.

Despite the falling temperature, our cheeks were burned rosy by the fire and hot rum cider. The moist, chilled winds gusted as we held hot dogs over the fire, watching their skin bubble and blacken and eating them straight from the sticks. Logs cracked and whistled, and Dalton's constant ambushes united the four of us, supplanting the doubts and prejudices we'd held against each other earlier in the night.

"Pass me the dogs," Dalton said with a full mouth, bits of meat spewing out as he spoke.

"That's your fifth one," Harry said with disdain.

"So?"

"So, do you know what's in these? I mean, one is bad enough, but five?"

"I'm growing!"

"Yeah, just not up," Ozzie chided, throwing the package to Dalton.

He quickly speared another dog and set it deep in the fire. "Okay, who can answer this one—"

"No," our group protested in unison.

Bette moved to refill his vodka Red Bull, but Dalton shook his head, shoving the hot dog in his mouth. He stood and grabbed a bag of marshmallows from the bench next to Ozzie. "I'm outtie. Aggs should be at her cabin by now."

Ozzie yelled after Dalton as he made his way up the hill, "Do you need a ride back Sunday?"

Bette groaned, and Harry hissed ferociously, "Shut up!"

They relaxed as Dalton yelled over his shoulder, "Nah, I'll find a ride home. See ya later, douchebags!"

As Dalton's heavy steps disappeared into silence, Harry sighed. "Ah, peace." He pulled a joint from his coat pocket and lit the tip, taking a long drag, then passed it to Ozzie. Bette made herself busy refilling our insulated tumblers with cocktails.

"I don't know how you're so patient with him." I could barely finish the sentence without laughing, thinking of the ridiculous subjects Dalton thought up and his uniquely crass way of delivering them.

Ozzie held smoke in his mouth, shrugging his shoulders. He blew out and smiled. "He's my brother. What can I do?"

After blowing out a billow of fragrant smoke above her head, Bette passed me the joint.

I had never smoked pot, and under normal circumstances, would have just passed the joint back to Harry. But normal circumstances had ended the moment I met Bette. Everything seemed like a good idea. So, instead, I took a long hit, held the smoke deep in my lungs, then began to choke. The smoke poured from me as I coughed uncontrollably. It burned my eyes and rose directly back up my nose.

Ozzie giggled and even through my watery vision, I could see Harry shake his head, laughing. Bette reached over and squeezed my hand, silently acknowledging the rite of passage.

Harry carefully removed the joint from my convulsing arm. He drew in another hit and peered at me through one open eye. "Speaking of brothers, you have one, right? What's the scoop? What is it like living in Marin Finch's home?"

Whether it was the drugs or the safety of the small bonfire, I didn't know, but my introverted tendencies fell away, and I began to talk.

I told them about the joys of growing up among cornfields. How Ty and I played hide and seek in the alfalfa crops. How we went to the county fair, where I got to ride atop my father's shoulders. The scary rush I got when I'd start to slip and his strong hands pressed my feet into his chest, anchoring me in place. How I marveled at the freedom of the Ferris wheel, the merry-go-round, the coveted stuffed animal prizes. How my mother did the ironing while watching late-morning soap operas. How the starch she used made the house smell clean and crisp. How she tucked me in at night, kissing my nose, pulling the blankets up tight around my neck. How my father had called me Princess, how my mother called me Munchkin, how Ty called me Martian.

The bake sales held at school and church, homemade pies and cakes and cookies still warm from the oven. How we sat in the bleachers to watch Ty's baseball games at the high school field, gorging ourselves on concession stand junk food—hot dogs and nachos and soda. How proud I'd been when he'd walk to the plate and knock the ball over the fence. How my father held my mother's hand.

How Ty went away to school. How he came home often at first, then less and less. How my parents began pecking and snapping, like selfish crows keeping each other at bay. How my father traveled more and more, and for longer stretches. How my mom grew increasingly irritable. How Ty was too busy to talk. How Sarah did all my thinking for me. And how relieved I was for that. How my parents' arguing became outright screaming. How my mother heaved a plate, my father calling her names, while I was just one thin wall away.

My father no longer smelled of cologne. He smelled of cheap perfume. Young perfume. My mother smelled of resentment and anxious sweat. Family dinners became cold cereal. Pizza. Whatever Sarah's parents were serving. Sarah. The neighbor girl who took me under her wing. The cool girl. The girl who made me believe we were friends and gave me hope, only to grow tired of and discard me like an outdated doll. My father moved out. Mother cried. Mother cried. Mother cried. I outgrew my clothes, jeans too short and shirtsleeves even shorter. No new clothes appeared. Sarah's family hugged me. They tsked with sympathy when I left the room.

Then things really changed, and Father smelled of baby powder while Mother smelled of poison. The house was always dark. Lights were left off. Muted colors faded into dirty colors. Mud. Mustard. Algae. My father stopped seeing me. My mother stopped seeing me. Sarah stopped seeing me. I could disappear and no one would know.

Finally, completely spent, I stopped talking. The group sat in silence, staring into the fire, as I quietly caught my breath. The words had come so swiftly and effortlessly, tumbling one after another, gaining momentum until I was just . . . done.

Harry slowly shook his head. "Tragic."

Bette's eyes lit up and she nodded enthusiastically. "It is tragic. Can you imagine Marin, our Marin, in that environment? Day in and day out? Suffocating? Here she is"—she gestured toward me—"this brilliant, blazing, starburst living in in that purgatory. In shackles. Tethered. It's a crime. Like a butterfly in a glass jar instead of free to ride the wind."

Harry's and my eyes flicked quickly to each other. I looked away first, refusing to allow him into my head. Instead, I seized Bette's words, inviting them to drip down me like honey. She'd transformed my history, had made my emotions sound poetic rather than pathetic. Had taken me from the quiet, shy girl living a drab existence to a colorful songbird in need of freedom.

"Can you imagine knowing you have so much more to offer but nowhere to go?" Bette's eyes were moist, face flushed with spiked spiced cider, her body an apparition glowing in the firelight. "You don't belong there, Marin. You never did."

But, Harry, his words made of steel razorblades, sliced through the illusion.

"No, that's not what I meant." Harry's voice was edgy. "It's tragic because she was a part of a family that went through a complete breakdown. It wasn't just her—they all suffered. It's *all* tragic."

Harry turned to me, compassion in his voice. "It was obviously painful. Lonely. I'm sorry you went through that," he sighed. "I can't imagine what your mother was going through. How scared she was to start over and be on her own. The embarrassment she must have endured. I'm sure your brother was pretty broken up, too. I doubt he meant to abandon you. Maybe he dove deeply into school as a coping mechanism."

He paused and turned his face to Bette. "People have strange ways of dealing with pain."

She bristled as he continued. "And I would wager your dad even struggled. It's not that hard to imagine a middle-aged man getting caught up in the excitement of a sexy, young—"

"Stop," I protested, tears rising uncontrollably.

"No, no, let me finish. He's a human being. Like all of us. I just mean that maybe what started out as a fling, as a momentary lapse in judgment, snowballed into something he never intended. And suddenly he had to make all these decisions. Maybe he doesn't even really love her or want to be with her, but with a baby on the way, he knew he needed to man up. He had to decide between his current family or a mistress who threatened to make his life a living hell if he didn't legitimize her and their new baby. I'm not excusing it, but that's heavy stuff. Maybe he's scared to death he now has two families and, at his age, a new baby."

He stopped to take a take a hit from the disappearing joint Ozzie offered.

"Marin, this is your family. Every single person was hurt. I understand you're hurt that no one was there to swoop in and make it all better for you but, my point is, it doesn't sound like anyone was in a state to be the savior. Normally, a family is there to help pull each other out of the mud pit. But that's not always possible. When we're struggling, we all think everyone else doesn't have it as bad. We can be blinded by our own wounds and not see the pain others are going through."

My head spun with rage that had been boiling under the surface for years. "Of course we were all in pain. Do you really think I didn't see it? I wasn't blind and I wasn't deaf. I watched Helen physically place herself where the malicious bitch knew she'd run into my mother, smiling smugly. I heard the screaming, the accusations, the pleading that occurred nightly in my house. I heard my mother railing against my father and her wailing over a destroyed marriage. My brother, my hero, disappeared. He was the only good man I knew, and he vanished. And my father, *my fucking father,* made his choice and never looked back. He didn't want to be pulled out of the mud pit. And he sure as hell wasn't going to get his hands dirty helping us. I don't know if he mourned anything.

But if he did, he mourned in silence."

I stood, jabbing my finger towards Harry's face. "You don't know a thing about me. You don't know what I went through. I didn't come from private planes or European royal titles. I wasn't whining; I was just trying to make it through. And I had to do it alone." I paused. "But you're right about one thing: No one could save anyone. That's why I finally left. Bette understands that."

I swayed and stumbled away from the fire. My mind blurred, minutes were lost, and suddenly I was inside the house again. One foot in front of the other, until I collapsed onto the living room couch.

Voices, gibberish, passed by in vague tones. The words were simply sounds with no meaning. Then they were gone. A comforting weight fell over my body. Butterfly wings fluttered on my cheek. Then my lips.

Sunlight momentarily blinded me, suddenly waking from a fetal position on the living room couch. My neck was stiff and pinched from sleeping in a cockeyed position. I winced, stretching out my misaligned body to its full length. Someone had placed a blanket over me during the night, and I wrapped it tightly around my shoulders as I heaved myself upright with a grunt.

Ozzie, perched on the coffee table, grinning mischievously, methodically tapped his finger on my forehead. I kicked him away playfully, and he pounced like a puppy, singing in my ear.

"Get up, lazy bug! Rise and shine!"

"No, it's so early," I wailed.

"Early? Sister, it's four o'clock! You slept about twenty hours straight."

I pulled the blanket over my head in embarrassment.

"Don't chastise me. I was drugged."

Ozzie rolled his eyes and waved me away. "You're such a lightweight. Anyway, we're setting the table. Thanksgiving feast is near!" He clapped his hands and pulled me to my feet.

I scratched my matted hair and reached for a stack of plates. Harry's eyes landed on me. Immediately, the previous night's tirade came back to me.

"Harry, I'm really sorry. I don't know why I—"

Harry waved me off with a slight nod and a wink.

Bette gave me a cool once-over. "I laid a dress out for you on the bed."

I took in the easy elegance of my friends: Bette's well-cut trousers and luxurious cashmere sweater, Harry's fine camel-hair sports coat, and the Sunday-best bow tie peeking from under Ozzie's apron. I quickly made my way to the bathroom to shower. Winding my hair into a sleek wet bun, I heard Ozzie crooning, the clink and clang and ping of cooking utensils and glass, a stainless whisk whipping against a metal bowl, the oven door slamming shut, and instructions being thrown back and forth.

I slipped into the bedroom and slowly fingered the silky floor-length dress. Oxblood red, long sleeves, striking neckline, minimalist aesthetic. And a perfect fit. A pair of kitten heels lay on the floor. Never had I dressed up for a holiday meal. In Kearney, we wore jeans and sweatshirts, tennis shoes and ball caps.

I swept back into the living room, transformed, standing taller.

"Thank you," I whispered into Bette's ear.

The table had been set with a mixture of China sets.

Even though the plates didn't match, everything melded into an exquisite tablescape: Silver candlesticks clustered in the center, a wine decanter filled and breathing, and embroidered napkins slipped into drinking glasses. The overhead lights were turned off, leaving a few floor and table lamps to cast a soft, yellow glow.

Emulating Bette, I sat at the table in silent reverence, watching Ozzie place one dish after another on the table. Apple and walnut dressing, savory mashed sweet potatoes, creamed corn and spinach, asparagus with hollandaise, fresh cranberries boiled with sugar. In the center of the table, left empty for the crowning achievement, Ozzie placed the turkey, half-carved, juice dripping and the skin a crispy, succulent caramel brown. Harry poured the wine as they applauded Ozzie.

"I have to say, I'm quite impressed," Harry ceded, eyeing the spread.

"Last year's baking courses got the best of me, I admit. But this year—" Ozzie smiled brightly, making a show of inhaling the scents of his glorious creations. "*This* year is gourmet comfort food. And that's what I'm all about."

I reached greedily for the bowl of garlic mashed potatoes when Bette placed her hand on my arm. "Not yet. First, thanks and gratitude. Harry, would you like to start?"

"Absolutely. This year, I am grateful for this meal." We cheered, nodding in agreement. "I am thankful for my schooling. I am thankful I have hope and future dreams. I am thankful for my parents and their generous and limitless support. I am thankful for my friends." Harry gestured around the table. "And, of course, I am thankful for love. A very colorful love with a very colorful man."

Blushing, he gently touched his lips to Ozzie's cheek, who beamed with appreciation.

"Me next!" Ozzie crowed. "I am thankful for my unruly family and for the deep love they give me and the deep love they allow me to give them. I am also thankful for my devoted friends." Ozzie blew air kisses all around. "And I am eternally grateful for my bae."

Harry sighed. "Don't call me that."

"Why not? You are!" Ozzie said indignantly.

"It's just not you. It's . . . it's affected."

I paused at Harry's comment. To my ears, the affected term was *completely* Ozzie. But Harry had said Bette morphed people into who she wanted them to be. Maybe there was a truer side of Ozzie, one that he kept hidden from Bette, from everyone besides Harry.

"What would you rather have me say?"

"Say what you mean. Not what's cutesy or in fashion."

"Okay." Ozzie stared at the ceiling for several moments, then turned to Harry, pensive and uncharacteristically serious. "What I should have said is that I'm thankful for the tangled compartments of my mind that you point out to me. I'm thankful you don't need to open them, only to observe that they are there. I am thankful for quiet moments when I see all your cracks, all your vulnerabilities, and all your fears. To me, they are glorious. I'm thankful for your honesty, your truth, and your sense of justice. I'm thankful that some days, when they're overwhelming, you drag all my shit out into the sunlight where it can't hide. And, without judgment, make me face it all. Because those are the moments I know I'm really being seen. Understood. Loved. And Harry, I'm thankful there is a God who said, 'These two lost souls should find each other.'"

Harry laced his hand with Ozzie's, tears pooling in his eyes.

"In other words," Ozzie continued, "you are my bae."

The table burst out laughing. And, for the first time, really, I understood why Harry and Ozzie were together. Because under all the layers of Harry's hardened demeanor and behind Ozzie's outrageous theatrics were two good people with good hearts, banding together to face the world.

"You're up." Bette whispered.

My comfortable lot in life was to watch from a corner where I wouldn't have eyes on me. But, not wanting to disappoint Bette, I took a deep breath. I had to close my eyes before I could speak for fear of stumbling over words or rambling inconsequential nonsense. When I opened my eyes, I looked at Harry and Ozzie, and felt their words still beating in my heart. No one had laughed at their speeches of gratitude. No one had rolled their eyes in judgement. There was only love and acceptance, and I knew in that moment that, if I didn't leap, I would never know whether or not a net waited to catch me.

So, I jumped.

"I am thankful for so much." I paused and looked at the faces around the table. "When I met you, I was scared. Really scared. I was so terrified of life, and I told myself I was protecting myself by keeping people at a distance, but really, I was just closing myself off. And now, I don't even know now what monster I was afraid of. I'm thankful for all I have learned, for how I have grown. I am thankful for everything you have shown me, taught me, and introduced me to. I'm deeply thankful for this meal. Not just because of the food"—I quickly looked up at Ozzie—"I mean, I am really stoked for the actual food, but what I'm grateful for is for the experience. The new traditions. Ones I want to be a part of for a long time. I've found a new life. I've found a new me. And I like her. And it's because of you three."

I lowered my eyes again, waiting for the laughter. But there was only silence. When I dared to look up, everyone had a glass in hand, raised; Bette's eyes were watery, and Ozzie's hand lay over his heart. But Harry had a strange look on his face. He was thinking hard. I could tell the thoughts were not good, but at least he kept them to himself.

We toasted and turned to Bette. Her voice quivered. "I don't know that I can follow these beautiful graces. So, I'll only say that my sentiments are the same as yours. And best summarized by Hemingway: *'We ate well and cheaply and drank well and cheaply and slept well and warm together and loved each other.'* I love each one of you. You are my heart." Bette took my hand as we raised our glasses again. "Happy Thanksgiving."

And, like Hemingway, we ate well, drank well, and loved. We lounged in our chairs past nightfall, sipping wine, picking at platters and bowls, laughing, sharing stories, and finding endless delight in each other. As I looked around at Ozzie and Harry's fingers entwined, Bette languid, her delicate kitten heel dangling off her foot, a wave of gratitude flooded me. This was not an image out of one of a celebrity magazine, not a moment created for social media posts. This was our life. A family.

Later, after the kitchen was cleaned and the leftovers neatly stored for the next day's turkey sandwiches, Bette and I curled up next to the fireplace, blankets thrown around our shoulders, sipping on snifters of brandy. Our bellies were full, bodies warm, and hearts safe. We all four fell asleep on the floor that night, curled into one another, nuzzling tenderly, cheek to cheek.

8

The rowboat was double wide. In theory, we should have had two people on each side with oars in the water to propel across the lake. But Oz, disgusted within minutes, stubbornly threw his oar to the boat floor.

"These arms are not meant for crew!"

"But think of how much stronger this will make you for whisking." Harry nudged him.

"You're the buff one. I'm the delicate swan. Remember?" Ozzie smiled demurely, fluttered his eyelashes, and lifted his delicate chin.

We floated leisurely, thick wool blankets pressed into our laps as a shield from the biting frost. The sun blinded us in the crisp, cold air, and where the cabin had seemed dark and rich on arrival, it had transformed into a bright Bob Ross painting.

Bette passed around a thermos of hot cider, and I shuddered as it seeped down my throat, warming my stomach.

We sat in amiable silence, enjoying the quiet stillness. I thought of summer lake days in Missouri when I was a kid. Our family—when it was still a family—would fill a day bag with thick sandwiches, cans of cold pop, Mom's cookies, and bags of salty potato chips. Beach towels, swimsuits, books, and headphones would go in a second bag. We'd set up folding chairs and a card table. My mother would spread out the bounty, and Ty and I would run eagerly toward the murky waters of Smithville Lake. We'd hesitate as we first stepped in, letting our feet sink into the muddy bottom, cold silt oozing between our toes, and then bravely plunge forward into the water.

The day would pass with Mother's warnings about sunscreen and Father arranging and re-arranging the camp's position as other families arrived and departed. Ty and I would play loud games of Marco Polo, King of the Mountain, and, if we were lucky enough, Keep-Away with other kids willing to join in. At the day's end, we'd sleep heavily in the back seat the whole way home, our skin sunburned, bodies drained from the sun and physical effort, our exhaustion and happiness well-earned.

"Marin? Hello?" Ozzie waved his hand back and forth in front of my face. He came into focus; I returned to the present. "You look so sad." His exaggerated frown forced me to laugh.

"Just remembering something." Shaking off the cobwebs, I inhaled a deep breath of icy air to clear my head. I couldn't understand why I continued to be pulled into the past, rehashing memories that left me melancholy. I took a second breath, determined to focus on the beautiful surroundings and activities of the present.

Harry gazed dreamily down the shoreline. "I love it here. From the first time I came, I loved it. I love the homes, the solid foundations, the quaintness." He paused, his smile growing. "Did you know that it was on my first visit here that I discovered I wanted to be an architect?"

"But you were already in school studying architecture," Ozzie said, surprised.

"I know. My parents influenced me, and I was testing that path, but I wasn't sold yet. I didn't have the enthusiasm or the fire for it. Everything was straight lines, ninety-degree angles, steel girders, and cold glass. But then I saw these cottages." Harry shook his head. "They settled me, and then it just clicked." He gestured to the homes sprawled in front of us. "See how people have added on? Architecturally, the changes don't even make sense. But they arose from so much thought and heart and purpose that they become appealing. Beautiful, even. These houses weren't built to win awards or to be featured in magazines. They were built with families in mind. These homes reflect their lives, their hearts, and souls, not some cool aesthetic ambition."

Ozzie swooned. "You're such a romantic." He turned to Bette. "Brilliant idea happening! He could design the salon."

Harry, still absorbed in a dreamy trance, smiled. "What salon?"

"The one Ozzie and I are opening after graduation."

Bette offered Harry a stony smile, her eyes narrow and harsh.

"Yes. We were going to rent or buy a space and just make do, but you could design and build it instead. It will be fantastic. A real old-fashioned salon! We're going to offer coffee and tea in the morning—"

"Don't forget your pastries," Bette prodded.

"Of course! I'll be the house chef and baker. Pastries in the morning. Light finger sandwiches and dainty salads for lunch. Brunch on Saturdays. Then, at night, it becomes private. Invitation only." Ozzie's enthusiasm gained momentum. "We'll be a hotbed of intellectual and artistic exchange, a breeding ground for new artists and writers and musicians. They'll gather for inspiration, for intellectual debate. We'll be the nucleus for the best and brightest creative talent in the country! Like Gertrude Stein and Alice Toklas."

Harry straightened his shoulders. "Oz, you never mentioned this before."

"It's all new! Bette and I began talking and, oh, Harry, doesn't it sound like the most amazing idea?" Ozzie's eyes glittered in anticipation.

"It sounds like something." Harry glared at Bette. "Then again, we could talk about other options."

"Such as?"

"Such as, there's a whole world out there. Don't you want to see it all? The salon might be like Paris, but it's not Paris."

"I've been to Paris, silly." Ozzie waved him off.

"But you haven't lived there. We could try it. Or the countryside of Japan. How about London?" A pleading note crept into Harry's voice.

Bette knew when to strike. "Why would Oz want to leave his home? Everyone he loves and who loves him is right here."

Harry turned on her. "I love him. I would be with him."

"You might be interested in him now, but Oz and I have been like siblings our whole lives. Can you say that? Can you guarantee that you'll still be around in twenty years? Ten? How about even two? He's my family. You don't leave family."

"Fucking bitch." Harry fumed.

Ozzie gasped. "Oh my God—that was unnecessary."

"Don't you see what she's doing?" Harry grasped Ozzie's hand.

Bette sat cool, still.

Harry spat, "He is not your possession. You can't tell him what to do or how he's going to live his life."

Bette held up her hands in surrender, her lips forming a wounded pout. "I haven't done anything, Harry, except dream about the future. We're just talking. I didn't know that was a crime."

Harry's finger jabbed the air at Bette's face. "Deal with your shit. He's not a replacement."

The cool façade left Bette's face, replaced by furious contempt. The boat had floated close to shore, and Bette threw her feet over the edge, plunging knee-deep into the frigid water. I called after her as she trudged up to the beach and off into the woods.

Ozzie whipped around to Harry. "How dare you? I am not her plaything. And I'm not yours, either. I wish you'd give me credit for knowing my own mind." Ozzie followed Bette's lead and jumped ship, heading toward the house, cursing that his new trousers were ruined.

Harry slammed both his fists against the seat in frustration.

"What was—" But before I could finish, Harry scrambled after Ozzie.

I sat alone, the last rowboat passenger, reviewing the scene in my mind. Some part of Harry's analysis of Bette, of her motivation, seemed right—the part about planting ideas, placing people where she wanted them, intentionally manipulating them to make her world appear effortlessly glamorous. But I knew Bette loved Ozzie dearly, and I wanted to believe any manipulation arose solely because she couldn't bear to have Ozzie live so far away from her. Confused, I took hold of a set of oars and made my way to shore.

Hours later, I found Bette sitting in an Adirondack chair at the far edge of the property. I took two heavy Native American blankets and joined her. Bette didn't move, didn't seem to know I was there, as I wrapped a blanket around her and silently lowered myself into the chair next to her. We sat together, watching the sunset, Bette in her world and I in another.

That night, alone in our bedroom, I fell asleep to the rising and falling sounds of Harry and Ozzie arguing in the kitchen, while Bette's bed remained empty. She hadn't returned from her chair. I tried to quiet the anxiety rising in my chest. I knew this particular tension; these hushed angry voices were different from my parents', but the intensity told the same story. The thought of my new family falling apart hurt as much as the collapse of my original family, if not more.

I awoke the next morning, last again, to the sounds of

chopping, stirring, clanging, and laughter. Tiptoeing to the door, I was reminded of walking on eggshells after one of my parents' fights. But after observing the three together in the kitchen, I was no longer fearful my friends might divorce each other. Perry Como drifted from the record player, fire burned in the oversized fireplace, and the windows were partially covered by frost—all the while, Harry read the *Financial Times* weekend edition aloud, alternating between derision and praise for the latest in fashion, literature, and architecture. Bette and Ozzie, in matching kimonos, carefully built pyramids of vegetables in bloody mary cocktail glasses.

Ozzie stepped back to admire his work. "Hmm. No, it's off-balance. I think I need another pickle spear to the left of the celery stick."

"How about an olive? To offset the green bean?" Bette and Ozzie analyzed the drinks as they would fine works of art.

I sighed with relief. How it had been suddenly resolved, I had no clue. But even in the midst of gratitude for peace, Harry's accusation tugged at my mind: *"He's not a replacement."* It had been the final fatal blow between Harry and Bette, and though I didn't know specifically what he meant, I was certain his words were at the center of the many questions I had about Bette. Instinct said it wasn't the time to ask questions, frightened another fight might rear its monstrous head again with an unintentional misstep, so I kept quiet and avoided the unspoken minefield. We'd be safe that way.

We leisured another day away, our vision rolling in and out of focus as we consumed cocktails—each spiked with more vodka as the hours passed—and grazed on the last of the leftover turkey and pumpkin pie. The fire crackled. We read books, shared passages aloud, initiated impromptu sing-alongs, and lazily drifted between naps.

The late afternoon sun had begun to set when Ozzie's eyes lit up.

"Oh my gosh! I believe it's time!" he shrieked as he ran into his bedroom.

"Wonderful." Bette clasped her hand together, a large smile overtaking her face.

Harry put down his book with a playful *thud*. "You've got to be kidding me. We're doing it again this year?"

Ozzie emerged with his bed sheets. "Of course! It's brilliant every year! Why would we stop?"

"So, 'brilliant' is what we're calling it—is that it?"

"Yes, it is." Ozzie blew a kiss over his shoulder as Bette helped him pin the sheets across the doorframes of our two adjacent bedrooms, pulling back the edges.

The jovial energy was contagious, and I laughed, "What's going on?"

Ozzie threw his arms out wide, then announced, "Talent show!"

And suddenly the picture came into focus: Curtains, a theater, showtime.

Ozzie closed the sheet curtains and disappeared off-stage into his bedroom. "Gotta get ready!"

Bette went into her room, and I turned to Harry. "Get ready for what? What are we supposed to do? Or—"

Harry shrugged. "This isn't really my thing, so I play the part of audience. I sit and clap or boo and hiss or sleep, depending on the quality of the act." He winked at me and whispered. "It's all just good fun. No pressure."

Bette opened the curtain to our room and poked her

head out. "I have you covered. Don't worry."

Ozzie yelled muffled directions. "Places, everyone! The show is about to begin!"

I stood, then sat, then stood. Harry gently took my arm, pulling me back onto the couch. "Believe me, they'll let you know what you're to do. Until then, just enjoy the carnival."

When a recording of Barry Manilow singing "Copacabana" began to play, Harry clapped wildly, whistled, and stomped his feet. Bette raced out and snuggled next to me, giggling. "I can't miss this!"

Ozzie's hand shot out from behind the curtain and fumbled for the light switches on the wall. He flipped off the main light and hit the hall spotlight, creating a perfect halo in front of the curtain.

In a whirl of color and glitter, Ozzie sprang from the bedroom, adorned with a tall headpiece made of tropical fruit, a bikini top and, below, a slinky mermaid skirt made entirely of sequins and fringe. The three of us exclaimed in sudden understanding of why Ozzie had brought so much luggage.

He gyrated his hips in tempo to the song, as the pyramid on his head threatened to tumble off. His garnet red lips and darkly rouged cheeks jumped out from his milky-pale skin. He lip-synched the words, and his attempt at heels, teetering on the verge of an ankle break, left the group laughing madly. He hopped from lap to lap, digging sequins into our knees and poking our eyes with the flailing bananas that protruded from his hat.

Ozzie ended his act by twirling, quite out of control, into a wall, jazz hands flailing and rubber fruit spilling to the floor. We applauded and whooped and hollered until our hands were beet red and our voices cracked. Ozzie bowed deeply, and then curtsied as backup, blowing kisses to his fans, feigning tears as he exited. "You love me! You really love me!"

Bette ran behind the curtain. "I'm up!"

Minutes later, with Ozzie wedged between Harry and me on the couch, his headpiece reaffixed, a scratchy tune began to play. It reminded me of my mother's old 45 records she used to listen to on Sunday mornings. Both Harry's and Ozzie's eyes lit up.

"What is it?" I asked.

"*Sweet and Slow*," Harry said.

"Fats Waller! It's the first song Harry and I danced to. I can't believe she remembered!" Ozzie sighed affectionately.

Bette drifted out from behind the curtains. She wore a shimmering cream lace gown with bell sleeves that fell nearly to her knees. Her hair circled her face in perfect pin-curl waves, and her heavily glossed lips sparkled in the soft hall light. She was angelic.

We swayed in our seats and cooed while she danced daintily, softly gliding to and fro, waltzing with herself. She moved toward the couch and took my hand, pulling me to my feet.

"Take your partner," she instructed.

Harry stood, the consummate gentleman, and extended his hand to Ozzie, who happily accepted, holding his mermaid skirt to the side as he slid into Harry's arms.

The familiar tug of anxiety appeared like an apparition, a twin shadow that nudged me back into my solitary cage of comfort. "I don't know how to dance. I mean, slow-dance." The moment was magical, and I was sure I would ruin it.

"Here." Bette gently placed my left hand on her shoulder and interlaced our fingers in the other hand. "Now, don't think. Just move." She put her hand on my waist and, by pressing and pulling with her fingers and palm, almost imperceptibly, she directed the movements. Bette tilted her head and smiled. "There, see? You have it."

She pressed her cheek against mine, and as my fearful, introverted shadow disappeared, we danced. Ozzie mouthed *thank you* to Bette. I closed my eyes, my cheek warm against Bette's, and marveled as my body followed her lead. Bette's chest expanded and contracted with each breath, the lithe muscles rippling in her arms and back, all falling into rhythm with mine. Our small steps quickly synced, and we glided smoothly, as if skating on ice. I barely noticed when the song came to an end.

Bette slowly pulled away and curtseyed deeply while everyone clapped with reverence and appreciation. But, instead of retreating behind the curtain, Bette grabbed my hand and hurriedly led me to the bedroom.

"Intermission! The show resumes in thirty minutes!" she shouted and quickly closed the curtain. "Are you ready?" she asked with glittering eyes.

I laughed nervously. "Ready for what?"

"To be found."

"Huh?"

Bette stood tall with a defiant look in her eye. "I see you haven't been reading much Thoreau. '*Not until we are lost do we begin to understand ourselves.*'"

I nodded slowly. "That's good."

"You're lost."

"I am."

"You don't understand yourself yet."

"I don't."

"But I do. I understand you perfectly." Bette raised an eyebrow slyly. "So, do you trust me?" From behind her back, she pulled out a large pair of shears, snipping the air once, then twice for effect.

"Please don't cut off my ear for 'art's sake.'"

Bette jumped up. "And no peeking until I'm done!"

I took a deep breath and sat up as straight as I could in the chair. There was the sound of the first clip of metal and then a long section of brown hair fell to the floor. I gasped, "Oh my God."

"Shut your eyes. It's like viewing a sculpture—it's better to see the finished product than the mess it is halfway through."

In the cabin bedroom, eyes shut, I could barely make out the low voices of Oz and Harry and the clinking of glasses as they mixed drinks. Bette hummed to herself as she snipped and shaped. She pulled and tugged, checked the length, then cut again. I opened my eyes only once. Bette was inches from my face as she measured the front ends of hair against each other. She smiled and kissed the tip of my nose. When at last she finished, I began to stand.

"No, not yet. Not done." She pushed me back into the chair and grabbed her makeup bag. Step by step, she painted. Meticulously. I watched her eyes flutter, her head tilt as she weighed and balanced. She gave small commands: "Close your lids," "Look up," "Rub your lips together."

I sat motionless, armpits sweaty, aware of the mix of excitement and expectation in the air, as I tried to convince myself that that Bette was capable of miracles and that I was a lucky recipient of her handiwork.

Bette stepped back, a strange look spreading across her face. "Take your clothes off."

I didn't move. "What?"

"Your clothes. They just aren't—"

"I know. They're horrible. Sorry."

Bette looked shocked. "No, they're not horrible. You're just . . ." Frustrated, she tugged at my shirt and pulled the white top sheet off the bed. I undressed to my underwear and stood self-consciously. Carefully, artfully, Bette swathed me, draping the end of the sheet delicately over one arm, leaving the other bare.

Bette didn't squeal and didn't clap enthusiastically. She didn't even smile. With a look of wonder, she took my hand and led me to the full-length mirror.

I froze.

Staring at the woman in front of me, I moved my hand back and forth, just to be sure it was my own reflection I saw. Old Marin, who had arrived with long stringy hair tied in a topknot, clothed in frayed jeans and a hoodie, had vanished. Framed in the mirror stood a siren in white. My hair was sharp, cut to the jawline in a sweeping line. Bangs fringed my eyebrows, a dark auburn frame for my face. Bette had powdered my skin, giving it a dewy, luminous glow, and my eyes were heavily charcoaled, mysterious, even ominous. My lips had become plum pillows full of invitation.

Bette stepped close and whispered, "Show the boys?"

I wanted to sprint to them to share the transformation,

but was so terrified of ruining Bette's work that I moved slowly, one foot in front of the other, like a bride walking down the aisle.

Bette walked out first, and I heard her quick, short directives to sit, be quiet, put drinks down. She flipped the ceiling spotlight back on and ran to sit by Ozzie.

"My lovely friends, for tonight's final act, I present to you: Marin. Okay, come in now!" Bette's voice electrified the air as I presented myself, breath held, to my most trusted friends. I expected Ozzie to throw himself at my feet, wailing with delight, awestruck. I expected Harry to wink and smile, and clap slowly with appreciation.

But no one moved. All three stared with identical expressions of disbelief: Harry's mouth frozen in an O, Ozzie slack-jawed. Had I not seen Bette's creation with my own eyes, I would have shrunk away, deciding I looked like a monster.

But I knew. I knew.

And at that moment, I awakened.

I wasn't sure I'd be able to sleep. It felt like I'd won the lottery. And the Pulitzer. And been given a pony for my birthday. Energy surged through me in waves. I'd grudgingly removed the makeup at Bette's insistence (*"You don't want to break out."*) and slipped into bed. Staring at the ceiling, I smiled, reliving the night in my mind. I screeched a silent exultation and wiggled my toes like a child, the charged excitement trying desperately to free itself.

Bette came out of the bathroom and slid in next to me. I moved over just far enough to let our legs tangle, to let our arms wrap around one another. We'd spent many nights together, giggling like schoolgirls, kissing each other's foreheads and sharing intimate secrets so freely that our bodies had learned how to fit together like human puzzle pieces. We knew where to place weight so edges touched without invading, so skin melted onto each other's without offending.

I faced Bette, unable to stop smiling. Bette smiled back and moved a piece of hair from my eyes.

"I don't know how to thank you."

"Why would you thank me?"

"Are you kidding?" I cried out. "I never knew I could feel like this or look like this or . . . I don't know. I'm a whole new person."

"But you're not a new person," Bette said quietly. "You're who you have always been. I just tried to adjust your glasses so you could see it for yourself." She lightly tapped my collarbone. "You've always been beautiful. I just hope you believe it now."

I closed my eyes and breathed in deeply the smells of Bette's lotion, the blankets, the cabin. Peace rippled through me. "I do."

"Will you always be my sister?"

"Of course."

"Do you promise?"

"I promise." I paused then added, "I hope you believe it now."

Bette rolled to her side, taking my arm and wrapping it around her like a blanket. Her back was pressed into my breasts and stomach as I hugged her tightly. She laced her fingers through mine and whispered into the dark. "I do."

9

O pening the door to my boarding room was like opening a tomb; the stale wallpapered walls, the bed I hadn't slept in for over a week, my cheap, scratchy acrylic comforter. I grimaced in distaste at Cassie's desk, with its feather-puff-topped pens and pink fabric binders. Smoothing my newly cropped hair, I shut the door behind me.

Cassie's head popped up from her pillow, eyes wide, while the lump under the covers next to her continued its undisturbed sleep.

"Holy shit," she whispered.

I smiled demurely. "Do you like it?"

"Yes. It's so different. Wow. I mean, it's really pretty. It just doesn't look like you. It's so . . . you look like a model."

"Really?" I beamed, knowing full well how good I looked. Humming to myself, I went to my side of the small closet and began to unpack my things. It was a newfound routine: Immediately unpack and repack, to be ready for whatever new adventure Bette had planned. Next to my sparse wardrobe hung a foreign garment bag. I pulled it out and laid it out flat on the floor.

"What's this?"

Cassie leaned over the edge of the bed to see. "Some guy dropped it off. Said he was told to deliver it from the store."

I unzipped the long black canvas bag and gasped.

"Well? What is it? I've been dying to peek." Cassie propped herself up on her elbows.

I stared at the mystery outfit: A black corset, embellished with triple-stitched glass beads and intricate loops of hand-sewn embroidery. A pair of sleek, skintight black leather pants. Stiletto-heeled boots had been thrown into the bottom of the bag, almost as an afterthought, but they were as elaborately made as the other pieces, adorned with gritty, weathered zippers and buckles. The outfit was the perfect combination of urban chic and feminine fierceness.

Lifting each item, I ran my hands over the roughness of the beads and breathed in the heavy scent of leather. Cassie was silent as she watched me try on the outfit, her eyes seeming to shift between curiosity, envy, and distrust.

When she finally spoke, I couldn't help but catch the hint of jealously in her voice. "Is there a note or card? Who do you think sent it to you?"

My cell phone rang in response.

"It's all beautiful. I just don't know what to say. I mean—" I was breathless.

"Please say you'll wear them tonight." The smile in Bette's voice came through the line.

"Where are we going?" I was giddy we had plans because the truth was I would have worn the new outfit and shown off the new hair and makeup at the campus cafeteria if that had been my only choice.

"An opening." Bette paused. "But come to my place first. I'll send a car now."

I set the phone down and put on the boots, swaying back and forth around the room, trying to gain balance on the impossibly high heels.

"Bette?" Cassie asked softly.

"Yes. Can you believe how nice she is?"

Cassie didn't answer, only replied, "So you're going out again?"

"A new gallery opening. Downtown."

Cassie cocked her head, and an uneasy darkness came over her. "You haven't been to any classes lately."

I kept my back to Cassie as I slowly unbuckled the boots.

"Are you going to skip class again tomorrow?" she pressed.

I silently began repacking the duffle.

"You better be careful. You could lose your scholarship."

Fingering my fringe of bangs, I bit my lip. I'd been ignoring the nagging voice in the back of my mind mimicking Cassie's sentiments. I'd worked hard to get into the school, to get away from my old life and arrive at a new one. Logically, I knew one misstep—let alone the many I'd made since arriving—would hurl me straight back. Yet, I couldn't help but wonder what it was all for if I couldn't enjoy the fruits of my labor. Everything I'd dreamed of was finally in front of me. Friends, experiences, adventure. Eve with a basket of apples, ready to devour them all.

I surveyed the growing pile of clothing at the bottom of the closet, clothes I wouldn't allow myself to wear anymore. As I unpacked my bag from Thanksgiving, I added a few more items. My already-small stash of clothes was becoming more and more sparse as my consciousness and comparison to Bette's style grew. I pulled a black turtleneck from my dresser, a piece that had already reviewed a nod of approval from Bette.

Cassie groaned and rolled over in bed away from me. "Ugh. More black. Shocker."

Ignoring the slight, I regarded my reflection in the mirror, reapplying the heavy eyeliner and dark lipstick. I'd left the leather pants and boots on, already too attached to remove them. My hand ran over my new bob, smoothing down stray hairs. It looked right. It felt right. *I* felt right.

For the first time ever, I was something more, and the environment around me was amiss. *I belong. I just don't belong here. Maybe that's what's been wrong all along.* I wanted to believe it so badly that I couldn't see how deftly my thoughts were being swayed or how blind I'd become to the real world around me—or the price I was paying.

"See ya later, Cass." I grabbed my bag and walked out of the house. A limo sat idling at the curb. I smirked, flattered by Bette's gesture. The car had attracted attention and a handful of students passing on the sidewalk gawked and pointed and peered into the blacked-out windows. But as I made my way to the back door, the stretch became the lesser attraction. The outfit fit me like a glove, my legs seemingly poured into the leather, the boots appearing to have been applied with paint. The effect was deadly, and I witnessed students stopped in their tracks, boys scratching their heads like confused puppies.

The driver opened the door, and I slid in. I was a queen, a goddess, who had just allowed the commoners and mere mortals a glimpse. The car drove away, leaving behind onlookers with astonished stares and open mouths.

Bette called out as I was unpacking my overnight bag. I had been designated my own drawers in the bedroom. *Our bedroom.* Bette continually asked me to keep permanent clothes at her place so I wouldn't need to lug a bag to and fro, but I still couldn't bring myself to verbalize that I only had three acceptable outfits left on rotation. It didn't seem to be of much consequence anyway, as I found myself in Bette's clothes more and more often, while she dressed me like a doll.

"I have drinks ready when you're done."

"Just a second more," I answered over my shoulder. As had become a habit, I went to Bette's dresser and silently slid open the top drawer. I sifted through Bette's delicate lingerie, fingering the lace and satin pieces that made my heart skip a beat, looking for an exquisite bra Bette had worn a few days before, hoping to slip it on before the evening event.

At the back of the drawer, my hand grazed a piece of paper. Curiosity taking the driver's seat, I pulled out the hidden Manila envelope and opened the flap. Inside was a motel key, the plastic fob attached worn and faded. *Southside Inn.* I shook the envelope again and a small stack of photographs slid out. The first photo was of two girls, one's head thrown back in laughter, the other with a large, satisfied smile. They appeared to be at a magical moment of girlhood, walking the tightrope of innocent youth and blooming sexuality. Their still-wispy bodies were clothed in bikinis, hip bones sharp, chests flat.

I recognized the beach they stood on. It was the same I had been on, watching the sun set next to Bette over Thanksgiving weekend. The beach where she'd sat catatonic, lost in her own mind.

The inscription on the back of the photo was a perfect cursive script. *Bette and Olivia ~ Age 14 ~*

A few other photos showed the girls, still side by side, but increasingly different. One girl vibrant, her head consistently tossed to the side with an air of confidence. The other girl, shoulders slouched, barely making eye contact with the camera. One sister completely in the other's shadow.

I flipped through the photos once more before returning the envelope to its resting place.

Bette's head rounded the bedroom doorframe. "What are you doing?"

Startled, I gave the easiest smile I could muster. "Just finished."

Bette looked at me and then her dresser.

I cleared my throat. "You caught me. I can't stand the thought of wearing my old cotton bra tonight. The outfit deserves better."

Bette rolled her eyes playfully and opened the drawer, one finger pulling out a black bralette consisting of barely three strands of fabric. She handed it to me with a wink. "Here you go, silly. But you can change later. Come with me now." And just like that, the envelope was forgotten, her magic charm washing all my anxiety and worry away. This was the Bette I knew. This was the truth I knew. A friend, a sister.

A fire roared, and to the side of the fireplace, a small side table held two crystal liqueur glasses filled with a green liquid. Silver, antique-looking utensils sat on top of the glasses. Bette gestured to the couch as she moved to the table.

"What is all this?" I asked.

"Absinthe."

"And that?"

"An absinthe spoon. And a sugar cube." She placed the cube on the spoon then poured water over the top. I watched in awe as the sugar melted into the glass and mixed with the alcohol. It swirled, turning a murky, milky-green color. It reminded me of the Disney movies I'd watched as a child, when the wicked witch would mix her poisonous concoctions for the princess to drink. I half-expected a noxious phantom skull and crossbones to float over the cup.

Bette removed the spoons and handed a glass to me, raising hers in the air.

"To us." She took a delicate sip, sighed happily, and slid in next to me on the couch.

"To us." I gingerly brought the glass to my lips. Pleasantly surprised, I took another small sip. "It tastes like licorice!"

We sat by the fire, content in the silence while watching the flames dance, throwing off light as it grew and receded. I accepted when Bette offered to mix another round of drinks, my body growing increasingly calm and heavy, as if a thick cocoon was slowly winding its layers around me. Out of the corner of my eye, I saw Bette crush a pill into the drink.

"Another step in the absinth prep?" I teased.

Bette didn't answer, but instead waxed lovingly about the first time she had tried absinthe. "People say it gives you hallucinations, but I don't believe it. I just think it's *really* strong." She gave a smile—the same one that had made my blood run cold with Harry at the bonfire—and I froze as my chest constricted. Slowly letting out my breath, trying to regain mental footing, I looked again at Bette and the menacing smile was gone, replaced by her beautiful, languid laugh.

I laughed along. "There might be something to the hallucinations."

Bette continued. "I was in Amsterdam the summer after high school. I'd been staying with an uncle who lived there and met some fascinating young artists. I ended up moving in with them for almost a month." Bette's eyes moved across the ceiling while she told her story, reliving the memory. "We did everything every young person does in Amsterdam"—she smirked—"and I'd become quite used to accepting whatever was put in my hand without questioning it. This one particular night, we went to a fabulous apartment. Very bohemian. All the local artists were there. Musicians, painters, writers. I remember a jazz album was playing on a record player and an argument had erupted over the merits of Coltrane versus Gillespie."

I immediately thought of Bette telling Ozzie her idea for a Parisian salon. She'd presented the venture as something entirely new and unique, a creation of her forward thinking, her own vision. But it wasn't. It was an imitation. A cut and paste. Just as Harry had stated.

"A man handed me a glass of absinthe. And then another. He kissed me, and I followed him into a bedroom." Bette never talked about her sexual encounters, not even sexual interests, and her sudden candor was unsettling. "Except it turned out that he wasn't a 'he.'" She smiled fondly. "He was a woman, just very androgynous. It was quite a wonderful night. And all thanks to the absinthe, I'd say."

Bette stared right at me, daring a reaction. I looked away, flushed, and remained silent.

Whether it was the roaring fire only a few feet away or the blunt discussion of sexuality, my legs suddenly felt like they were ablaze under the leather pants. I vigorously rubbed my hands on my thighs, breaking up the heat and taking out my misplaced anxiety. Instantly, the material transformed, softer than before, smoother under my touch. Back and forth, my fingers methodically moved, and the rubbing turned to caressing. I forgot the heat and found myself fixated on the sensation of my skin grazing the leather. Euphoric sensory overload. Bette was right; the absinthe was strong.

I looked up to find Bette had inched closer. Her fingers fell in time with mine, running up and down my leg, our eyes both following the pattern in a trance.

"What did you put in my drink?"

Bette, her face close to mine, didn't confirm or deny

but put her finger to my lips.

And then her mouth was on mine.

I pulled away. "What are you doing?"

Bette kissed me again, harder, impassioned, pulling at my neckline, at the waist of my pants. There was a ferocity in her that ignited a spark. I didn't stop to think. I didn't analyze the situation. I didn't pause, wondering if I was making the right moves or if I was embarrassing myself. I didn't pause to consider what was happening at all. I let myself go, swept up in her breath, in her lips on my neck, in the softness of her breast.

I didn't think.

I allowed.

I reciprocated.

Entangled, Bette's hands flew over my body in a frenzy while our clothing was tossed to the floor.

Bette had pressed against me many times before, had kissed my cheeks and stroked my hair. But it had been altogether different. In an instant, the same skin and lips were foreign. New. My body was on fire, fueled with each touch. We acted as insatiable monsters, grabbing and pulling with violent need.

I slipped in and out of consciousness, each time emerging to a new place of flesh.

Exhausted, we slowed our movements, weak and shaking, relishing raw lips and bruised hip bones. Bette brought the glass of absinthe to my lips, and I took a contented sip, allowing it to run down my chin. Bette licked it off, resting her mouth on mine. I watched her blonde halo of hair as she laid her head on my chest.

Sex was something I hadn't had experience with. Boys. Thoughtless, dull, and fleeting. They were simply something I knew I was supposed to talk about and be interested in. And I had in theory. But it was suddenly apparent I'd been going through the motions before, feeling nothing.

I knew I'd never be able to share the night with anyone. *This is just the absinthe. This isn't going to happen again.* Like so much of my new life, it would remain a secret, one more step away from my old life and family. Looking down, I observed a peaceful Bette, her softness radiating through my skin. Softness that I coveted for myself.

Like a lazy cat, Bette pushed herself up with both arms, back arching and stretched toward the ceiling. She sighed dreamily as she lowered herself back onto my stomach and looked at me, ice-blue eyes twinkling mischievously. "Time to get dressed. We have a big night ahead."

The sound system in the limo blared EDM, and Bette's eyes were already a mix of wild anticipation and intoxicated chaos, but her movements were slow and methodical. She was a tsunami simmering under a glass-smooth surface. Wordlessly, she pulled out a mirror from her purse, reapplied her lipstick, then sealed it with a kiss. She poured a sloppy serving of vodka into a tumbler and sipped. Only then did she really look at me, taking in the makeover from head to toe. My leather pants had somehow made it back on, and the corset was pulled tight, pushing my breasts up to enormous heights.

"Perfection."

"Are Oz and Harry meeting us there?"

Bette said nothing, ignoring my question.

By the time the car pulled up in front of the gallery, the world had begun to change colors. Neon lasers, flashes of star beams, streaks of ice. Flash bulbs popped, opening the late-night sky and spotlighting the artists, reviewers, and performers attending the opening. A thick red velvet rope kept back large groups on either side of the sidewalk leading to the doorway. A lanky giant of a man stood next to a giraffe-sized girl, both holding clipboards loosely in their hands, yet never actually looking at them. They seemed to know by sight who to wave through and who to reject.

The driver opened the Mercedes door and, like a swan, Bette emerged from the car. She wore a barely-there white mini dress adorned with so many crystals and sequins that her body seemed to glow. I followed, and we walked slowly forward, hand in hand, black and white, devil and angel. The cameras splashed light. Both fashionable sentries nodded as we strode past, no hesitation in our gait, already confident of their approval.

Inside, the venue exploded. Music pounded with a thumping, fiery bass. A dizzying kaleidoscope of colors spun from overhead, threatening vertigo with every swivel of the light machine. Overwhelmed and intoxicated, I swayed in the swarm of people buzzing with energy. One group would part slightly, only to envelop another. With every turn, there were camera-ready smiles, flirtatious glances, and explosive laughter.

"Who is the artist?" I yelled over the music.

"Simon Duchamp."

I quickly glanced at a wall of oversized photographs. New Orleans neighborhoods and their residents. The French Quarter. Whites, Blacks, Haitians, French Creoles. Wrinkles on their faces and a glint in their eyes. Real.

Bette greeted a few people, introducing me as her sister. She paraded me from artist to writer to musician, and for the first time in my life, I was more than happy to be the center of attention. I was invincible in my new skin.

Moments later, a thick girl with stick-straight hair grabbed Bette by the elbow. She could have been anybody's brash college sorority sister, and her heavy Southern drawl was as shocking as her hot pink shift dress.

"Oh my God! Bette! Do you remember me? Poppy. Poppy Montgomery." She slurred her words, and her bright blue cocktail sloshed over the side of the glass, running down her tanned wrist into her heavy gold charm bracelet. Bette straightened her shoulders and a familiar iciness washed over her face.

"Don't you remember? We met last year? At Simon's last showing?" Poppy's jaw hung low, incredulous that Bette didn't seem to recognize her. I knew Bette's game. She recognized this girl, but was simply letting her dangle for dramatic effect. "We all went out afterwards? Then ended up at Simon's friend's house? Then your place?"

I bristled. Of course, Bette had friends before we'd met, but a pang of jealousy jolted me, nonetheless. Had this girl also lazed on the couch? Worn Bette's clothes? Slept in her bed? I had to stop obsessing. We had shared an intimate moment, that's all. We were not suddenly tied to each other, any more than we had been before the night began, and I had no right to analyze Bette's past. I tried to play it cool, stepping closer to Bette.

A smile edged across Bette's mouth. "I do remember that night. Wow, I had almost forgotten all about it. Talk about wild."

As calm as I attempted to be, I couldn't stand to see the gratification on Poppy's face for a second more, and didn't appreciate being Bette's sidekick without even the courtesy of an introduction. Poppy began talking again, moving closer to Bette. I interjected. "I'm going to get a drink. Want one?"

Bette smiled innocently. "Go ahead. I'm going to catch up with Poppy."

I turned on my heel, refusing to react to the rebuff.

I wandered around the gallery, trying not to pick at my nails, feeling vulnerable and misplaced without Bette at my side.

I stopped to take in a photograph of a young Haitian girl, full-lipped and slightly agitated. Stepping backward to move out of the way of passing partiers, I bumped into a handsome, gray-haired man. He smiled, and his eyes crinkled so warmly he temporarily took my breath away. He gestured toward the portrait.

"It took a lot of prodding to convince her."

Confused, I looked at the man. He was still staring at the photo, a smile of remembrance on his face.

"Most teenagers love having their photo taken. They clamor to be chosen. And I usually have to shoo them on afterward. Can't get enough of seeing themselves. But this girl was different."

"You took this photograph?"

The gentleman nodded and turned. "If I was smart, I'd have waited until you offered up some opinion of the work. I suppose I'd rather you know it was mine and lie and say you liked it." He chuckled, holding out his hand. "I'm Simon."

Shaking his hand, I blushed. "I'm Marin. And I would have said how much I like the photo."

I looked at the girl's image again. "She's just being her. I like that."

"Plainness worth studying." Simon chewed on the thought. "I'm going to take that as quite the compliment."

"I really don't know anything about art, but I hope you do know it was a compliment." I shifted, nervous I might have inadvertently insulted him. My earlier confidence was quickly losing its grip on me. *Why did you even open your mouth? Stupid.*

"Oh, I do. And you know more than you think you do." He paused. "I saw you once."

My heart skipped.

He continued. "At the Zette House opening. Your hair was longer, though. And you weren't quite so—" He hesitated. "Your edges were softer."

I fingered the tips of my bob, astounded such an important artist would remember me. Yet, there was nothing sexual or flirtatious in his demeanor. I couldn't be sure, but he sounded downcast, almost melancholy.

"In fact, I remember thinking, 'Now, there's an unusual creature.'"

He began to say something else when a small cluster of admirers swallowed him up, shaking his hand and asking him about his work. I slowly backed away, waving. He waved back while graciously answering the many questions from his group of fans.

I bobbed and weaved through the crowd until I found Bette.

"I just met Simon Duchamp! The artist. From this show!" I exclaimed, breathless.

Bette waved off the excitement with one hand while she accepted a champagne flute from a waiter. "Simon is a sweetheart. I've known him for years."

"He said he remembered me from Zette House."

Bette rolled her eyes. "That sounds like something he'd say."

The old feeling was seeping back in. I was dangling off a precipice, close to falling into the realm of outcast.

I tried to lighten the mood and winked playfully. "Feeling jealous?"

Bette turned and bore her eyes in before walking away. "Why would I ever be jealous of you?"

I pulled my corset down and smoothed my hair, trying not to cry. What had happened from the afternoon to now? Maybe it was a fleeting moment, a drunken transgression, but we had shared *something*. Even if it had been nothing to Bette, our friendship meant the world to me, and I needed to know why I was suddenly being thrown aside like a used piece of trash.

Bette turned and began speaking to a young man. He put his hand on her waist then pulled her closer to his chest. Bette glanced at me and winked. He ran his finger down her side, just as I had hours before. She stepped closer to him, pressing her pelvis against his, giving her best come-hither smile.

I couldn't stand to watch the scene any longer. I turned as hot tears freefell down my cheeks. Suddenly, the strobe lights were too bright, and the hot air suffocating as Harry's words echoed: *She doesn't feel the same about you. As you do about her.* He had been right all along. And if he was right about that, what else was he right about?

10

Sheltered in the confines of the boarding house, I needed time to clear my head and sort through everything that had happened. I pushed my physical encounter with Bette aside. We had been drunk on absinthe and whatever pill she had put in my drink. It had been a recipe for disaster, no matter what. But Bette's hot and cold demeanor was something I could no longer hold space for. I rehearsed a litany of outrages, determined to stand my ground.

However, I knew myself.

Please meet at Les Mots? I'm horrid. When Bette finally reached out, I caved.

I had wanted a best friend and had gained so much more. I didn't want to admit out loud how much I enjoyed being dressed up, made up, and taken out. An addiction of sorts was forming.

Maybe I wasn't her court "favorite" anymore, but I didn't want to risk losing it all.

Bette was already at the café when I arrived, slumped into a velvet couch and looking haggard. She cried. "I know you're upset with me."

I gathered all my courage. "Bette, you really hurt my feelings."

"Please, you have to tell me what I did."

"Are you kidding me? First of all, you blew me off in front of that girl—"

"Poppy? She's just this flake I've known forever. She's not—"

"Then I was so excited to meet Simon and you acted like it was nothing."

Bette rolled her eyes. "He's just an artist—"

Tears threatened to return. "And then, that . . . that *guy*, who you were throwing yourself at—"

Bette waved me off. "I don't even know who that was."

"That's actually worse! Bette, I can't be thrown aside whenever you feel you're not the center of attention."

Bette pulled back, her eyes suddenly wet with tears. "Thrown to the side? Marin, you are my world."

"You are your own world," I said, my raised voice seeming to surprise her. Harry's assessment crept in and took hold. "You cannot treat me as a possession. I'm your friend because I want to be your friend, not because you *allow* me to be. My life is not governed by your whims. But you can't seem to appreciate that, and I deserve a friend who does."

I'd felt powerful, telling Bette the truth, and allowing the hurt to come pouring out. Maybe it was for the best that we ended our friendship. The more the reel played in my mind, the more I was embarrassed by our escapade in her living room. My imagination played out over and over with what would happen if Bette told Ozzie and Harry. Or my family. I secretly wished it had never happened. A part of me wanted to walk away from Bette right then and there. The farther away I could distance myself, the better.

I pulled off the scarf, the same scarf she had given me as a gift, and began to fiddle with the saltshaker. I focused on turning it over and over, catching the falling granules while not making eye contact.

"Do you remember the first time we met at the library? I didn't know anything. I mean, nothing. I didn't know about art or philosophy, about clothes or food. I didn't know restaurants or cocktails or galleries or classical music. I didn't know about architecture or design or literature. I didn't even know how to talk to someone. Not without sweating, anyway. I'd never experienced anything outside of my hometown. I thought if I came to a school where I was forced to find my own way, make my own decisions, I'd stumble onto something I could call my own. But I didn't. I just did the same thing I've done my entire life: I followed. Then I met you. And it seemed so great. But you know what? I just followed you, too. And I didn't even realize it."

Bette choked. "But it *is* great. I love you."

I froze, stopped cold in the denseness of the moment as once again Harry's words echoed in my head. *Are you in love with her?*

Bette continued to cry. "Please. Please, you have to forgive me." She held my face, kissed my cheeks, and frantically stroked my hair. "You have to. You have to."

I was dumbfounded at the shift in power, unsure if I should trust her apologies or if it was a trap to pin me to the ground even harder than before.

In the end, I held Bette. Like so many times before, we laced our fingers together. We sat silently, understanding for the first time both the strength and the weight of the friendship. How easily we could be wholly perfect together or destroy each other completely.

Both scared me.

We fell all too easily back into our nightly pattern of drinks and outings. But we had changed since the fight. Bette became more careful with me. Not more gentle or agreeable, but more guarded and watchful. If anything, Bette pushed to party more, to attend more functions to expand our circle of friends. She was pushing my limits. And I began to watch Bette, too. We were in the middle of a dangerous new waltz, circling each other while holding on tightly.

We rarely saw Ozzie and Harry. Whenever I asked Bette, she would either say they had other plans or would ignore the question completely. Any text to Ozzie would result in a reply with different variations of *Thanks for checking in, sweetie. Harry has assignments to finish/a test to study for, then we're going to the cabin this weekend/going to a party at Harry's parents' house/visiting my idiot brother at school.* Sometimes I forgot that we were all still college students. I'd sent Harry messages too, but he never replied.

There was no need to dwell too long on their absence. The extremely extroverted Southerner, Poppy Montgomery, became a permanent fixture at our sides. She was like a yipping dog who seemed to barely catch her breath between exclaiming one opinion or another to everyone within earshot. According to Poppy, even though she and Bette had met only the year before, their mothers, as budding national socialites, had been friendly from a young age. Poppy's father, Buckley, was originally from Chicago, while her mother, Georgia, or Gigi to her friends, was a die-hard Texan. Poppy's family was raised in Dallas and had relocated to downtown Chicago four years earlier. Only a few months after the move, Poppy's father succumbed to cancer, a battle he'd kept hidden from his family until the very end.

"I finally said to her, like, 'Seriously! Stop bringing dresses into the fitting room.' I totally don't even like teal. I just happened to grab one stupid skirt that had a streak of teal down the side and this girl is all, 'Oh! That's this season's color! Blah blah, teal this, teal that.' Whatever. Like teal would ever be a season's color." Poppy paused a moment to inhale a long line of cocaine from the glossy cover of a fashion magazine. "I fucking hate teal."

We were in the back of a limo on the way to Poppy's mother's Lake Shore Drive penthouse. Gigi was hosting a large fundraiser and insisted we attend. Actually, she'd insisted that Poppy attend, and Poppy insisted that Bette go with her. Bette, as usual, had refused to step out in public without me at her side. However, I sensed that Poppy was less than thrilled to have me along, breaking up what, in Poppy's mind, could have been the perfect pair of best friends. She rarely missed the chance to drop a name, bring up an event, or pass along a piece of gossip that only she and Bette could appreciate. She used their mutual understanding of upper-class wealth to exclude me, driving home the point that no matter how hard I tried, I was an outsider.

Poppy carefully passed the magazine to Bette, who swiftly separated a line from the massive white pile with a credit card and inhaled through a snipped-off soda straw. I saw it was coming around and put up my palm. "No thanks."

Bette's expression didn't change, nor did she take back the magazine. She just stared at me with a dare in her eye. It was a look she was using more and more often. As she held it out, I looked to her, then to Poppy, who raised her eyebrows smugly. Unbelievably, I was intimidated by the loud-mouthed girl who moved like an ox, but my possessiveness for Bette was still so overwhelming, I was ready to fight for best friend status, even though I couldn't say with certainty that's who I was anymore.

Setting down my cocktail, I smoothly slid shoulder-to-shoulder with Bette, picked up the straw and bent over the magazine, inhaling deeply. I blinked once, twice, my sinuses growing instantly cold, and a quiver, just under my skin, rippled throughout my entire body. I straightened my back, stretched out my arms, and smiled at Bette. Unimpressed, Poppy took back the magazine and began to separate another line for herself. I quickly took a large drink of vodka in hopes of washing away the acidic taste running down the back of my throat.

"How much further?" I asked.

"Why? You got some other big plans to run to?" Poppy barked. She laughed with a squawk that reminded me of an irritated parrot. Bette deftly wiped the side of my nose and winked. "Another thirty. Forty-five maybe."

The magazine passed faster and faster between us. With every mile, our speech became more exuberant, our behavior more manic. Heart pounding in my throat, I was unable to stop my knee from bobbing up and down. I placed my head on Bette's lap, taking deep breaths, trying to slow my nervous system, which was running like a freight train powered by jet fuel. Bette stroked my hair rhythmically while Poppy rambled on.

"So, how about chartering a sailboat during spring break this year? Wouldn't that just be the *coolest*?!"

My senses were overwhelmed, teeth chattering, nose running, and body convulsing in sporadic waves of shivers. Yet, the feeling was euphoric. I laced one hand under Bette's thigh and one over, fastening myself tightly to her lap, anchoring myself so I wouldn't drown. Bette squeezed her legs together, hugging my hands, then seamlessly draped one of her arms over my rib cage, resting her hand on my breast.

"We could go to the Med. I mean, everybody, like *everybody,* says Ibiza is the shit, but Ibiza is *lame!*" Poppy droned on, oblivious that she was speaking solely to herself.

Bette's finger ran over my nipple. I inhaled shakily.

Time seemed to stop as the drugs stole any sense of reality. My fingers dug into the soft flesh of Bette's thigh while she teased me with her featherweight touch. I could have stayed in that moment forever.

But Poppy's frenzied shriek ripped us from our trance: "We're here!" She took another line of coke, then passed it for one last round.

Poppy threw open her door and recklessly launched herself onto the traffic-laden street. Our driver scampered after her, leading her safely from the middle of the road as cars whizzed past, their horns blaring. Bette and I remained in the car in a dazed stupor.

Without thinking, we did the last line of cocaine, carefully smoothed our hair and skirts and stumbled out to meet Poppy near the building's doorman. His eyes bore into us, disapproving of our obviously intoxicated state. For a fleeting, paranoid moment, I sensed he could see right into our drug-saturated souls.

In the elevator, Bette linked pinkies with me; my stomach flipped. Poppy had yet to stop talking, bouncing from one subject to the next without slowing down as she primped and fussed with her hair in the mirrored paneling of the elevator. She wiped her nose vigorously a few times and then shuddered from head to toe, as if she could shake off the drugs and alcohol. She might have pulled it off had she been able to walk without teetering.

"Let's go!" she yelled, too loudly, into my ear as the elevator doors opened to reveal a grand black marble foyer.

I followed Bette's lead and walked slowly, taking measured steps, trying in vain to focus my eyes. As the scene adjusted itself, I shrank. This was no gallery opening, no club. There was no house music or strobe lights or gangly models in black cat suits. And there was nowhere for me to hide.

I found myself face to face with Chanel suits, sleek Armani gowns, pearls the size of jawbreakers, and diamond rings that could easily be used as weapons. Lilies lined the hallways and sat on corner tables, heavily scenting the air. Men in crisp tuxedos offered hors d'oeuvres off silver trays and pricey champagne in crystal flutes with paper-thin stems. The male guests were older than middle-aged, yet dressed in expensive, modern suits with peaked lapels and pocket squares. A string quartet played lilting classical pieces from a nook just to the right of the party.

Bette, sensing my anxiety, directed a firm smile my way. "You're fine. Just try to say as little as possible."

Thankfully, Poppy drew all the attention away from the two of us. "Mama!" she barked into a group of women of indeterminate age. One head lifted slightly and raised an eyebrow. She floated toward Poppy, arms open as if she were royalty. I held my breath, willing no noise to escape, all the while wishing we had more cocaine, certain it would help the situation.

"My darlin' Poppy." The woman's voice dripped like sugary sap, though her tightly pulled face seemed unable to exhibit any expression of recognition. Her drawl was just as thick as Poppy's, but she had to fight to lift her weightless voice above a murmur. "I am so happy you could come and bring your adorable friends." She squinted her eyes, attempting a smile, and then tilted her head as if she were addressing an infant.

Poppy gestured toward the woman while scanning the room. "This is my mama, Gigi."

Bette tenderly took one of Gigi's excessively bejeweled hands and matched her saccharine voice. "Thank you so much for hosting us. It was incredibly gracious of you. Your home is divine. My mother, Eleanor, sends her love."

I began to giggle at Bette's affected delivery until I realized that Gigi was captivated. Gathering myself, still peering from one open eye to focus, I took Gigi's other hand. "Mrs. Montgomery."

What came out of my mouth was a nonsensical mix of

accents—upper-class English and deep Southern drawl. I couldn't contain my voice, so I simply let the words flow, hoping there'd never be cause to speak to Gigi again. Bette gave a puzzled squint then giggled herself, shaking her head. I plowed ahead.

"I really love your"—my eyes darted across the room—"piano." The drugs had commandeered both my body and brain.

Gigi smiled brightly. "Well, aren't you the sweetest thing. Thank you. I do love a Fazioli Brunei."

"Ah, yes, as do I," I answered with a knowing nod of my head.

"Do you play, dear?"

"Ah, no." I shook my head solemnly. We nodded and continued to look at each other with nothing left to say, Gigi's face frozen by Botox and mine frozen by drugs

We stood, awkwardly, until a tuxedoed waiter arrived with a tray of champagne. We simultaneously offered thanks and shared well-mannered toasts to the evening. Gigi drifted away to greet other guests and Poppy stumbled off, presumably to a bathroom with a clean, flat surface. Bette and I threw back our champagne in gulps.

"I'm going to find Poppy. You come in about two minutes." Bette's pupils were dilated, her eyes bloodshot, swimming with intoxication. I knew there would be no slowing down on the night's partying. Not that I minded—instead, I relished the escape from my self-consciousness. Fueled by liquor and cocaine, I had no intention of slowing down that night either. Just as I was about to go track down Bette and Poppy, a pair of eyes locked with mine.

Simon Duchamp winked and smiled. Despite my state of mind, I was elated to see him again. Per usual, he stood in the middle of a large group, all pawing and purring, clamoring for his undivided attention. Simon waved me over and all heads followed, their eyes sizing me up. I lowered my head, avoiding their scrutiny.

Simon wrapped his arms around me in a bear hug. "So nice to see that friendly smile again."

I melted in his embrace. "I didn't know you were going to be here."

"Gigi is an old friend of mine, so I've come to support her latest endeavor."

"And what is that, exactly?" I hiccupped while Simon gave me a curious glance.

A young man, with a striking, angular face and chiseled athletic body turned around. His dark brown eyes sparkled. "That would be me." His Russian accent was thick and deep.

My mouth opened, then closed. Then opened again. Then closed again.

The young man laughed and turned to Simon. "She is like fish!"

I shrank as Simon laughed, then wrapped his arm protectively around me.

"Marin, this is Sergei Karsavina. Sergei is a visiting artist from Moscow," he explained, "and hasn't quite learned how to be a gracious guest." Simon raised his eyebrows in a gentle reprimand. "Sergei, this is Marin. She is beautiful but delicate. You must be gentle."

I stopped at this, both touched and surprised.

Sergei stepped forward before I could think further. "You come to my showing?" Sergei took my hand and began to walk me away from the crowd.

Over my shoulder, I looked uneasily at Simon. "Go on. I'll keep the wolves at bay." He turned cheerfully to the aging group of leeches in pearls and launched into a story, drawing their attention away.

Stopping at small side table crowded with flowers and empty champagne glasses, Sergei lifted a finger toward one of the waiters, who hurriedly brought two fresh glasses. Sergei sipped slowly and regarded me over the rim. "You are very beautiful woman."

My cheeks burned. "Oh, no. No. I'm not, really." I took a large sip of champagne, then another, and stammered on. "It's, um, it's makeup. And this new haircut." I fidgeted with my bangs, looking everywhere to avoid his eyes. When Sergei said nothing, I dared to glance up at him.

His features softened and he grinned like a little boy. "I like you! You are very different." He sighed loudly, his mind searching. "What is the word I look for?" He paused and then set his gaze directly on me again. "You are—rare." He lowered his voice and leaned in. "Yes. Rare." He continued to stare as I shifted my feet.

"I'm not." I swayed on unsteady feet.

Sergei rolled his eyes, smiling brightly. "See? I tell you, you are rare. You say not rare. That is why you are rare!" He gestured around the room. "All these people, they say what I say, do what I do. I say, 'I like,' they say 'Oh! I like, too!' See? Not rare. Not extra special."

Charmed by his accent, I mimicked him. "So now I'm rare and extra special?" My laugh trailed off as he stepped in again, closer.

"Yes. You are."

I swallowed hard as his hand traced my arm from shoulder to wrist. The drugs amplified every nerve ending, and I shivered.

He took my hand. "Please say you will come to my showing."

"I think I have to go now."

"Again!" he exclaimed. "So honest. Come, I must get my coat." He led me by the waist, ignoring the other guests and their attempts to capture his attention. Hands reached out for him, but he walked past like a king brushing off peasants. Only when Gigi's wispy voice floated above the rest of the hum did he pause.

"My darlin' Sergei, how are you? Are you comfortable? Do you need anything?"

Sergei might have withheld his good manners from other guests, but he knew where his bread was buttered. A large smile broke across his face as he took Gigi's hand, pressing his soft lips against its dry surface.

"I am in heaven and you have put me here. Thank you, Angel."

Gigi blushed, tittered, and waved him off. "Dear boy, you are a peach!" Gigi's watery eyes looked past him. "Have you seen Simon recently?"

"Yes!" Sergei exclaimed. "He was looking for you. By front room."

A flicker of excitement crossed Gigi's face. "I'd better go see what he needs." She left quickly, without looking back.

Sergei grinned and took my hand. We wove through a back hallway, past a bustling and chaotic catering kitchen, and finally entered a side wing. Silently, we crossed through a large siting room into a massive bedroom filled with lacquered antique dressers, gilded mirrors, and heavy chintz draperies.

I turned to Sergei. "I don't see any coats."

"This very strange. I think all coats has been taken." he said, tapping his lip with his finger, feigning confusion.

I raised an eyebrow playfully. "Oh my! Someone stole the coats?"

"Yes!" he nodded enthusiastically.

"All the coats?" I asked, attempting to match his false dramatic flair.

"Exactly! All the coats stolen. Who would do such terrible crime? Hold me, I'm scared!" He threw his arms around me, and we toppled onto the bed, laughing.

Sergei lay on top of me, kissing me gently. A nibble here, a taste there. His hands slowly ran down my side, reaching my hip. Then in a rush, he clenched my thighs and kissed me hard. My heart beat out of my chest. Animal instincts fired deep in me, and in that moment, I wanted nothing more than all of Sergei. But instead, I paused, quickly looking around the room, "Sergei. we shouldn't—"

Sergei did not chide or make light. He did not move as my pulse raced under the weight of his body. "What do you want?"

I looked into his eyes and fingered the muscles of his back. I knew. The pent-up energy that had begun in the car came screaming out of me. I ripped at his shirt, his pants, biting his lip as he bit back. His hands slid up under my skirt, grabbing my flesh, pulling me closer. I gasped and moaned, unable to contain myself, as he kissed my stomach, running his tongue lower and lower down my abdomen.

I screamed internally with pleasure. My back arched, overtaken, and I turned, burying my face in the pillow, nails digging into Sergei's shoulders.

My eyes opened for an instant, and I went cold.

Bette. Her left shoulder leaning on the doorjamb. Watching.

I bucked without thinking, pushing Sergei off. But when I looked back to the doorway, Bette was gone.

"What?" Sergei asked, panting.

"I, it's, um," I gestured to the door, stammering.

Sergei smiled mischievously. "You afraid someone see? So, let them see." He tapped my chin with a finger. "I'm not hiding anything."

"It was Bette."

"Who is Bette?"

"My friend. She was standing there. Just now. Watching."

Sergei smiled again. "Maybe she is jealous, no?" I looked at him, his hair rumpled, his muscles tense with desire, an extraordinary mix of boyish charm and coarse sexuality.

"Maybe," I whispered.

"If she is not, she should be," he breathed, gently biting my inner thigh.

Sergei stayed stock still, stunning, his muscles taut, ready to pounce. *Yes, she should be,* I thought as I gave myself to him, allowing his affection to wash over and through me, basking in a moment that was all mine.

We emerged, hair back in place, clothing smoothed, as people were beginning their goodbyes. I looked for Bette in the remaining crowd, but could find only Poppy. She obviously had continued her party, with pupils the size of platters as she tipped from side to side.

"Oh God! She left like forever ago," Poppy said, spittle spraying from her lips as she spoke. "Want to stay over with me?" She raised her voice for effect, directing her words toward a group of finely coiffed women. "My bitch of a mom won't let me take the car home!"

Gigi was out of view, but her faint whisper came through the crowd. "Darlin' Poppy, whatever will I do with you?"

"No, thanks. I have class tomorrow," I lied, hugging Poppy. I hadn't been to any of my classes in weeks and was certain I wouldn't be able to power through the inevitable hangover the next morning for calculus. I slid out quickly and caught a cab.

"Where did you go?" I tried to sound nonchalant as Bette answered the call.

"I couldn't find you, so I thought I'd take off. The party was getting so tedious." She paused. "Don't you think?"

I held my breath, unsure how to answer. Bette was lying, and she knew it. We both knew it.

"Yes," I agreed, matching her bored tone, "completely tedious." I paused. "I'm in a cab. Should I come to you?" The question was odd and unnatural on my lips, as I'd practically been living with Bette, only going to my place occasionally for an odd piece of clothing or personal item.

"I'm really tired. I think I'll just go to bed." It wasn't a direct answer, but it was an answer.

I asked the driver to head north, toward campus.

Later that night, I thrashed and writhed in my lumpy twin-sized bed, the sheets twisting around my torso like a straitjacket. The mix of drugs and anxiety was overpowering, despite the Xanax I'd taken to offset the cocaine high. Bette had given me a bottle of the sedatives after I'd complained of trouble sleeping, cold sweats, and general twitchiness. I swerved among vibrant dreams—radical shifts from contented highs to agonizing lows. They involved my family, smiling and happy one moment, miserable and despondent the next. Bette, warm and embracing; Sarah, laughing and dancing down the corridors of a high school.

But then the dreams melted into nightmares: My father screaming profanities, Bette pushing me down a flight of stairs, finding myself walking, naked and lost, down the streets of Chicago. A fourteen-year-old Olivia, drowning, screaming out my name to save her. I woke repeatedly, panting and sweating, terrified, until I remembered where I was.

My eyes flickered open a few times, foggy and crusted, and sporadically caught glimpses of Cassie coming back from class. I heard her murmuring, then leaving again, slamming the door. I ignored messages from my mother and Ty asking where I was, if I was all right, to please call back. But I was simply too wasted, physically and mentally, to successfully navigate around their treacherous questions. I had lied outright so many times during the semester, omitted so many truths and failed to disclose so many bad acts that I needed all my faculties just to carry on a seemingly ordinary conversation with them.

Two days passed with no word from Bette or Sergei, so I decided to go to class.

That, too, was a mistake.

I walked out of a classic literature lecture after

realizing the class was almost finished with Thoreau's *Walden*. I couldn't remember when it had been assigned, hadn't read a single page of it, and so had absolutely no idea what the discussion meant. My only Thoreau reference was Bette's comment before her makeover of me at Thanksgiving. Unenthusiastically, I tried attending my other classes and was met with the same disastrous outcomes. The TA for my biology lab wouldn't let me join in with them. Neither he nor the other students even knew my name.

I milled about the cafeteria and nibbled on dry cereal while watching the students come and go. In my new world, they were aliens, dressed in jeans and purple soccer shorts, mascot-emblazoned T-shirts, and sweatshirts with big embroidered Greek letters.

A group of backward-cap-wearing boys flirted relentlessly with two girls, their eyes lined with thick blue shadow, wearing oversized sweatshirts and yoga pants, feet encased in ridiculous lamb's wool moccasin boots. They laughed vapidly as the young men showed off, playfully throwing dinner rolls at each other.

It was a typical college scene, but all I saw was provincial, unpolished, uncultured Neanderthals. Red plastic cups, kegs of beer, boys vomiting on sidewalks, and girls weeping in dirty bathrooms. I overheard conversational threads about apathetic boyfriends, sex with hot girlfriends, the cool band playing that weekend, and the anticipation of getting wasted.

I spied Cassie and Chad, along with a boy whose name I couldn't remember. He hadn't been worth remembering. Cassie, Chad, the boy, the other students—they all blended together into one humdrum whole. Sheep.

Very, very bland sheep.

And none of them saw me.

Slumped in an orange plastic chair at a cafeteria table, I checked my phone every few minutes, hoping for some word from Bette. I tried to brush away the thoughts that I was still seeking Bette's approval, that Bette's opinions were the backbone of my own. But as I pressed refresh over and over on my phone, I knew I was lying to myself. Our relationship had become a toxic cocktail that I couldn't stop drinking.

It was an addiction that had taken over my life and clouded all my thoughts save one. And that thought was becoming crystal clear: I was going to flunk out.

My phone pinged: *Les Mots? 6ish?*

It had been days since I'd heard from Bette. Dread and elation collided at once. The sane side of my brain said winter break was approaching, stay put, continue sorting out the mess I'd created and find a way to salvage my scholastic life. Unfortunately, the obsessed side of my brain won, and I sprinted all the way to my room, eager to wash off the stench of the cafeteria.

Walking to the café, I pulled my winter coat tight around my chest as the wind picked up. I had worn a thin black top of Bette's. Her favorite. Once inside the dimly lit Les Mots, I scanned the patrons. Then froze.

Knee to knee, nose to nose, sat Bette and Sergei, sunk deeply into the velvet couch, engrossed in whispered conversation. My jaw hung slack, and my forehead screwed together in confusion.

Sergei noticed me first and jumped to his feet, his face glowing with enthusiastic recognition. Bette glanced up with the same chilly nonchalance she used to employ when we first met. I looked away quickly, down at my feet, then at a waiter in a corner of the café. Anywhere but the cold abyss of Bette's eyes. When I dared to steal another glance, the callousness had vanished, and Bette clapped her hands together as if celebrating. I had just witnessed two separate souls battling over the occupation of Bette's physical body, and this time, the kind soul was the temporary victor.

"Are you surprised?" Bette cheered.

Sergei grabbed my hand and pulled me onto the couch between them. "Bette called me, and I came to see you."

I took a deep breath. "I didn't know you two knew each other."

Bette didn't crack but smiled innocently, responding evenly. "We didn't. But since you and Sergei seemed to hit it off so well, I thought he and I should be friends, too." The steel gaze behind Bette's happy façade didn't fool me for one minute, but I tried to match her smile. I shoved my hands under my thighs so Bette couldn't see them quiver.

"Yes!" Sergei exclaimed. "I told Bette that I am ah, what was word?"

"Smitten," Bette filled in, her smile fading slightly.

"Yes! Such sweet word." Sergei kissed my shoulder. "I am smitten."

While Sergei held one hand, Bette took my other. She softened visibly and rested her chin on the spot between my shoulder and collarbone.

She whispered, "Forgive me? I was jealous. I didn't want someone to come between us." She sighed breathily. "I thought maybe we could all be friends . . ." her voice trailed off.

I should have walked out. I should have paid attention to the thousand signs dangling in front of my eyes, all flashing red warnings. But in that moment, all I could focus on was the lilt of her whispers. I longed to hear the heartbreaking pleading in Bette's voice. I needed to be needed.

Kissing Bette's soft white-blond curls, I smiled demurely. "We can all be friends." I then turned to Sergei, emboldened, and kissed him.

I spent as much time as possible at Bette's apartment in the week leading up to Sergei's art opening. It wasn't unusual for Bette, Sergei, and I to collapse together into one bed, and more than once, I awakened to find myself completely naked alongside them. I could recall only certain moments of those nights, as blackouts became normal occurrences. I was losing myself in their lifestyle, willingly succumbing to the physical and mental destruction that was slowly eating me alive. But at the same time, there was freedom in the constant flow of drugs and alcohol. Freedom from anxiety, freedom from worry. It was a false confidence, but I craved it with an insatiable hunger.

The night of Sergei's opening was filled with palpable electricity.

Bette zipped up my dress while I sipped a martini. "Fits like a glove."

I glanced at myself in the full-length mirror. My ribs jutted out, creating deep shadows on my chest. My arms looked like baby bird wings. Our life was taking its toll.

Bette smoothed my bottom hem. "Turn around, let me fix your eyeliner." Nose to nose, I examined her bloodshot eyes. Dilated pupils. She ran her fingers through my hair, placing it perfectly around my jawline. After applying my lipstick, I took the tube from her and softly ran it over her lips. A crackle of energy, a quick short circuit, physically passed over her face. I had broken a rule. She was in charge and was creating me, not the other way around. Satisfied that I'd had a moment of power, I smiled sweetly.

"There. Now we're sisters again."

A stretch town car provided by the gallery sat idling. Once inside, Sergei turned up the volume of the music until it was deafening, the thundering bass adding to our already-heightened state. Drinks were mixed and distributed. We clinked glasses with wishes of good luck and threw back the martinis, along with a tablet of ecstasy. And why not? We had no reason to slow down.

The car pulled up directly in front of the gallery entrance. Sergei stepped out first, and the cameras began to dance, flashes exploding like fireworks. He held out his hand, and Bette stepped out. More photos. Then he held out his hand for me. The cold air hit my skin as I swung out one long naked leg. More photos. I stepped fully out of the car and Sergei pulled me in for a kiss. More photos. The three of us stood together, the city lights behind us serving as a perfect backdrop. The flashes blazed from all around.

Then from a photographer: "Hey, blondie, move to the side."

I saw Bette pause, her expression unfazed, then saunter inside, air kissing the two girls manning the door and guest list.

The evening was a whirlwind of introductions, cheek kisses, cocktails, and photographs. I was never far from

Sergei's side. Finally able to locate Bette, I pulled her back into the fold, and we spent the remainder of the night that way: Bette holding one of my hands and Sergei holding the other.

I was scrutinized by every person in the room, observed and judged from every angle, and for the first time in my life, I did not falter or shrink once during the evening. I flourished. My spine straightened, my shoulders thrown back, my chin lifted. That night, Sergei was the darling prince, and I was his princess. We were royalty.

Eventually, I blacked out and lost the remainder of the evening and early morning. I was already accustomed to losing time, brushing off the tiresome nagging voice that asked how far I had gone the night before. There was no judgment, no shock. I reasoned that everyone else was experiencing the same loss of time and self. If no one could remember, no one could point a finger.

tepping out of the Uber, I looked past the cracked sidewalk and saw my childhood home. Cold, flat, matte. It reminded me of a "before" picture on a house renovation show. The shutter paint curled and peeled. A shrub covering a section of exposed concrete, where the lawn had eroded away, was brown and dying from the underside up. Sighing heavily, I put my key into the weather-beaten lock on the front door. Winter break already felt like a prison sentence.

Mother sat at the kitchen table and quickly rose when I caught her attention. She paused just a beat before approaching.

Tenderly, she touched the tips of my hair and attempted a smile. "You're so thin." Her eyes welled and she pulled me in, her tight hug filled with desperation. "I'm glad you're home."

I hugged her back, the familiarity of her smell causing a fissure in my heart. "Me, too."

Unpacking my suitcase, I heard plates and glasses being set out.

"Smells good," I yelled from my room. "Rosemary chicken?"

"Of course. What kind of mother would I be if I didn't make my daughter's favorite meal?"

The kind of mother who doesn't have a clue what's going on in her daughter's life, I thought, guiltily.

When we finally sat across from each other at the kitchen table, I pushed limp green beans and overcooked macaroni around my plate. My stomach hadn't had a true meal in weeks and was cramping in want of a drink. Thankfully, Mother didn't seem to notice.

"How have classes been?"

"Um, good. You know, hard. Harder than community college." I faked a laugh.

"I bet! How do you think you did on your finals?"

I blew air between my lips in a *They got the best of me* way and that seemed to appease her. She went on, "I haven't heard much about friends. How is your roommate? Cassie, right? Are you two still getting along? How about the boys?" Her face lit up in expectation.

Dinner moved at an excruciatingly slow pace. Mother continued to ask the questions I knew she would, and I answered in the way she expected. It was a boring game of tennis. A seemingly infinite and tiresome lobbing of conversation.

Back in the doldrums of Missouri, I lay sprawled on the worn, dirty brown tweed couch, absentmindedly flipping channels on the remote. I'd check my phone. No texts. No calls. No events to attend. Nothing for which to dress. No art gallery opening in Kearney, Missouri.

The tedium of being home, coupled with my abrupt withdrawal from drugs and alcohol, was getting the best of me. I had bitten my nails down to the quick and paced the house, trying to exorcise the negative nervous energy. My body would tremble from time to time as it attempted to purge the previous months' worth of debauchery. At those moments, I would quietly slip into the kitchen and down a small glass of boxed chardonnay from the fridge.

Ty's visit home afforded the sole relief during holiday break. Although he only stayed for three days, he was a joyous distraction. Per usual, the household atmosphere changed immediately on his arrival. Mother spent the entire morning baking cookies and hummed along to the Christmas carols playing on the local radio station. A group of her friends, all teachers she worked with, came by for drinks and appetizers—pigs-in-a-blanket and crab dip. They made elaborate Christmas-themed cocktails with peppermint schnapps and Kahlua and cream. I made myself heavily spiked versions when no one was watching. My mother dressed in what I supposed was her finest holiday attire: A thin gold-sequined sweater and matching gold trousers. I shrank in humiliation, imagining what Bette would have to say about it all.

Father came over the next day to take Ty out to lunch.

"Marin." He greeted me like a long-forgotten colleague. I was ready for him to stick his hand out for a hearty shake, but instead was given a lukewarm hug. Civil.

He waited by the front door while Ty grabbed a coat.

"How about a trip to the mall while you're home?"

Mother suddenly appeared at my side, and he quickly dropped the subject.

I didn't see my father again while I was home.

Ty and I slipped out on Christmas Eve, sitting across from each other at the same truck stop café where our parents' last dismal interaction regarding my college future had taken place two years earlier. It had been an abysmal argument that had dissolved into yet another opportunity for me to become a pawn in their divorce battle. It seemed like a lifetime ago.

My appetite had finally returned, and I spoke between large mouthfuls of a greasy cheeseburger. "It's a lot harder than I thought it would be. Balancing it all."

"Don't bullshit a bullshitter." Ty leveled his gaze while biting down on a fry.

"What?"

"Listen, I know I was busy before you left for school. I wasn't the greatest big brother. But you haven't returned any calls, no texts, no emails. Not even an Instagram post since you arrived in Chicago. That's not like you."

I dropped my eyes and picked at a piece of lettuce, trying my best to breathe evenly.

"I've been in school for a while now," Ty went on. "I've seen lots of students come and go. I know the look."

I shoved a pickle in my mouth, assuming the most nonchalant face I could muster. "And what is the look, oh wise one?"

"The look of someone who has drowned themselves in partying and is about to drop out."

Nausea bubbled up. I was found out. It was inevitable, but it was still a shock. At home, with no communication from Bette or Sergei, I only had now-sober thoughts to revel in. I had begun to second-guess every aspect of myself. Self-doubt had seeped in, filling my head with questions. What would I do when the axe came down on the scholarship?

For a fantastical moment, I convinced myself that I would return to school, take responsibility, and turn over a new leaf. I would meet with my advisor, abandon the philosophy plans, and return to my world of numbers and equations. I would take out a new loan, solely in my name. Most importantly, I would disappear from Bette's world. I knew I would have to if I ever wanted to redeem myself academically. I'd thrown away the entire semester believing in Bette's fairy-tale world, believing I played a part in it. But the cold, harsh wind of reality was blowing it all away, and I chastised myself for being swept up so easily in the first place.

Ty went on. "You look like shit."

I remained focused on my plate. "Thanks a lot." I paused. "I'm going to fix it."

"You want to live with Mom another year?" Ty raised an eyebrow and smirked.

"Oh my God, no." I poured another mound of ketchup between us. "I mean, I feel bad leaving her. But then again, I couldn't have stayed. I may be drowning now, but I was drowning here, too. Worse. You were gone, my friends all went away. Dad hasn't wasted any opportunities to remind me how he bent over backward to sign on my initial school loan. And he's so into his new kid. It's like I'm a bother for just existing."

Ty took my hand and locked eyes. "You are not a bother. And Dad can suck it."

"Easy for you to say, Golden Child."

"No, I'm serious. He signed his name on a loan to help his daughter go to school. Big whoop. He can afford it. That's not bending over backward." Ty sighed, taking a fry off the plate. "All I'm saying is, it's your life. And life changes. You wanted to go, you figured out a way, and you did. And now maybe you're in over your head. I'm worried about your health, that's all. Past that, you don't owe anyone an explanation."

"You know Mom and Dad will want one. If I screw this up? It'll be a huge point of contention."

"Everything is a point of contention between them. They may use your school as an excuse, but they're not fighting because of you. They're just fighting."

We ate our lunch while watching the truckers meander in and out. Ty knocked his knee against mine under the table. "Want dessert?"

"Duh."

We dug into hot apple pie with vanilla ice cream melting over the sides.

"So, philosophy, huh?"

I groaned. "It's so stupid. I don't know what I was thinking. I guess it just sounded cooler than math." I stared at the table. "Have you ever looked back at your decisions and just—" I shook my head, unable to completely divulge all that had happened over the last few months.

Thankfully, Ty didn't press further. "I'm the one who finished law school, then realized I needed to start all over again. So, yes, I know that feeling."

I put my fork down and leaned back against the plastic booth. "I'm pretty sure I failed all my classes this semester."

Ty eyed me.

"I still have no idea how I even got in. And I never really considered what would happen once I was there."

"You've been partying. You're not keeping up because of that, not because you're not capable. You just have to put your head down and—"

"You don't understand. I don't belong there. A person like me was not supposed to go to a school like that. I don't really have any hobbies, I'm not good at any sport, I'm not wealthy, I'm not socially—"

Ty shook his head. "Stop."

"But—"

"No. Stop." Ty wiped his mouth and leaned forward. "You're rattling off old, untrue assumptions that you got from God knows where." He held up his fingers as he ticked items off. "Fact. You don't have designer clothes and you aren't the star of varsity lacrosse, and you aren't valedictorian."

"Oh, please, no more compliments. I won't be able to get my big head out the door."

"You wouldn't be going there if it wasn't for this one scholarship—"

"You suck at cheering people up, you know that?"

"But also fact: You are beautiful, Marin. And smart and kind and thoughtful. You're easy to be with, and believe me, not everyone is. And you are in Chicago, so why not treat it like what it is? An amazing opportunity. I think if you give yourself a chance, you'll surprise everyone. You'll surprise you."

I pushed the plate of pie toward Ty. "Okay, you do have a decent bedside manner after all."

Maybe Ty was right. And maybe Bette was right. Maybe I was coming out of my cocoon, and this was just the price that had to be paid to emerge. Self-doubt. Challenge. Maybe I was worthy. And maybe not all was lost. I smiled to myself as I brushed crumbs off my lap. Maybe, just maybe, I was going to pull it all off.

Ty returned to school the day after Christmas, leaving me with three more weeks alone with Mother. The night he left, my mom put on a happy face. "Movie night?"

We rented *Sixteen Candles* and spent the evening curled up in pajamas, reciting our favorite lines in unison and unapologetically shoveling popcorn into our mouths. The weight of school lifted, and the smell of my mother's lotion when she put her hand on my arm as she laughed made me nostalgic for the time before the divorce. It was odd to be at home but still be homesick.

The next day, I woke to overhear Mother on the phone, speaking tersely with Helen. "I understand he's a busy man. I was married to him once, you know. I'm a busy woman, as well. But I'm sure he can spare five seconds to sign a check. It's not like the alimony amount is going to break your bank account."

The delicate bubble from the night before had already burst.

The only beacon of light in those long days were short bursts of texts that would sporadically appear:

Sergei: *My Pastila, so busy. I am sorry I am such a bad man for you right now. So many meetings, so many showings—I cannot wait to share all I have seen and so many exciting news. I also miss your skin. I want to eat you like piroshky! ;)*

Bette: *Hello, lovely. Honestly, could this break be any longer? Was with Oz a few days ago . . .did Xmas in St. Bart's . . .we were both in tears over your and Harry's absence! Let this last half of vacay fly by . . .I'm missing you desperately . . .my bed is cold, and I have no one to speak with.*

Ozzie: *DOLLFACE! OMG! West Indies was AMAZING! And Dalton actually came & we talked Mom into coming, too!!! No joke, traveling with my family is like being with the superstars of Looney Tunes but SOOOOOO fun!!! Off to Portofino! Ciao!*

I answered the texts immediately, only to sit staring at the phone, waiting for a response that never came. Bette was heaviest on my mind. When I would pass a mirror, Bette was there, in my own reflection, pulling me back. I had brought home only my old clothes—jeans, T-shirts, sweatshirt—and had left behind all traces of urban life. I stopped wearing makeup and sculpting my hair into its edgy cut. After continuous critical scrutiny from my mother, it was easiest just to wash it, tuck it behind my ears, and be done with it. Simple and conventional were what Mother could process.

But for me, returning to disheveled, plain, and ordinary was grueling. I no longer saw myself as my mother and brother saw me. I saw myself as Bette did, and the two were not compatible body-mates. My outfit of track pants and high school hoodie was a necessary disguise, because how could I present my new life to those at home without acknowledging Bette, Sergei, and Oz? So, the new me had to stay hidden until I could make my escape, silently living the lie and counting down the minutes until I could leave. The push and pull of knowing what was in the best interest of my future, of distancing myself from the life of the past few months and of wanting to satisfy the instant gratification craving that Bette had created, of the adrenaline high from our escapades, warred on continually.

"I haven't seen your grades yet. I've been checking the mailbox every day. How do you think you did?" Mother asked, smiling in between bites of leftover casserole.

"They email the grades now. You know, electronic over paper. Save the planet and all that stuff. I'll send them to you when I get them. And I think I did pretty well. I mean, considering it was my first semester and everything." When she said nothing, I filled the empty space. "Don't you guys post online now?"

Mother sighed. "The district is slowly switching over, but you know how it is getting those things implemented. There are holdouts that don't want to learn the technology, there are budget issues—"

I moved the creamed chicken around my plate, feigning interest, before interrupting, "Can I have the keys? I'm going to the gym."

I hadn't lied about grades being posted online. I had simply omitted that they already were out. I had failed three of my classes and the other two were graded simply on attendance. Obviously, one of those two teachers had not been noting absences accurately, since he passed me.

I left in a hurry and drove several miles toward a neighboring town until I reached Watkins Mill, a historic landmark set within a state park. An hour passed on a snowy bank of the park's one-hundred-acre lake, pacing until my legs were numb and my lungs burned in the cold air. I hated lying to my mother. I hated that I had failed so spectacularly. I hated the voice in my head saying that all the self-manipulation in the world didn't change the fact that I was a fraud. I was losing my grip and needed to get away from the atomic bomb that was set to blow at any moment.

Shivering as I pulled back into the driveway, my back stiffened. Standing at the front door was Sarah. For a split second, I thought of immediately pulling back out and racing away. But she turned, her brow furrowed, then smiled broadly and waved. Taking a deep breath, I got out of the car.

"Talk about great timing!" She looked the same.

"Wow. Yeah. Nice to see you." I straightened my bangs quickly, aware of my baggy, bedraggled appearance.

"I thought you might still be back for break."

"Um. Yeah." I shifted from one foot to the other. "I'm here."

"How are you? How's school?"

I could feel the fingers of irritation digging in. I hadn't heard from her since high school graduation. Not even a goodbye when she left for Stanford. It seemed a malicious cosmic joke to plant her in front of me once again.

"It's great!" I said a little too brightly. "But, I mean, hard."

Sarah nodded in agreement.

"I mean, there are so many parties. And it's Chicago, ya know? There's always something going on in the city. Like football games and concerts and . . . yeah, so—" My rambling had returned, and I wished for the Earth to swallow me up and save me from the hole I was digging.

"I bet." Sarah nodded.

"Yeah, and there are like so many guys, too." The words felt like drool escaping my mouth. Sarah gave me a quick once-over and smiled again. I paused, trying to regain my footing. "How's school for you?"

"It's been really good. Busy. Between the sorority, rowing, and studying, there's not a lot of time left for much else." Her self-confidence only amplified my insecurity. "Are you doing any extracurriculars? Did you end up joining a sorority?"

"No. I mean, I had some girls that *really* wanted me to join. Like, they begged me. But I'm just too busy."

"Right. All the parties and boys." The smirk on Sarah's face confirmed I had pushed too far. My lie was laid bare. "Anyway, I just wanted to say hi." She stepped past me and began to walk away. She threw over her shoulder, "If you ever come out to California, give me a call."

I closed the front door behind me, and tears sprang to my eyes. From an upper kitchen cabinet, I grabbed a bottle of cheap whisky that had been Mother's go-to the first year after the divorce and flopped on the couch, ready to settle in for an afternoon of self-loathing,

The saving grace came later that evening in a text. I read it with liquor-laden vision.

Bette: *My love, pack your bag as fast as you can! Swimsuits, sunglasses, and a wide-brimmed hat! I'm sending you a ticket for tomorrow.*

Me: *What? Yes! I'll find a way to talk my mom into it. Where are we going?? And I can't even talk about the state of my old swimsuit . . . I don't have a hat.*

Bette: *Just tell your mom you're going. Don't ask. You're covered on packing; I'll bring enough for us both! And you're flying into Midway. It's a surprise from there. ;) Look for an e-ticket, should be in your email already. Miss your beautiful face . . . can't wait!*

12

I landed in Chicago, white-knuckled and grateful to be on solid ground, to find a driver holding up a sign bearing my name. I settled in the back of the sedan. We left from the commercial arrival gate and circled around the airport to arrive a few minutes later at the private jet terminal. Small knapsack in hand, I warily stepped into a small-but-tidy lobby. Clean-cut pilots in uniform, checking their text messages and completing paperwork, mingled with attendants manning the counter. A few men in expensive-looking suits and heavy cashmere overcoats stood near the automatic door leading to the tarmac. A young Hispanic woman, presumably a nanny, attempted to corral three rambunctious children as a polished woman in her mid-forties chatted idly on her phone, wholly unaware of the disorder.

I scanned the crowd until my eyes settled on a leather couch in the corner.

Bette and Sergei saw me at the same moment and simultaneously rose to their feet. My heart raced like a lovestruck schoolgirl at the sight of them both. I tried to stay composed as my mind whirled with delight. From the moment Bette's text beckoned me, I had fallen back into daydreams of her make-believe world. It pressed hard against the logic of school and the reality of student loans and family obligations. Hard enough that the fantasy had won, and all rationality left. I had swallowed the pill of Bette's influence once again, before I'd even seen her.

Sergei wrapped his arms tightly around me as I breathed in his cologne.

"I can't believe you're here. I thought you had another few weeks of shows?"

"I did, *Uebok*. I did. But I had so many, and I want to be smart. Not give everyone everything. Besides, I am tired." He stroked my hair. "So much talking and talking and shaking hands and making so nice to all peoples." He smiled mischievously. "And I miss you."

I flushed. "I missed you, too."

Over Sergei's shoulder, my gaze met Bette's. In a flick of an instant, I watched Bette's eyes shift from icy hardness to irresistible warmth. *She missed me and is jealous. That's all.* I pulled away from Sergei and threw myself at Bette. She giggled as we teetered backward, narrowly missing the luggage stacked around us. Bette took my hands and kissed both cheeks. I breathed her in as I had Sergei, her scent equal parts excitement and comfort. She smelled like true home to me.

"Okay, you two. What's going on?"

Bette nodded over my shoulder where a voice sounded seemingly out of nowhere.

"So, this is the motley crew I'm in charge of, huh?"

I turned to see Simon, his eyes as bright as ever. The strong, perfectly balanced features were enhanced by his outfit—worn khaki field pants and a faded blue chambray shirt. Surrounded by official-looking men in business suits and pilot uniforms, he looked like a modern Teddy Roosevelt, rugged and ready to lead a big game hunting expedition in Africa. I could not hug him fast enough.

"Simon, please tell me what's happening? No one here will—"

"Wait." Bette stepped up and took my hand again, leading me away. She grabbed one of the small designer duffels from the pile. "First, a change of clothes." She swiftly surveyed my outfit as we walked toward the bathroom. I shrank, feeling the defeated load of Kearney like a stinking odor I couldn't wash off, no matter how hard I scrubbed.

"Here, take that thing off."

Inside the small, immaculate bathroom, I looked around with awe. A pile of thick, neatly folded towels sat next to a basket overflowing with small bottles of toiletries—mouthwash, toothpaste, self-misting spray— and tampons. Even a couch and coffee table, in case you needed to rest a moment before returning to your private plane, I supposed. I'd never seen a public bathroom so beautiful.

I stripped to my underwear. "Ah, already better," Bette said, stroking the line from my shoulder to the hand that held my shirt. Gently, Bette took the blouse and deftly threw it in the trash can. A small corner of my heart tightened. The blouse was without a doubt terrible, with bright, petite flowers and a Peter Pan collar. But Mother had just given it to me for Christmas. She had been so excited that morning when she saw me wearing it. I turned away quickly, afraid if I looked back at the sad heap of fabric, my conscience would compel me to snatch the shirt from the trash and run.

Bette reached into the duffel and pulled out a black slip dress.

"Take off your bra," she instructed. I hesitated briefly, and Bette cocked her head. "You're not embarrassed, are you? It's me." She stepped closer. Bette took another step forward, our faces inches apart. Without looking away from my eyes, Bette reached around with both her arms and unclasped my bra. The straps slid down my shoulders, and I stood in front of her, arms at my sides, frozen. Bette frowned and handed me the dress.

"Are you angry with me?" Bette's bottom lip pouted slightly, and she fumbled around the bag until she found shoes.

"No," I stammered, pulling on the dress, grasping for an excuse. "I think I'm just confused. What is all this? Where are we going?"

Bette quickly came nose to nose again. "But you're not angry with me?"

"Not at all. Why would I be?"

Bette released a relieved sigh and placed her head on my shoulder, wrapping her arms around me again.

"I missed you. I was very alone during break. I needed you."

"I missed you, too. But we're here together now."

Bette pulled away, recomposed. "Yes, we are." She ran smoothing gel through my windblown hair. As she had done so many times, Bette primped and preened me until she was satisfied.

Reaching into her bag, she handed me a thin fur stole and sealed the transformation with a small kiss. Unfortunately, along with the silky chemise dress, strappy high heel sandals, and sleek hair came a return of my false confidence. While Bette adjusted my hem, I pushed away my conversation with Ty and my promise that I would turn my life around. When I turned to see Bette's handiwork in the mirror, new Marin stared back. And that was all it took for me to forget about my family's concern, the failing grades, and the crumpled blouse in the wastebasket.

The private jet rolled slowly down the tarmac, filing into the line of planes positioned for takeoff. The cabin bounced slightly as we rolled over bumps on the runway. I clutched the armrest, rapidly shifting between states of dreamy disbelief and bloodcurdling fear.

"Are you all right? You look a little pale." Simon eyed me carefully, an eyebrow raised. "There's a small bathroom in the back if you're feeling ill."

I shook my head and gripped the armrests tighter.

"Yes, if you are to get sick, go in bathroom. Don't sit here," Sergei added with distaste in his voice.

"I'm not sick," I snapped, more harshly than I intended.

Bette cocked her head. "Oh, darling. You've never flown before?"

"I've flown. I flew here, remember?" Through clenched teeth, I added, "I just don't like it."

"Another one of your anxieties, huh?"

I ignored the comment, unsure if it was a dig or merely an observation. Bette moved to the front of the plane and began to open drawers with swift familiarity. She returned, dispensing drinks all around.

"A screwdriver makes everything better," she said, taking a sip and perching on an armrest. I downed the cocktail in three gulps. Bette lifted an eyebrow. "Another it is," she said, taking my glass to refill it.

I took a deep breath, waiting for the vodka to kick in. "Simon, is this your plane?"

Simon chuckled. "I'm not that good an artist, sweetheart." He set his untouched drink in the cupholder. "No, it belongs to our dear friend Gigi. We'll be meeting her later today."

"We'll be meeting her *where*?" I prodded, clueless where the airborne death trap was taking us.

"You scoundrels didn't tell her where we're going?"

"Mystery is everything!" Bette exclaimed, theatrically presenting a refreshed drink.

I noticed Sergei tapping away at his phone, completely uninterested in the conversation until Bette spoke. At her voice, his eyes shot up. He winked and then went back to his texts. An unpleasant flutter rippled through my heart, but another small bump in the cabin quickly refocused me.

"Key West."

"Simon!" Bette protested.

"Seriously?" I asked.

Bette sighed, defeated. "Yes. We're staying on Gigi's boat for New Year's. The yacht was supposed to sail to St. Tropez, and that would have been fab, but Sergei has to run to Miami for a few days. Gigi insisted we travel to

Florida to accommodate."

"Don't blame it all on me," Sergei protested. "I'm not the only one who must fly off."

"True. I'm sorry, dear." Bette turned. "I have to meet with Terrence McMillan about the upcoming poetry collection."

My brow furrowed. "Who is Terrence? What collection? You're leaving, too?"

Bette sat on Sergei's lap, her knees pressed together, and leaned forward, taking my hand. "Only for a day or so. Sergei and I are sharing a small charter plane to Miami. I'll be back as quickly as I can."

Simon glanced at me with a look I couldn't read.

The turbulence of the flight, the knowledge that Sergei and Bette were going off together, and Bette's kinship with Sergei, familiar and endearing, conspired with the vodka. I became detached, like an observer watching things happen from yards away. Goosebumps formed on my arms, and I shivered in the thin dress. My eyelids became heavy, and a familiar thought crossed my mind: *Bette put something in my drink.* But I knew better than to ask. I wouldn't be given a truthful answer.

Before closing my eyes, I dared one more glance out the window. Clouds billowed like soft groups of marshmallows, and I imagined myself jumping from the plane and bouncing, cushioned and protected, from one puffy sphere to another. Bette continued to sit on Sergei's lap, giggling, as she sipped her drink. Simon seemed lost in thought, his face fixed toward his small porthole to the outside world. I wondered if he, too, was jumping across the clouds, letting them carry him away.

The rest of the flight flew by in an alcohol-induced

blur as we made our way through the bottle of vodka. The little I remembered was sparse and hazy.

The plane landed at Key West International, where a stately white-haired man in uniform met us at the private section. I stumbled into a shuttle, saying nothing. My tongue was thick and immovable, my thoughts dull and out of my control. The gentleman drove our group directly to a dock, where our bags were loaded onto a cart. I faintly remembered Sergei asking if we were going to be thrown into the ocean for bad behavior. Bette and I had roared with laughter, exaggerated and inappropriate. I still wore the fur stole, despite the humid tropical air. Bette grabbed my arm, kissing my hand, before jumping on Sergei's back for a piggyback ride. They earned curious looks from passersby, but took no serious notice.

What did finally catch my attention stopped me in my tracks. I teetered backward in astonishment.

"Why are they . . . they're going . . ." I couldn't finish the sentence, but Simon knew what I was attempting to ask as he steadied me.

"That's where we're staying. It's Gigi's boat."

"Fuck!" I exclaimed too loudly.

Simon quickly ushered me up the gangway with a shush. "Dear, I think we need to get all of you inside." He motioned to the captain, who steered Bette and Sergei toward the boat.

Gigi's boat was a two hundred-foot mega yacht named *Echapper*. A stewardess greeted us on the main deck with champagne, which we happily consumed while touring the ship. We entered the main salon, an expansive retreat, through double-glassed doors. The walls were raised-panel, finished in dark, satin-lacquered mahogany, carved with old-world precision. Expensive art hung in every room, even the cabins and down the long corridors. Sergei was like a kid at Christmas, exclaiming, "It's a Koons! A Warhol!"

We continued the tour, misbehaving everywhere. In our bedroom, Sergei threw me on the crisp cotton bedding; in the movie theater, we climbed over seats to find the best view; in the wheelhouse, we pretended to drive the ship; and as we made our way to the top sun deck, we repeatedly motioned to have our glasses refilled.

Bette fell leisurely into one of the lounge chairs, purring. "What time is dinner, darling?"

The stewardess, Morgan, didn't flinch at the ill-mannered antics. Instead, she smiled professionally. "I believe Mr. Duchamp called for appetizers at eight p.m. and dinner at nine."

"Marvelous," Bette said breezily.

We didn't make it to dinner, nor did we see Simon the rest of the night. The moment Morgan disappeared down the back stairs, Bette grabbed Sergei and me, pulling us into the small lavatory. On the sink, she portioned out six lines of cocaine for the three of us to share. We inhaled them all within seconds. Sprawling on lounge chairs and crowding into the bathroom long after dark, hours passed as quickly as minutes. At one point in the night, I came to long enough to realize we were all naked in the hot tub.

Sporadic blackouts continued over the following days.

In our minds, we three young adults were entitled rock stars and behaved as such. When not parading around the island, we wreaked havoc on Gigi's boat. We awoke to mimosas and continued drinking until we passed out in the next morning's early hours, with glasses of whisky and bourbon spilling into our laps and Gigi's cashmere carpeting. We rudely blasted music, had outlandish sex on the sun cushions, and harassed the crew members with outrageous demands. All the while, carelessly popping pills of all varieties, even those passed to us by strangers at the street parties.

We were part of the beautiful "in" crowd. We were the lucky ones. Sergei smiled at me. Bette smiled at me. The world smiled upon us all. We were untouchable.

A few days after New Year's, I awoke on the floor of my bathroom surrounded by vomit. The heated tiles had warmed the pool until its putrid smell filled every atom in the room. My head pounded like it had been cleaved in two. Shaking violently, I called out for Sergei. When he didn't answer, I called louder, but the force of my raised voice only triggered another round of gut-wrenching projectile bile. I began to cry, moaning Bette's name.

Mercifully, the door opened. It was Simon who, to his credit, paused for only a moment when the rancid smell hit him. He knelt and gently wrapped his arms around me, "You poor sweetheart." Slowly, he lifted me to my feet, guiding me to the bed, and tucking me under covers. Somehow, I was simultaneously burning up and freezing to death.

"I'm . . . I'm . . ." I gulped back the vomit rising in my throat. Simon quickly grabbed a small wastebasket by the writing desk and slid it under me just as my mouth filled past capacity. He stroked my back as I heaved over and over. The tears came again. "Simon, I'm so sorry. I think something is really wrong with me."

A sympathetic grin passed over Simon's face. "Yes, my dear, it's called 'way too much indulgence.' We've all had the virus at one point or another."

"Where is Bette?"

"She and Sergei left for Miami. They said they should be back in a couple days."

At once, I wasn't just sick but also deeply anxious. Simon read it on my face. "Don't worry. We'll get you rehydrated and feeling better, then we'll find a way to pass the time."

I didn't respond. My mind was racing, filled with thoughts of dread. Things had been off at the airport, and a voice in the back of my head had warned of the newfound friendship between Bette and Sergei. But I had faltered for just a moment too long, and now it was too late. I knew I'd be living with worst-case scenarios playing out through my imagination until they returned.

I spent the rest of the day in bed. Morgan brought me seltzer to sip, but I vomited after each attempt to drink. When I was finally able to hold down a few swallows, Morgan brought electrolytes. I slowly drank the bottle, then ravished four more in quick succession, unable to drink fast enough to quench my thirst. During one bout of fitful sleep, Morgan cleaned the wastebasket and bathroom. Incredibly, the room again smelled of lilies.

I was still shivering in bed the next day, the drugs and alcohol slowly leaving my body, when Morgan quietly entered and set a bowl of chicken noodle soup, rich and thick, on the nightstand. "Mr. Duchamp thought you might enjoy this."

Humiliated, I smiled weakly and thanked her, suddenly sober and aware that I had not eaten a single true meal since arriving on the boat days earlier. It wasn't a stretch to surmise that our behavior must have been atrocious. However, Simon was right. The soup was delicious.

I felt less than human, but at least could finally get out of bed. Taking a scalding hot shower, I emerged reborn. Reborn on a mysterious new planet. I went to the closet and found it fully stocked. I had no idea who had arranged our luggage, nor did I remember seeing any of the clothing before. Foggily, I recalled noticing Bette had an overly large bag as the crew took the luggage upon arrival.

I chose a long flowing sundress and sandals, then made my way up a flight of stairs. A young woman with a European accent and uniform met me at the top, smiling cheerfully. "May I ask you to remove your shoes? I'll leave them by the door in case you'd like to depart the boat."

"Um, yes, thank you."

"Lovely to see you're feeling better!" she chirped. I nodded and flushed, embarrassed that, surely, I had met this woman several times but in the light of day could not pick her out of a lineup. I looked around for a moment with no idea where to go. The girl nodded toward another set of stairs. "Mr. Duchamp is having breakfast on the bridge deck lounge if you would like to join him."

One floor up, I walked through sliding glass doors and was slapped by blinding light and sweltering humidity.

"There she is." Simon rose and pulled out a chair.

Had I sat at this table before? Had I even visited this level? I couldn't remember. Newspapers were strewn across the table, along with an extensive buffet. Bacon, fruit, scrambled eggs, muffins, croissants, and sausages. My mouth salivated.

Morgan emerged and poured a glass of orange juice. "Would you like some French toast? Waffles? An omelet? Chef Henry is quite talented."

Simon nodded in agreement. "I recommend the Montmorency cherry crepes."

I thrilled at the thought. "Yes, please. That sounds amazing."

Simon took the liberty of filling a small plate high with pastries and miniature quiches. I added a few pieces of bacon and dug in. Simon, mercifully, read the paper and left me alone while I ate. I covertly observed him. His hair wasn't an ordinary matte gray; it was more like silver flecks shimmering as they caught the sunlight. But his face, his eyes, reflected a youthful zest.

I thought of our first encounter and his kindness. It was the same kindness he was showing me now, without judgement or reproach. I noticed that the table was only set for the two, and my thoughts jumped to Bette and Sergei. There was no denying it—all was not as it seemed. Or worse, maybe it was. The small monster of anxiety was desperately trying to find a place to sink its claws into, a tiny hold where it could latch on. I refused. Deflect and ignore, my greatest defense. I smoothed my hair and lowered the sunglasses perched on my head to cover my eyes, gaining confidence behind the black lenses.

People idled on the dock, pointing at the boats, wondering which celebrities or tycoons might be on board. *Me. That's who is on board.* My father would never be invited on a yacht. Sarah would never have fit in. But I did. I was there, on the back of the ship, leisurely sipping strong French roast coffee, paying no mind to the strangers who gaped awkwardly. I even allowed myself a haughty nod in their direction, imagining they might mistake me for the owner. Had paparazzi already photographed me on the boat? Maybe I would be featured in a tabloid as the unidentified statuesque brunette cavorting in the playground of the rich and famous.

Simon cleared his throat, jolting me from my posturing. "I'm going for a walk. Join me?"

I sashayed down the dock, arm linked in Simon's, callously avoiding the smiles of people we passed, while Simon graciously returned hellos. We walked down Duval Street, stepping over gutters full of confetti and plastic cups from the previous night's festivities. I hopped daintily around streams of water where storeowners hosed away unidentifiable garbage from the sidewalks. Every few steps, Simon stopped to point out a local's artwork. I scoffed, but Simon was quick to point out the unique characteristics of the work, validating the talents of each artist.

Stopping in front of a bar, Simon gestured to the entrance. "I need to have a beer with a couple of friends."

"It's ten a.m.!" I laughed, following Simon in.

Simon turned, smirking. "You, my dear, have no room to talk about when and when not to have a drink."

"Touché," I conceded.

As soon as my eyes adjusted, I stopped following.

If, in a far-reaching universe, there were a polar-opposite galaxy, a disgusting parallel world that held the nemesis of Les Mots, this was it. Every inch of space, floor to ceiling, wall to wall, was covered in dollar bills, posters, newspaper clippings, license plates, and bras. A thick layer of sticky oil blanketed the exposed wooden surfaces. Was it grease? Lacquer? I didn't want to know and hesitated in the doorway.

Simon smiled at my trepidation. "Come on in and have a seat." When I didn't move, he added, "Or stay there and welcome people as they come in." He gestured past me, to two rough-looking women waiting to enter. They wore their hair in crew cuts; one wore jeans, the other cargo shorts, and both well-worn leather sandals. I mumbled apologies and hurried to meet Simon at the bar, trying to sit with as little of my body as possible touching the stool, keeping my hands in my lap.

The bartender looked to be in his mid-seventies, haggard and squat. He greeted Simon fondly, pushing a frosty mug of beer toward him. His friendliness vanished when he saw me. He waited three counts before barking, "Well?"

"Just give her the same, Buzz." The bartender harrumphed and slid a mug across the bar. Simon took a long drink and wiped his mouth with the back of his hand. "You seen Mike recently?"

"Naw," Buzz answered, drying a glass with a worn gray rag that looked as if it hadn't been washed in years. "That cocksucker still owes me two hundred forty-five bucks. Won't see him for a while. How long you down for?"

The place was filling up. The number of morning drinkers at Tony's was astounding. An early mimosa was one thing, but I counted at least six whisky glasses already sitting on the bar, a wretched-looking soul curled over each. I wondered why Simon would choose to frequent a dump that drew so many losers in ragged clothes and missing teeth. Especially when we had a little Shangri-La waiting at the end of the dock.

"Couple of weeks, I think."

"You working on anything new?"

"Yup." Simon's easy demeanor fused perfectly with the relaxed surroundings. "I'll bring it by as soon as it's presentable."

"Ah, don't bother," Buzz waved off Simon. "I ain't got the funds right now. It's been a slow winter."

"Who said it was for sale? Besides, you need something to class up this joint." The two men grinned at each other. At his last exhibit, every one of his photographs that sold had gone for at least six figures. I couldn't imagine he'd give away a photograph that valuable for nothing.

Simon noticed my untouched beer and turned to Buzz. "Pirate Punch for the lady."

I'd spent the past few months drinking specialty martinis and French champagne. I no longer drank beer. Or ate stale peanuts from a warped wooden bowl sitting on a gummy bar top. And I wasn't keen on any drink called Pirate Punch.

Buzz put a well-worn glass in front of me filled with a mix of pale pink and peach, a sort of sickly nude color, and shoved a thin plastic straw stuck through a piece of orange and a maraschino cherry as garnish. I envisioned a muumuu and flower lei as fitting attire. Audibly sighing, I surrendered, and took a sip.

The concoction was delicious, whatever it was. Simon keenly observed the second-long draw of liquid and went back to chatting with the bartender.

"Thought Frankie would be here."

"That asshole didn't leave until four this morning." Buzz's derogatory comments were tinged with obvious affection and fondness, like pet names for sweethearts. "I'm sure he'll be in soon."

"Who's Frankie?" I scooted back fully on the barstool, making myself comfortable.

"He's a pirate."

"A what?"

"The real deal," Buzz chimed in.

"Truth," Simon continued. "He does some unsavory swindling on the sea, makes enough to live for a while, and spends the rest of his time here bullshitting with these guys. We don't ask specifics of what he does, and he provides us with some pretty great entertainment." Buzz agreed with what sounded like an energetic tribal yelp.

"So, where's this pirate from?" I pushed the empty plastic cup forward and Buzz pushed a refill back.

Simon shrugged. "No one knows." He eyed my drink, "Take it slow. Trust me."

I nodded understanding and asked for a diet soda. "Where does he live?"

"On his boat."

"And he just hangs around here when he's not . . . pirating?"

"Right on that seat you're sitting on." Buzz gestured to my stool.

I giggled. "A pirate named Frankie. That's one of the funniest things I've ever heard!"

"And what would a proper pirate name be, then?" A

gravelly voice boomed into my ear. The smell of sweaty alcohol and putrid musk filled my nostrils. Simon and Buzz laughed as I examined the man I presumed to be Frankie. Dirty, dishwater blond hair verging on natural dreadlocks, deeply tanned skin, dark stains seemingly ground deep into the wrinkles of his skin. A T-shirt so used it was translucent from repeated wear—definitely not from over-washing—tattered and ripped at the collar. Surprisingly fresh-looking board shorts. No shoes.

His dark hazel eyes stared at me. "That's my seat."

I quickly hopped off the stool, no questions asked, and moved to the other side of Simon.

"You forgot your girly drink," he growled. I whisked the two cups from the spot in front of him. The men howled.

"Frankie, you're such a dick. No wonder you can't ever get laid." Buzz poured a generous quantity of whisky into a tumbler and banged it down in front of Frankie.

Frankie looked pained. "Now, that wasn't very nice. That pretty thing would go back to my boat with me. Wouldn't ya, dollface?" He raised his glass and I smiled wanly, raising mine in return.

Simon winked. "Don't worry—he's not serious." He swiveled on his stool. "Frankie, this is my friend Marin. We were telling her about your profession."

"Oh shit, that's what you were 'pirating' about, huh?" Frankie rolled his eyes. "Don't believe a word of it, girly. I'm no pirate. I'm a fisherman. I fish, I sell my fish."

"What do you fish?"

"Well," Frankie looked around as if the answer was written on a wall somewhere, "I throw out my hook. Whatever it snags, I reel in, and it becomes mine."

"Snapper? Grouper?" I prodded.

"Jesus, girl!" Buzz shouted, exasperated. "He's a pirate. He waits until people leave their boats unattended and then he steals whatever he can. Hooking? Snagging? Sells his 'fish?' Get it?"

Frankie gasped. "I am offended, sir! I am a fisherman!" He placed his hand over his heart, fingers spread. Throwing back the last of his drink, he smacked his glass on the counter twice. Buzz was ready, the bottle raised to pour. He gestured with the bottle at Frankie's shorts. "Awfully fancy."

"Yeah. I thought so too. Liked the color."

"Where'd you find 'em?"

I chimed in. "Let me guess. You went fishing and happened to catch them on your line?" The men roared goodheartedly, slapping the countertop while Simon gave me a high five.

"So, Princess, tell me what world-changing things you're going to do with your life," Frankie taunted with a wink. "And pirating is already taken, so you can't use that."

"Oh"—I straightened in my chair and fingered my bangs—"I'm going into philosophy."

Buzz raised an eyebrow to ask Simon. "Is she serious?"

Frankie smacked his empty glass on the counter, nodding for another. "What the fuck do you do with philosophy?"

I had repeatedly asked myself the same question. I knew the pursuit of knowledge, to nurture and expand minds, was a worthwhile thing, because it's empowering, it civilizes humans, and in general makes people better. I knew that because of watching Ty. And because Bette had drilled it into me. I just had no clue what role philosophy played in that. Or how it would pay my bills. That question was becoming more pertinent as the reality of student loans loomed large with the possibility of no degree to show for it.

"I'm still trying to figure it out. My friend Bette talked me into a double major." It was the first time I had conceded that the choice might not have fully been my own.

Buzz pointed a calloused finger in my face. "One lesson I learned over the years: Listen to your own voice. People can sell you a load of shit all day, but you're the only one who can buy it."

Frankie nodded his head emphatically. "Damn straight. So, what does your own voice say?" The men fell silent, waiting for an answer, as my throat went dry, stripped naked of all the false bravado I'd been building up over the past few months.

Simon, seeing me frozen, came to the rescue. "You could teach."

Frankie answered, as if he were considering the profession for himself. "What? And spend your day with a bunch of snot-nosed, sticky-handed, loud-mouthed brats?"

"Sounds like my job," Buzz said under his breath.

Frankie pressed on. "Not teaching—no way. What're ya good at?"

"I'm good at math. Also, I spent a summer a few years back reorganizing and categorizing the sales and accounting files at my dad's car dealership. I did a pretty good job with that." Even though my father had barely mumbled a "thank you," I had walked away with a huge sense of pride and accomplishment.

Suddenly, Frankie bellowed, "Hey, Jacob, you asshole! You owe me two hundred dollars."

A young man at the end of the bar, as leathered as Frankie, snipped back. "Go blow yourself, Frankie. I don't owe you shit."

Frankie turned back to the group with a smile and shrugged his shoulders. "Worth a try."

We sat at the bar for two more hours, listening to tales of Frankie's fantastic adventures. Of getting lost at sea, truly lost, while storms whipped him off-course and incipient hurricanes threatened to splinter his small boat. He told us about a few of the saltier dogs he had encountered, some wild and eccentric, some just plain dangerous. He spoke of an especially perfect day when the sun shone brightly but, oddly, did not overpower and a strong cool breeze blew as he fell asleep on the bow of a boat drifting out to sea. He said it was the closest he had ever been to God.

"A religious pirate?" I quipped.

Frankie answered with unexpected seriousness, "I commune with God daily. Whoever and whatever God might be. The important part is to remember that life is bigger than ourselves."

Walking back to the boat with Simon, I sipped a bottle of water and looked out over the ocean. I could imagine Frankie, calm and content with nothing, floating aimlessly, with God smiling down on him. I couldn't shake the sense of cracking resolve that I'd experienced earlier in the day at the bar. There was an unsettling in me as I realized that the pirate and bedraggled bartender, in one afternoon, had seen the forest through the trees in a way that I hadn't been able to. It was becoming clearer that Bette was blurring my already-shaky vision and, for the first time, I was sure that Bette's "help" was anything but.

That night, I dialed Bette's number. It went straight to voicemail. I immediately tried Sergei, with the same result.

Simon led me on a different route, through neighborhoods no tourist would come to see, with humble one- and two-bedroom cottages lining the narrow streets. An elderly Haitian man waved to us from a front porch cluttered with dying plants, rusted folding chairs, and twisted pieces of scrap window treatment. I smiled and waved back, telling Simon about the job I once had at the Williams-Washburn Nursing Home. I had volunteered as a kitchen worker for extracurricular credits.

While Sarah had been given the uplifting task of playing bingo with the seniors, bringing them smiles, laughter, and joy, I was put to work clearing trays of pureed peas, creamed corn, and mashed corned beef. I removed trays from empty tables, scraped the remains in the back, and sprayed off any crusty remnants.

The women working in the kitchen were furiously bitter with the world and, because I was volunteering, believed I was one of the many privileged students who rotated through the doors. I was met daily with scowls and cold shoulders, despite the fact my menial job fell far below theirs.

The first month I worked at the care center, I arrived, did my job, and left. I kept my eyes forward, reasoning that if I did a good job I would be rewarded with the cooks' approval and an agreeable nod from a college. My plan was working until midway through the summer, when an elderly woman, known for her incoherent moaning and grunting, grabbed my hand as I bent to take her tray. Startled, I tried to pull away, but the woman held tight. She was staring at me, pleading with watering eyes.

My heart split and I sat next to the elderly woman, keeping my hand in hers. The woman whimpered and nodded until an orderly came and rolled her wheelchair away, apologizing as if the woman had somehow been a nuisance. "Clara can be a handful."

From then on, I spent less time in the kitchen. I made excuses of going to collect trays, then walked the cafeteria and sat with lonely residents who simply wanted to see a fresh smile or to experience touch from another human. I took time with Clara every day, holding her hand and giving her attention as she cooed in appreciation. At every pair of eyes that pleaded, I would stop to let them know I saw them, that they mattered.

A month into the newfound happiness at work, I was called into the head chef's office, where I was curtly told that my volunteer services were no longer needed.

When I protested, the chef took no time in putting me in my place, punctuating the fact that I wasn't doing the job I had been assigned and that they didn't hand out credit hours for nothing. After that, I ended up at my father's office, head hanging, filing papers.

Simon stopped walking and turned. "So, when we asked you what you were good at, why did you say math and organization?"

I shrugged.

"I may not know much, but I'll tell you this. You might be good at alphabetizing files and punching at a calculator, but that is not a talent."

"Oh."

"Not *your* talent."

"No?"

"No. Your talent is kindness. Empathy. You'd be surprised how hard that is to find in people anymore."

Simon turned and began walking. I caught up quickly, a smile tugging at my lips.

As I quickly checked my phone again, Simon spoke softly. "But the kindness you have may not be appreciated by everyone. And it's not going to make either of them answer the phone. They're different than you."

I knew Simon wanted me to respond. But I couldn't. I didn't want to hear the truth, so I turned my face away, ashamed at how transparent the situation was. Mercifully, Simon cleared his throat, checking his watch.

"We should start getting back. Dinner will be served soon."

After a quiet meal, I took a deep breath and finally addressed Simon's observation directed at Bette and Sergei. "I just hope they're okay." I looked to Simon for reassurance. He ignored the comment and, instead, smiled at the stewardess.

"The filet was delicious. Please tell the chef thank you." He dabbed the sides of his mouth with a linen napkin.

"How exactly do you know Bette? You never said."

"I know her family through Gigi."

"You seem to spend a lot of time with Gigi."

Simon smirked. "Nothing like that. Gigi and I are friends. That's it."

"I think she has a crush on you."

"That's for sure. She's never been short on crushes. But we're just friends." Simon took another long draw off his beer. "Eleanor came to me a few years ago for art lessons."

A shot of adrenaline swept through me. "The big paintings. The slash marked ones."

"Yes."

"The ones she said were like therapy."

"Yes."

"The ones she painted after Olivia died."

Simon paused. "Yes."

A rush of relief came at the opportunity to finally speak to someone who had insight into Bette's history, someone who could finally settle the questions left unanswered after Eleanor confided in me.

I knew I had to be delicate and dipped my toe in, testing the water.

"I can't imagine what that was like for the family."

"I can't either. I know the pain I saw through Eleanor's eyes in her paintings, but what she and Thomas endured in their hearts must have been hell."

"For Bette, too."

Again, he paused. "Most definitely. I think she lives in a hell of her own."

"Right! I think that going through a trauma like that must change a person. Makes them react differently to situations?"

Simon looked at me thoughtfully.

I prodded. "I mean, wouldn't you think?"

"Yes. A person can experience tragedy and come out changed. But in this case—" He spoke slowly. "I didn't know Bette prior to Olivia's death. It's possible, I suppose."

"What are you saying, Simon?"

His brow creased. "I'm not saying anything." He paused. "Has Bette ever discussed Olivia with you? Any of what happened?"

I was an open book to Bette, almost embarrassingly so. But what did I know about Bette? I knew what cocktails she preferred, what designer clothing she favored, what artists she deemed worthy and what musicians she did not. I knew every curve of her body, every freckle that peppered her skin, every speckled shade of blue in her eyes. On the surface, I knew her definitively. Before Simon sat in front of me, asking if Bette had shared the most traumatic moment of her life, a moment that everyone seemed to know about, I would have said we were as intimate as two people could be. But as I glanced again at the blank message screen on my phone, reality hit me with a disturbing thud. It wasn't that I didn't know everything about Bette Winston. It was that I knew nothing.

The next morning, I again found Simon at the dining table, reading the paper, but no dishes had been set out.

"Would you like to join me for breakfast?"

"Where to?"

"Ah, that's a surprise. I'll meet you downstairs in ten minutes."

Quickly, I went to my room to dress, rifling through the dresser drawers for a pair of shorts, something plain, not couture, that Bette might have packed. Instead, I found an envelope delicately placed between silk trousers and a linen sweater. My name was on the front in Bette's handwriting. Inside was a hefty stack of cash. I counted two thousand dollars. Bette must have known in advance she was going away for more than a couple days. Had Sergei known?

My skin prickled. I went to the closet, dressed robotically, and straightened my bangs. Bangs that I'd let Bette cut. The night we swore to stay sisters.

Simon stepped around a rooster strutting down the sidewalk as we neared the restaurant, which resembled a rundown tiki hut. I noticed several chickens follow us in and laughed. Simon was greeted by name, and we were immediately seated at an outdoor table.

"Ah, this is the stuff," Simon said as he filled our glasses after an ice-cold pitcher was brought.

"What is it?"

"Iced tea. But real iced tea. Sun-brewed. It's spectacular."

Simon was right. The crisp tea hit my lips, and I gulped down the glass. Simon refilled the cup.

I mumbled my praise through swallows.

"My friend Maria owns this place, and she makes me a batch whenever she knows I'm coming to town."

"Oh? Maria? Who is *Maria*?" I teased.

"She's just a friend," Simon said, waving me off.

"My mom says best friends make the best spouses."

"Uh-huh. And didn't you also say your parents are going through a nasty divorce?"

"*Went* through it. Already done and dead as a doornail. But in fairness to my mom, I don't think they were ever best friends to begin with." I realized it was the first time I'd spoken about my parents' relationship without immediately slipping into doldrums. I gave myself a mental pat on the back. Progress.

"A lot of people seem to know you down here."

Simon nodded. "I live here part of the year. My cottage is just a couple of blocks over."

"You live here? Then why are you staying on the boat with us?"

"Like I told you, I've known Bette for a long time," Simon said passively. "I just wanted to make sure you guys were all right."

Before I could press him for more details, he changed the subject. "I do most of my painting here. I find the atmosphere is ideal."

A waiter brought out plates of food.

"Paint? I didn't know you were a painter." I took a bite of pancake and sighed as it melted in my mouth. Without the constant intake of drugs, I'd been eating nonstop.

Simon gestured with his fork to a painting on the wall behind me. It was an oil, depicting a muscular man and round woman intertwined and dressed in Renaissance clothing. Had I seen it in a museum, I would have sworn it had been done by a master. It looked like it should have hung in a museum, not a dirt-floored café.

"You're blowing my mind." I gaped.

"Most people don't know. I don't exhibit or sell them."

"What? Why not? You could make a fortune."

Simon laughed. "I already make a fortune. I do this for me." He shrugged. "Then, I give them away."

I thought back to the conversation at Captain Tony's when Simon told Buzz he had a piece for him. I'd assumed he was referring to a photograph. "That's fine, but seriously, I think everyone would eat this up."

"I appreciate that. I really do. But people have an image of me. They want gritty photographs. They want a gritty photographer. And they want wall-sized black and white shots made large so strobe lights can bounce off the images and fall onto the beautiful faces of partiers drinking champagne to bass lines of club music."

"I get it," I said dryly. "You don't like the scene."

"I'm not biting the hand that feeds me. It's just that people don't necessarily want the art. They want the package. They want that whole image. And this"—he gestured to the ornate depiction of lovers intertwined—"is not a part of that image." He paused. "And you're right. I don't like the scene."

Simon smiled broadly. "But I'm glad you like the painting."

"So, I told you everything about me. What about you?"

"What about me?" Simon continued to eat.

"Well, first of all, I didn't know you were a painter. There's more, I'm sure. I'm intrigued. What's your story?"

"Well, I'm from Indiana originally. My mother was a nurse, my father an insurance salesman. When I was about ten, we moved to Utah. My mother, Irene, loved it. My father did not and, not long after the move, he went on a sales call and never came back."

The lighthearted aura that had surrounded us vanished for me. In its place was the sunken hole in my heart that had emerged long ago when my father moved out. "I'm sorry."

Simon shrugged. "It is what it is. At my age, I've seen enough to know that circumstances could have been worse."

I changed the subject, refusing to allow myself to fall back into a funk. "Did you ever marry? Long-term girlfriend? One of your 'friends'?" I waggled my eyebrows and Simon grinned, shaking his head.

"Nope. No wife. No steady."

"Oh, come on. There had to have been women."

"Plenty of women. I said 'steady.'" He took a sip. "And I have a daughter."

I choked, sputtering. "What? You have a daughter? Where is she?"

Simon seemed meek in answering. "I don't know where. I wasn't a part of her life. I got a letter from her mother saying she had given birth to a baby girl, she had named her Kate, and she didn't want anything. She said that it just seemed right I should know."

"So, you didn't try to go find her?"

"I wish I could tell you yes. But my mindset at the time wasn't ready for the responsibility or weight of that kind of love."

"Do you ever regret not trying to find her? I mean— she's your daughter."

Simon paused and poured us each another glass of tea. "There was an artist in the Midwest I knew. We crossed paths here and there. Not a bad fellow, in small doses. He was married to a darling girl. She had gone through it all with him, from his slow start as a struggling artist through his rise to great success. She was pragmatic and strong-willed, yet gave him a very long leash. And, being a typical egotistical artist, he took advantage of that. He was a known philanderer, drank himself into deep depressions, screamed at anyone who dared try to right him. In short, he was hard to love. But she did, and she stood by him. Then one day, he met a young, buxom fan of his work and decided she was his muse sent from God. He had to be with her and filed for divorce.

"His wife had a strong reaction. Obviously. But not how you would think. She could have taken out a full-page spread in *The New York Times*, calling him a bastard and spelling out every one of his indiscretions. But she knew that wouldn't bother him. He would brush it off without a second thought. She knew, in fact, that he would probably welcome it. Free publicity and all." Simon leaned in. "She knew there was only one true way to get revenge."

I could detect a hint of secret admiration in Simon's voice as he continued. "His wife waited until he left town for a weekend, and then she held a garage sale. She dug up every piece of his art she could find and put it on their front lawn. Mind you, he had a large work shed in the back of their property, where he stored many paintings and paper casts for which he was famous. Some were finished, some were still mid-creation. She didn't care—they all came out. She put stickers on every single piece. Ten dollars on some; fifteen on others. The newer pieces, the ones she realized were styled after the mistress, she priced at twenty-five cents. She sold every single piece. And within the course of three hours, the value of his art plummeted to zero. His work suddenly had no value. She ruined him."

"I hate to say it but . . . wow. That was kind of brilliant."

"She was angry."

"No shit. I totally get why you aren't attached now. I mean, to know that someone could crush a person's career like that, just destroy his life's work, that's scary. I don't blame you for not wanting to take the risk."

Simon smiled sadly and shook his head. "No, it's not that. I don't fear my artwork losing value. I'm afraid of hurting someone so much that they would want to destroy me. I fear the power of that kind of love. I don't trust myself with that kind of power."

Simon paused, then took a long sip of tea. A crease formed on his brow as he went on. "Do I wish I had a relationship with my daughter? Now, yes, I do. I wish I could have a conversation with her, like the one I'm having with you now. I wish I could be a gentle father and a good listener and advisor.

"But that's not the person I was at the time. If I had tried to be a father—hell, if I had tried to be anything for anyone else at all—I would have ended up wounding both Kate and her mother. Whatever love they would have tried to give me would have been wasted. I would have turned it into poison. Looking back at the choice I had, to make a bad situation worse or to jump ship and flee, I can only hope I chose the lesser of two evils."

A strange sensation bubbled up. Suddenly, I missed home. More pointedly, I missed my father. I missed the smell of his skin in the summer, a slightly musky, sweaty scent that I'd inhale when he'd throw me on his shoulders. Missed his horrible jokes, his golf shirts, the way he'd stretch like a cat when waking from a nap. I missed being able to hug him. But I also knew that those memories were only that. Memories. And to think any of it was possible again was a fantasy on my part. He was what Simon had feared to become. Someone who took love and turned it to poison.

I knew what that poison felt like, knew how much power a toxic person held over someone who simply wanted love. It had become a pattern in my life and for all my best intentions, there I was—repeating the pattern with Bette.

We ate in silence, Simon caught up in his thought while my mood soured.

Chickens pecked at our feet, and I pulled off small corners from a slice of banana bread to toss to them.

"Don't feed the birds," Simon lightly admonished, taking a bite of shrimp and grits. I slumped in my chair, sulking. "The conditions are great today. Want to go fishing with Frankie and me?"

"No."

"What would you like to do? There are some galleries, or you can see some of the tourist attractions for a bit of fun. There's the dolphin show, if you're into that kind of thing." Simon smiled good-naturedly.

"No, thanks," I said solemnly as I stared at the phone.

Simon looked over his fork. "You all right?"

"You're really not worried?" I asked.

"They're adults, dear. Well, sort of. Adult enough they can make their own decisions." He took another bite and said under his breath, "Even if they're bad ones."

"I'm not talking about decisions, Simon. I'm talking about what if something happened to them? What if they got hurt, and they've just been waiting for us to help? What if they're in a hospital somewhere?"

Simon slowly set down his fork and settled his gaze on me.

"I know you and Sergei are dating. But I think it's safe to assume, at this point, that you might be more committed to your relationship than he is."

"What are you saying?"

"Nothing you haven't already thought. I'm saying that while you might be in a monogamous relationship with Sergei, he might not be in one with you."

"I never said I was in a steady relationship with Sergei."

"How about with Bette?"

I flushed, unable to directly answer his question. "Bette would never do that to me."

"I've known Bette longer than you have." He took another bite of shrimp and added cautiously, "I know Sergei very well, too."

My breath was coming in short spurts. "You keep saying you've known her for so long, but you don't know her like I know her. She's my sister."

Simon spoke slowly. "She is not your sister. I know how close you and Bette are. But she is not family. You have a family, Marin. A family that loves you. You might be angry with them right now, they may be in a dark place, or you all might still be in a state of flux. But that doesn't mean they aren't yours. Work through this hard time, then make peace with the outcome, whatever it is. You can't just run away from it. No matter how far you run, at some point you will have to face it."

I shook with anger. "Who are you to talk about facing your past? You don't even know your own daughter."

He winced. "That's true. But I'm sixty years old. I've spent many years dealing with my past. I'm not proud of who I was, of my choices, and I wish I could change some of them, but I've dealt with it. And I'm at peace with it."

"You're full of shit." Pushing my chair back away from the table, I sputtered. "I—I mean, my parents have nothing to do with Sergei and Bette going missing. They're *missing*. And it's like you don't even care."

I had never seen Simon angry until that moment. His face reddened, fighting back the urge to yell. "Marin, face the facts. Bette and Sergei went away. Together. And it's important for you to stop and think about the reality of the friendships you have with these people and the damage they could do to you. I know them. And this is not going to end well for you."

"How Simon? Tell me how it's not going to end well for me. How is my best friend, who loves me, going to hurt me?"

"Yes, exactly," Simon hissed. "It's exactly that love that might hurt you. It's the same love she had for Olivia, and now Olivia is dead."

My mouth opened, but no retort came.

"I thought that was what you were trying to ask me the other day. About Bette. About the rumors."

The air rushed from my lungs. "What rumors?"

Simon sighed as the anger visibly left his body. "There are a lot of unanswered questions."

"No."

"There were witnesses—"

"I don't believe you."

"—some contradictory accounts of the night—"

"I don't believe you."

Tears sprang to my eyes, and I rushed from the restaurant's courtyard and straight to the boat, throwing my clothes into a duffle along with the money Bette had left. Part of me expected Simon to follow and talk some sense into me, but the end of the gangway remained empty.

The Greyhound bus station was bustling with souvenir-laden tourists and families with crying babies. I bought a ticket for the next bus to Chicago, and forty-eight hours later, I was hailing a cab in a frigid snowstorm. As the taxi pulled away, bound for the boarding house, my mind fixated on how different the journey home had been from the trip to Key West. No limo, no private plane, and no friends. Utterly alone. I had arrived filled with excitement and a sense of unstoppable adventure. But in the cab, with an oppressive gray sky closing around, there was only a dark void.

14

Classes had started the week before, and I found myself exactly where I'd left off the previous semester. Lost. Only this time, the consequences were staring at me in the face.

Cassie greeted me at our bedroom door with a cold stare. "Wow, I didn't think you'd even be back this semester."

I didn't have any fight left. "Yeah. I'm not sure I am back." I walked to my desk, defeated. "But I can't go home right now." I said, sliding into the chair, my head in my hands.

Cassie remained motionless. I swallowed the small amount of pride I had left.

"Can I ask a favor? Can I just stay here for a little bit? I mean, I don't even think I'm still enrolled. I failed all my classes last semester and—"

"Sure," Cassie interrupted.

"Thank you. Thank you so much. I won't bother you. I promise."

"Whatever." Cassie ended the conversation and walked out the door.

I curled myself into a ball on my bed and closed my eyes. On the bus ride back from Key West, I had been able to distract myself with people-watching, but back in the room, alone with my thoughts, all I could focus on was Bette and Olivia. I replayed the conversation with Simon a million times. There was no mistaking what he had said and that he was warning me. On one hand, I felt I was betraying Bette in even entertaining such a horrific rumor. But on the other hand, I'd let the small idea creep in, wondering if it carried weight. *What do I really know about Bette?*

I went back to the first days of meeting her and the hours in the library spent pouring out our pasts, dreams, and fears. But it hadn't been "ours." Bette hadn't shared hers at all. She pulled out conversation and in the elation of being heard, I never thought to ask the reciprocal questions. Again, Harry's warnings that I was simply a butterfly for Bette to pin in a collection sent a chill down my spine.

Then there were the pills. So many pills. Some, I knew, were street drugs, but then there were the others. Strange prescriptions. Quickly, I picked up her phone and began to search the internet for "blue pill," "yellow pill" and then finally, "anti-psychotic drugs." The lists were endless, and I chastised myself for not paying closer attention to what I had popped in my own mouth without a second thought. Eleanor's worrisome pleading, *If she starts acting strange, if she becomes a danger* rang in my ears as if she were standing right next to me.

With shaking hands, I plugged in the next search: Olivia Winston. Several newspaper articles came up, and I quickly scrolled through, looking for anything out of the ordinary, but they all remained factual: *Olivia Winston, age 14, drowned.* I began to sift through faster, sure that there had to be some blog or post that mentioned the "rumor." Nothing. I began adding words to the search. Olivia Winston Bette Winston. Olivia Winston Bette Drowning. Olivia Bette Winston Lake Drowning. Olivia Winston Murder. All I could find were accounts of a young teenage girl taken too early in life and the anguish of a twin sister's loss. I felt like a traitor.

My stomach rumbled, having only eaten vending machine food since leaving the yacht. Walking to campus toward the cafeteria, I saw the students in a completely different light than I had just weeks before. They were no longer bubblegum simpletons, no longer ballcap-wearing Neanderthals. They were not common. They were normal.

What I had so quickly dismissed as a life lived sublevel was suddenly all I could ask for. I had thought I'd had the weight of the world on my shoulders when first walking onto campus, consumed with the worry of grades and maneuvering a new school and hoping to find a group of friends to eat pizza with. As I watched students laughing in huddles as they braved the snowfall, I craved those worries, ached to have my greatest agony being left out of a concert.

The cafeteria buzzed like a beehive, with kids flying left and right, grabbing trays of sandwiches and salads. I had hoped to hit a lull and find a quiet corner to eat and think, but no such luck. The student working the register gave me a friendly smile as she scanned the cheeseburger, fries, and soda. I smiled back and attempted not to cry for the hundredth time that day.

That could be me. I could have stayed the course, studied, gotten a job to supplement my scholarship. But I let it all slip away. Why couldn't I be the girl working the register?

The girl frowned and I froze. If I was no longer a student, that meant I no longer had a food allowance. I hadn't factored in trying to figure out how to eat on top of everything else. I couldn't call my parents yet, couldn't alert them to the fact that anything was wrong, let alone that I had flunked out. I needed time. The safety of the campus house and cafeteria food was crucial. In every sense, I couldn't afford anything else.

"Ah!" The girl rolled her eyes and giggled. "I accidently pressed credit, not student debit. My bad!" She passed the student ID back, and I exhaled with relief. I'd slipped by that time, but didn't know how long the luck would continue to run. It only amplified my urgency to come up with a plan fast.

I'd spent the bulk of the money Bette had left on the ticket for the bus ride home. There were small bits of cash left in various envelopes, and I tried to calculate how much I had in total and how far it could be stretched out. I thought of the bedroom doors constantly left open in the house. Trusting girls who used those open doors as an invitation to come visit, gossip, and discuss their communications papers.

I'd never taken any of them up on those unspoken invitations and doubted many of them would even know my name if I did pop in. I would need to start watching.

Five minutes would be all it took to slip into a room and make a quick sweep of their small desks, scooping up loose bills and change, anything that they might not notice right away. This was what I was to become. A thief. My mind raced as I calculated how far a box of dry cereal could be stretched, how long I could sustain myself on—

The manic thoughts were interrupted by a low, terse voice. "Marin."

"Harry. What are you doing here?"

Harry raised an eyebrow and nodded toward the tray in his hands. "Despite popular belief, I do not live solely off vials of blood and the heads of bats."

"Right." I shifted uncomfortably. I had never been alone with Harry, except for our one conversation at the lake over Thanksgiving, and was wary of how to proceed.

Fortunately, he took charge of the situation. "Want to have lunch together?"

I smiled appreciatively, and we found a table for two near a large window overlooking a square of snow-covered lawn. To anyone else, we seemed like a cute couple trying to carve out a little alone time. In reality, the air could be cut with a knife.

Harry drizzled dressing over his salad and began to toss it unenthusiastically. He glanced at my tray overflowing with junk food.

I blushed. "I was kind of hungry. I don't always eat like this."

"It looks good. I'm jealous." To my surprise, he smiled warmly. "My head says get the salad, but my heart screams fries!"

I gently moved the overflowing container of French

fries between us. "Share?"

Harry snapped his fingers excitedly. "I thought you'd never ask." He moved his salad to the side, and we sat for a few minutes, picking at the fries in silence. I opened a bagged cookie and put that between us as well.

Harry broke the ice. "How was your Christmas?"

I answered mid-cheeseburger bite. "Good, I guess. My brother swooped in and graced everyone with his presence. My dad barely acknowledged me. And my mom graded papers the whole time. You?"

"Really great. My parents and I went to Europe to see my grandparents, and then Ozzie met me in Portofino for the rest of break."

"I thought he was in St. Barts with Bette?"

"He was, but he left right after Christmas. He was exhausted when he got to Italy. We literally spent the entire week on a rock beach, sunning ourselves and eating boatloads of pasta." Harry chewed a piece of cookie. "Don't get me wrong, I think he had a great time in St. Barts, but you can only go out to night clubs so much, and Bette tends to treat those nights like it's the last night on Earth."

I laughed. "Believe me, I get it." Harry held up his salad and I took a cherry tomato off the top. A shift was happening between us, one I had not foreseen.

"This is nice," I said, reaching for a bite of cucumber.

Harry shrugged his shoulders. "Well, we're friends. Why wouldn't it be?"

I chuckled lightly. "I honestly thought you hated me."

"Why?"

"Let's see." I ticked off the reasons with my fingers. "There are the scowls, the derogatory comments, the eye-rolling—"

Harry smirked. "What can I say? I have resting bitch face."

I laughed. "Yes. Yes, you do."

Harry glanced up. "I heard you guys went to Key West."

When I only nodded, he prompted, "And how did it go?"

Something about the tone of Harry's voice said he knew exactly how it went. It came as a relief. He seemed to be opening the door to pick up our conversation where it ended on the beach. And it didn't scare me this time. I needed answers and replied carefully, testing the waters.

"Key West was interesting. I'd never been before."

Harry nodded and slowly chewed a fry, waiting for more.

"Got to see some local joints. Had a few rum punches." I smiled, trying to lighten the mood. "Stayed on a yacht, which was crazy."

"When did Bette and Sergei leave?" The comment, said so flippantly, was a punch to the gut. My reaction was confirmation. Harry placed his hand on mine. "Are you okay?"

The unexpected show of empathy threw me off-kilter, and I began to cry. *How did he know?* Angry and embarrassed, I tried to wipe the tears away. "I'm fine. They just went to Miami to go work on their projects. That's all."

When I dared to look straight at Harry, his face was soft. The cold stare I had become so accustomed to was gone, and his eyes radiated with a sympathy I'd only seen once before. At Tessa's art show. The night Bette first showed her dark, cruel side. The night Ozzie said she could be a coiled snake waiting to strike when least expected.

Harry's forehead wrinkled with concern. "I'm sorry this is happening to you."

Delicately, in a hushed whisper, I asked, "What *is* happening?"

Harry pulled his hand away and looked around the cafeteria. It had quieted significantly. He leaned in. "When I told you that Bette collects people, makes them into who she wants them to be, uses them to create her world, it was from experience. I've seen her do it with Oz. You know about that. But I've seen her do it to others, too."

"What 'others'?"

"Other friends. Girls."

The notion of another female sharing Bette's attention seemed even more of a betrayal than the possibility of Sergei stepping into my place. I didn't know how to ask Harry the painful question. Mercifully, he seemed to sense it even though his words left me cold.

"She's had close friends. I'm sure it hurts to hear but you deserve to know the truth. I was teasing you before, at the cabin, when I asked you if you were in love with her. Because honestly, I didn't think you were. I thought you were smart enough not to get caught up in her trap. I assumed you were just having fun. Maybe getting a taste of a life you'd never experienced before." Harry's words sped up as he gained momentum. "But then Oz told me you two hooked up at some point, then she spilt with Sergei, and that's when I knew she was doing it again. I just don't want to see you get hurt." He paused. "But I guess it's a little late for that, isn't it?"

Blood rushed from my face and a lightheaded sensation overtook my body, as if I was floating away, pulling me from the table. They'd been talking about me. About "us." He referred to it as a "hook-up," nothing with relevance. Is that what Bette had relayed? And there had been others before? As painful as the revelation was, I knew there was more. Harry's grave concern seemed too dramatic for a simple broken heart. Simon's warning thundered through my head, and suddenly the room began to spin.

I could barely breathe. "Tell me. Everything."

Harry suddenly seemed to realize how in the dark I'd been kept. He continued with kid gloves. "So, I guess there are two things. There are the facts, and there are my opinions. The facts are that she's had other close friends in the past—girls that she takes under her wing, all to different degrees, but all of them changed significantly from when we first met them."

I thought back to our first meeting at Les Mots. The way Bette had displayed me like a new *object d'art*, and the way Harry had dismissed me, refusing to close any emotional distance. In hindsight, it was clear he'd been protecting himself from an emotional investment that he knew would end up fruitless.

"They were always attractive, but always naïve," Harry continued. "Always in a perilous situation at home so that Bette could become the girl's world. She would pamper the girl, dress her, fawn over her like a pet. She'd totally immerse the girl into her life. But never vice versa. The girl would idolize Bette. And then they would become

. . . close."

I could see how uncomfortable Harry was, knowing he was circling a raw wound. "Then the girl would disappear."

"What do you mean?"

"Exactly that. They just go away. There's always a reason, whether they'd move or switch schools or just vanish. But the info always come from Bette. There's never a goodbye." Harry unscrewed his water and took a sip. "Those are the facts."

I was biting my lip, using the pain to keep focused as my mind railed. "So what is your *opinion*?"

"My *opinion* is you are a cool chick. I like you. A lot. And I don't want you to disappear."

"Well, I've recently realized that I need to get Bette out of my life. But she's not going to scare me or piss me off enough that I would stop talking to you or Ozzie."

Harry stared long and hard. "I'm not sure it's up to you whether you disappear or not." His voice lowered again. "That's also my opinion."

My voice matched Harry's, both barely audible. "Like Olivia?"

Harry nodded. "Like Olivia." He paused, as if weighing whether to continue. "She told Ozzie once. He said they were drunk at his house, just the two of them, and she told him a story about the night Olivia died . . ." His voice trailed off.

"Well?"

"Oz wouldn't tell me what she said. He started to, then just shut down. He said she probably made the whole thing up and it wasn't worth repeating, that I should forget he ever brought it up. But I—I'm telling you, he wasn't being flippant. He was *scared*."

We walked to the cafeteria exit together in silence. As we placed our trays in the bin, Harry turned. "It's not you that I'm trying to keep Ozzie from."

I nodded, numb. "I get that now."

"That's a big part of why I want to move Ozzie away from here: I'm afraid of what she might do to him. To me. I don't know how to stop her. I mean, there's no hard evidence, nothing tangible I could use. So, for now, I just watch her like a hawk." Harry paused. "You should, too."

Harry turned to leave, then swiveled back and hugged me hard. I pressed my forehead into his shoulder, grateful for the feel of something solid.

I was restless with Harry's revelation ringing in my ears—I needed a release. I desperately wished I was back in Key West with Simon, able to talk to him about everything that had been left on the table and about all I had learned. Cassie and I were officially not on speaking terms, passing silently as she skittered from class to class, looking through me like I was a ghost. Chad would only shrug his shoulders in defeat, understanding that, somehow, I had fallen from grace.

For a brief moment, I considered calling Ty, reasoning he'd be able to explain everything away with a quick quip, but decided against it at the last minute. It would mean explaining why I had again blown off classes and had hidden rather than make amends and start over. I didn't have an explanation yet.

I picked up my phone, ignoring the umpteenth text from my mom: *How was your trip? How are classes? The weather here is horrible. How about there?*

I was suddenly very, very desperate to talk to someone. Someone who was of my current world. Someone who might be willing to give me information.

As the line rang, I paced my room, impatiently chewing a hangnail.

"*Hey!*" Poppy answered. She perpetually sounded as if she were three hours into a college tailgate party.

"Hi, Poppy. It's Marin. From your mom's party. I'm friends with—"

"Duh!" she shrieked. "I have your number in my phone. You gave it to me that night! Remember?"

No. I didn't remember much from most of my nights out, but played it off. "Oh yeah, that's right. Anyway, I'm just wondering what you're doing tonight."

Her voice pierced my eardrum. "OMG! Nothing! Why? Is there a party? We should totally go. Is Bette going? O! M! G! What a blast!"

"No—no, Bette's not—I mean, I don't think she's in town right now. I don't really know. I just thought we could go out and do something. Maybe talk—" I stumbled on my words. I realized that, of course, Poppy would assume I was calling with party plans. That was how girls like Poppy operated. That was how Bette operated. Always with the inside scoop, closed doors thrown wide open for them. Life was one big party.

Fortunately, Poppy didn't seem to notice. "Hey, I just remembered! There's this new club opening up next month, but they're throwing, like, these rager parties every night to get people all jacked up and talking about it. I totally have an open invite. Let's go!" Doors thrown wide open. Poppy's family had known Bette's for a long time. There could be answers—if I could get Poppy to settle down long enough to open up.

A town car picked me up, then Poppy from her mother's. I had tried to hide my face from the doorman as he opened the passenger door, but he recognized me with a cold, "Good evening." Once inside the car, Poppy handed me a premade cocktail. I shouldn't have been surprised. Hoping to keep her happy, I took a long drink and thanked her.

"Where's that whore?" Poppy bellowed, obviously referring to Bette. I had learned that Poppy's terms of endearment ran an unusual gamut.

"I don't know." I shrugged, taking another drink from the heavily poured concoction. After two weeks of no drugs or alcohol in my system, the drink immediately hit. "Listen, speaking of Bette—"

"Fuck, who cares? Her loss. We're gonna rock out with our cocks out!"

Poppy quickly pulled out a small glass cylinder and scooped out a small portion of cocaine. She held it to my nose, but I pulled back. She gave me an exasperated look. "What the fuck?"

Knowing there was a fine line between keeping Poppy's attention and getting thrown out of the car, I smiled amicably and took the spoonful. "Thanks." The familiar sting in my nose felt worse than ever.

"Hey!" Poppy bellowed at the driver, "you missed the place. Back up. Back up!"

I looked at the plain brick building and unmarked rusted steel door. "Where?"

"They don't want to put the sign out until, like, an hour before they officially open. You know, drama!"

I rolled my eyes in solidarity and accepted another

spoonful of powder. I reached for my drink, swaying slightly, but found it empty. I was already losing track of time.

Poppy sent a quick text, and within moments, the secret red door swung open. We hurried inside as a hulk of a man closed the door behind us. My eyes adjusted to the dark room, and an inebriated smile spread across my face. A monstrous crowd of people swam in front of me, tangled, enmeshed, slithering happily past one another in the closest of quarters. The music was pounding, making it too loud to talk, and the electric house rhythms set my teeth on edge.

I had failed miserably in my plan to course Poppy into a serious conversation, but was relieved for a break from the sea of anxiety I'd been swimming in. Strobe and laser-beam lights flooded the two-story dance floor, illuminating the whites of teeth, eyes, and breasts for fractions of seconds, creating a live moving mosaic. Strobes bounced off two gigantic chandeliers, large enough to span the length of the dance floor. The brick walls were covered with twelve-foot black-and-white photos of infamous rock stars and DJs. The energy was palpable, and when Poppy placed a small piece of paper, no larger than the size of a pencil eraser, on my tongue, I didn't think twice.

"What was that?" I yelled into Poppy's ear as the paper melted in my mouth.

"You're swallowing a party, baby!" Poppy threw her arms in the air and began thrusting her hips to and fro, forcing a pathway to the bar. I saw a young, clear-cut man with stockbroker swagger grab her backside. Poppy turned on her heel and winked at him, then disappeared as the crowd swallowed her whole. She returned with four drinks.

"Who's this for?"

"Us! Down the first one, and then you can drink the second like a civilized person!" she yelled, throwing her head back in laughter. In my hazy state, I thought that, while Poppy did not fit into Bette's definition of a chic, polished, cultural elitist, she was actually fun. I found myself laughing along with her zany, Southern devil-may-care humor and cheered with abandon when she passed along a Jell-O shot. We tapped our mini plastic cups in cheers, squeezing the sickly-sweet gelatin into our mouths.

Four shots later, we were proudly showing off bright red tongues to anyone who would look. More than once, I turned to see Poppy stick her tongue out at some brawny boy, then shove it down his throat.

For a moment, I thought I saw a flash of blonde curls. *Bette.* Then the vision disappeared.

More drinks and more trips to the bathroom for cocaine. The music stopped rattling my brain and instead became a part of it, my body swaying in anticipation of the frenetic beats. Incredibly, more bodies packed into the club, making it impossible to move without knees slipping between thighs and breasts swiping along backs. The mixture of drugs kicked into high gear, and I found myself lost in the throng of grabbing hands, caressing and fondling, the sense of skin jumping between satin and sandpaper. Warm lips nibbled at my neck, and I laughed, sensually leaning into strangers.

I longed for everyone and, at the same time, for no one in particular. Bette and Sergei had blissfully floated away from my realm of conscious thought as the room became one large amoeba, everyone singing, jumping, arms in the air.

An arm slipped around my stomach, slowly pulling me backward until a large body spooned my own, rhythmically moving with me. I let out a faint moan and pushed my backside into his pelvis. He held me tighter. When I opened my eyes, still facing away from the stranger, I found that we had swayed away from Poppy and into a dark corner. One arm remained around my waist, an oddly secure feeling, while the other offered me a cocktail, which I drank down in four large gulps. He took the empty cup and began to run his fingers through my hair, kissing my neck.

I tried to turn, to kiss him head on, but he forced my face forward with aggressive kisses to the nape of my neck, his body coiled around mine. The room was becoming a blur of colors, electric blues and reds, swirling into each other. Like our bodies pressed together, I had trouble deciphering where one line began and another ended

One massive hand grasped my breast, firm and lustful, while his other hand moved to my short skirt as he began to grind against me. The hand moved up the inside of my thigh, higher and higher, deftly maneuvering my underwear out of the way. I was quickly losing consciousness, my thoughts flickering in and out.

My awareness was fuzzy, then brightly focused, then black.

Pulled through a hallway.

Slipping on spilled drinks.

Falling.

A grimy, wet bathroom.

Facing the stall wall.
Graffiti.
My skirt pulled up from behind.
Voices.
"Sell it to Hoover."
Pain.
The club dance floor.
Dancing.
Singing.
Falling.
Drinks.
Shots.
Pills.
Car.
Bed.
Voices.
"He can take it deep."
Blackout.

I woke with bile spilling out my mouth. My vision blurred, and as I tried to blink to focus, my stomach heaved, projecting vomit onto my cheek and face. Directions were tipsy turvy. *Sideways? No, not sideways. I'm on my back.* A garish collage of brown and yellow flowers spread before me.

Hoover. Deep.

I had no idea where I was. A dark-paneled wall. A cheap dresser with peeling wood edges. My eyes drifted up. A spackled ceiling. I couldn't move, couldn't command my body to do anything.

My heart beat rapidly, and tears sprang to my eyes. *Where am I?* When I was able to push myself up, a searing pain raged through my torso and daggers shot through my head as I vomited violently again. The cheap bedspread was covered in noxious bile, as was my hair and clothing. Curled into a ball, I waited for the nausea to pass. Frantically, I scanned the room.

Where is Poppy? Where am I? What the hell happened? Get out of here, Marin. Get out of here!

I forced myself to the door, locked it, and sank to my knees. Crawling towards the bathroom, I spilled bile on the dark green shag carpet. My gauzy blouse stuck to my skin as I pulled it off, as did my skirt that was pushed up above my waist, exposing blotchy, red, and bruising thighs.

The florescent light of the bathroom blinded me as I threw my clothes into the wastebasket and sunk into the shower, letting the hot water wash over while I hugged myself on the tub floor. Desperately, I tried to piece together the events of the night before. Poppy, the club, Bette. Was it Bette? It looked like Bette. Drugs and alcohol. The strange man. Bette.

Take it deep. Sell it to Hoover.

None of the fragments made sense. Everything was disjointed. The only clear thought in my mind was that I had seen this room before. *Scott's exhibit. The videos we had watched.* Bette had said it was art. But what if it hadn't been?

Had Bette known? Was she a part of it? My gut clenched with animal instinct.

Gingerly, I towel-dried and wrapped myself in a threadbare robe from the closet, scratchy and stained. I walked around the room briefly and was astonished to see my phone on the dresser. The screen was lit up with notifications: Facebook, Instagram, Snapchat.

I wasn't popular on social media—a few scattered "friends" here and there. And the little online interaction I'd had before meeting Bette ended when she stated social media was a pastime for simpletons. But here was name after name, more being added by the second, following me as a "friend," tagging me in pictures. I frowned at the unfamiliar usernames and hurried out the door.

Squinting from early-morning sunlight, I walked straight into an aging woman wearing sweatpants and a dingy tie-dye T-shirt. In one hand, she held a cleaning bucket overflowing with a dirty rag, cleaning solutions, and a yellow-stained toilet brush. The housekeeper gave me an emotionless once-over, shook her head, and sighed.

I asked her where we were, desperate to order an Uber, and she threw her head in the direction of the half-lit neon motel sign: *Southside Inn*. The name registered for a moment, the image of a keychain bearing the same name, but the physical pain and pressing fear immediately drove away the fleeting memory.

When the car arrived, I gingerly slid into the back seat. For once, I was grateful for the oppressive high-blasting heat as my body shook violently, though it was more likely from an adrenaline-induced fight-or-flight response than from the cold. The driver's dark eyes looked concerned as he examined me through the rear-view mirror.

Tears streamed down my face as bile fought its way up my throat again. I gulped air to calm myself and tried to think rationally. The housekeeper hadn't seemed to be shocked at the appearance of a girl outside in a robe mid-January. Maybe I wasn't the first girl she had seen.

How many had there been?

The car turned onto the expressway, and I pulled out my phone again. Opening Instagram, I found the pictures I had been tagged in. They were all from different people's accounts and all from the night before in the club. I cringed. The first photo was me standing atop the bar, holding a shot glass in the air, screaming at the sky with some guy's hand inching up my thigh. Other inebriated partygoers surrounded me and, fortunately, I didn't stand out too bad. In that photo. In others, I was sticking my tongue down a random boy's throat as multiple hands groped my breasts, straddling another girl while she held a tequila bottle to my mouth, offering my bare backside to a young man's waist. In every picture I was tagged, there were ten other people tagged, as well. The same ten people every picture.

I began to go through them, clicking each name, but each was set up for privacy except one. It was an anonymous profile face, a picture of the *David*, and all the photos were of major parties and club scenes. I clicked on a picture taken months before and saw that the same ten people were tagged. Each picture, different people, the same names tagged. Panicking, I logged into Facebook and found the exact same situation. Same photos, same names. None of the accounts linked to the names seemed to be real people. I tried deleting the pictures, with no luck. I untagged myself, but the images lived on. I reddened at the thought of my brother seeing me in those club shots, a party girl, loose, out of control.

Google provided no answers, either, as I entered the names—random, common names, thousands of hits with no connection linking any of them—until one name finally produced a crack of information. In the midst of insurance salesmen's LinkedIn profiles and posted fantasy football results, "K. Hoover," one of the names tagged over and over in the photos, provided a solitary link but no description. *Hoover*. I clicked and was directed to another link, then another. Finally, a dead end came with denied access. A simple white page appeared with the word *ONION* across it. Exhausted, I sank further into the crusty green leather bench seat.

Back in my room, I couldn't separate the feelings of anger and guilt from confusion and dread. I showered again, trying to scrub away the pain and shame. Dressing took an exorbitantly long time, my thoughts taking over, my brain and body going into lockdown as I sifted through the events of the night, trying to piece together some meaning. Tears came in waves, hard and fast. Recovering a pair of sweatpants from the bottom of my closet, I pulled them up to my knees as I began to weep again.

Cassie entered with an aloof, "Hey." She began to say more, then caught a glimpse of me. Concern immediately overtook her animosity.

"Oh God. What happened to you?" She gently bent down and helped me pull my pants up.

I tried to piece words together in between sobs, but none came.

Cassie whipped her phone from her back pocket. Her voice was steadfast, but I could see the fear in her eyes. "I'm calling the police."

At the hospital, the police officer shifted in her chair. Her demeanor had visibly softened from when she'd first led me into the consultation room at the hospital. "Can you tell me again, from when you arrived at the club, what you remember?"

I stared blankly at the Formica tabletop as the officer's eyes took in the flowering bruise on my cheek. The real damage was somewhere she couldn't see. I had spent the last three hours being poked and prodded and swabbed by nurses who said it would be weeks to get the results back. I'd had every inch of my body photographed. I didn't want to be touched again, didn't want to answer more questions. I just wanted to go back to bed and try to quiet my racing mind.

Instead, I picked up my phone and went to the Instagram account, holding it up to show the officer. "I was tagged in all these photos from the club I was at last night. I don't know who posted them, and I can't find anything out past that. And then there are these other people who are tagged in all the pictures, too. But all their profiles are private, so I can't see who they really are. Except this one name, K. Hoover. And I'm trying to find him—or her—but the only link that seems to have any relevance just keeps sending me in different direction and always ends with me not having 'access' and every blocked access point shows a gray key icon—"

The officer's eyebrows raised slightly and leaned in closer. "It sounds like an onion account."

Her tone and quick response made my skin prickle. "What's that?"

"Onion accounts are a part of the Tor network. It's the deep web."

I froze. *Take it deep.* The sentence, uttered the night before, thundered in my head.

A crease formed on the officer's forehead. "It's internet

space for illegal activity."

"Like what?" My voice quivered. I shoved the phone into the woman's hands, showing her everything and begging her for information on how to access the links I couldn't get around.

"I wish I could help, but it's encrypted. You need special software. I'm happy to take your phone to the precinct. They can send it to the FBI and see what they can find about whatever network this is." Her face was drawn but sympathetic.

Setting her notebook on the table, she paused, then spoke softly. "I wouldn't start poking around, though. There's some messed-up shit on there—child pornography, Nazi support groups, sadomasochistic fetish, snuff films—"

I began to shake.

"I have a little sister about your age. The thought of her seeing the things on there . . ." Her voice trailed off as she shook her head. "You don't want those images in your head."

I stammered quietly, "So, these accounts—to find them—"

The police officer sat back up straight. "Here's the deal: I really doubt these people even exist. They're probably just cover names. You know, like a code word, so creeps, when they see it, know something new is out to look at. Kind of like an online advertising campaign."

My attempt to blink back fresh tears failed. Somewhere out there was a video of me. A video that demented, perverse people were buying and watching. Getting off to. I was helpless, and it was becoming clear that the police didn't have the resources to stop the video, either.

Even if they could take down the video and destroy it, another would be made. There would be another victim.

The officer pushed a box of tissues across the table. "Let's start at the beginning again and see if it jogs anything in your memory, anything that might lead us to the person who did this to you."

There was nothing else to remember. And I didn't want to relive each moment again. A wave of shivers overtook me. I shook all the way back to my room, where I stayed in bed for the remainder of the weekend.

No word came from Bette, and I stewed over the image of her at the club. Why had Bette been there? I was certain she had set me up. She'd drugged my drinks before, so she could have easily slipped something into one of the drinks that night. *Easily,* I thought and admonished myself for allowing myself to again be pulled into such debauchery. I didn't want to admit it, but I was beginning to believe Simon's theory. Oz and Harry were still keeping their distance, a plan I wished I had followed.

Under the covers, I did the only thing I could think of and deleted all my social media accounts. Logically, I knew it was all still out there, the photos, the video, my body. But at that moment, "out of sight, out of mind" was what I needed. If I couldn't see it, if my family couldn't see it, if my classmates couldn't see it, it didn't exist. I needed it not to exist.

Although my soul felt as raw as my body, I pushed and pushed and pushed until the night at the club was a pinprick of a memory, nothing more than a hazy half-dream. I had to. I put it away, to bed, buried it deep in a steel coffin into the cold ground of denial.

15

My flower! I have returned. So much great work, so much to get ready for exhibit. I miss you so. Please, bring me your skin, your smell.

I had spent time planning how I'd react if Sergei reached out. Although rage surged through my veins, I'd play it cool and pretend I had barely noticed his absence. I knew I could find out the truth, and I knew the only way to do that was to act like nothing was wrong. I needed to play into his ego.

Immediately replying to his text, I wrote that I was relieved he'd written, that I'd missed his smell, too, and that I couldn't wait to see him. Twenty minutes later, I was in a cab on my way to his apartment, focused on one thing: The truth.

When I arrived, music was seeping through the doorframe to Sergei's loft.

Loud, angry techno music with a heavy, thundering bass. I wasn't sure he could even hear me knock, but he unlatched the metal door and slid it open as if waiting to pounce. He stood in front of me, shirt off, his normal creamy complexion tanned golden. His jeans were slung low on his hips. Observing him through clear eyes, I saw the sexual trap he was setting. It made my stomach turn over.

In one movement, he pulled me into his arms and into a kiss. His hands gripped tightly and slid down until he held me from behind, pulling my hips to his. I winced with pain, legs still tender and bruised, but he took it as longing. He began slowly stepping backward, making his way toward the bed.

I recoiled with nausea, my body rejecting physical contact and disgusted by his touch. The thought of sex made me ill in a very literal sense, but I had to stick to the script, play the part correctly or risk blowing it all. Bette had taught me how to pretend to be a character, and it was time to use that talent.

"No." I pulled myself from Sergei's grip, pouting.

"My *Uebok*? What?"

"No. I'm mad at you. Really mad."

"Why?"

"You left me. Remember? Key West?" I ran a finger down his chest. "I really wanted you."

He waved his hand and sighed. "Ah, that. I told you I had to work. So much to do." His eyes began to sparkle, and he smiled brightly. "The exhibit is going to be monument. This, my best work, and so many patrons and galleries are interested. I had so many meetings, created so many new pieces. The whole show took new form. Better form. Huge form!"

I walked over to giraffe-tall pieces tilted against the wall, hidden under large sheets of white cloth. The frames that housed the photographs were visible. The pieces were ready for showing. I honestly didn't know if he had gone to Miami to work or if he'd gone off with Bette, but I knew one thing: He was the link I needed to find the answer I was searching for. And the pieces of artwork were what would make the plan happen.

I reached for one of the sheets, and Sergei snapped, "*Nyet*! No! No, no. Not yet." He pulled the sheet from my fingers, hiding his masterpiece once more. "No one must see yet."

"Okay, sorry."

Softening, Sergei tugged at my hand, leading me toward his bed. "Please, don't be mad at me. I was only working." He kissed my neck. "I will make up to you."

I pulled back.

"So, where was Bette while you were in Miami?"

He shrugged. "I don't know." Before I could ask any more questions, he kissed me hard, and his hands ran down my leg, but I winced and pushed back again.

"What is this?" He gestured to the purple streak running up my thigh.

I lied, locking my knees together. "I fell. Off a barstool. Hit my legs."

Sergei eyed me suspiciously, then smirked. "Is okay, we can do other things. Your mouth is not bruised, no?" He laughed.

My mouth watered with quickly-forming vomit, but I managed a lighthearted giggle. "Could we just . . . Maybe we could just hang out, okay?"

"I see, you punish me. Okay, okay, but not for too long!" He smacked my rear playfully and went into the kitchen, pulling a bottle of vodka from the freezer. I breathed a sigh of relief, wondering how long I could keep him at bay. "I ordered food. Stay with me? Forgive me?"

I mixed martinis. Sergei's filled to the rim with cold vodka, mine with water. Then I mixed him another. And another.

"To your exhibit." I purred, touching my glass to his. Vodka sloshed and dripped down his forearm. The alcohol was working.

"To benefactors." He winked as he downed his drink.

A young man knocked at the door, spoke with Sergei, and quickly left. Sergei came back to the bedroom, a mischievous grin on his face and two plastic baggies in his hand. Soon, he was in a cocaine and ecstasy frenzy, while I became deft at snorting air and sticking pills under my tongue only to spit them out moments later, with Sergei never the wiser.

"—and Rodolpho said it will be bigger than Basquiat. More bigger than Warhol!"

"You don't say?" I cooed, batting my lashes. Sergei's ego was growing larger by the hour, which was exactly what I had hoped for.

"You must be next to me tonight. You must!" Sergei exclaimed, his eyes dilated black.

"I can't wait." I was in.

And just like that, I was again Chicago's darling, dressed in black patent leather, arm in arm with Sergei, cameras capturing our every move as we kicked off his exhibit weekend. I managed to hide in the bathroom for the bulk of the evening.

The next morning, as we stretched out lazily in bed, Sergei murmured, his eyes still closed, "You need call Bette."

I sat up on my elbows and smiled to myself. I had counted on Bette seeing the pictures of Sergei with me on his arm from the night before. It was the push she needed to emerge from the shadows. I was ready.

Affecting an offended tone, I responded, "Why? I don't want to chase her down anymore. Frankly, I don't care if I ever see her again."

"She is your best friend. You must invite her to the exhibit. She should be there."

"If you're so concerned about it, why don't you invite her?" I snipped.

Sergei shook his head. "Don't act like brat. Why she upset, I don't know. She text me and beg for you to call her." He sighed with boredom. "Flower, you are the beautiful one. I am yours. The whole city will be loving you. So, you be the nice one. Call her and invite."

He tossed my phone to me as he went into the bathroom. I sat staring at the wall. The plan to lure Bette back out from hiding, to place her where she could finally be confronted, was working. Still, Harry's words continued to loop in my mind.

Bette is a coiled rattlesnake. She'll wait until you think she's surely out of your life, or you've simply forgotten she was ever angry with you. And right at that moment, she'll strike.

In truth, I was scared of her.

Bette answered on the first ring.

"Marin?" There was desperation in her voice. "Oh God. Where are you? I need to see you." She sounded like she was crying.

I remained wary. "Where are you? I've been trying to get hold of you for two weeks, Bette." I tried to keep my voice steady.

"It's bad. I need to see you," Bette sobbed. It reminded me of her breakdown at her parents' house. Oz had warned she would disappear. This is what she did, with no thought of anyone else's feelings.

"You didn't answer my question, Bette. Where were you?"

"I need to—"

"Stop, just stop. I know you need. You always *need*."

"I—"

I calmed my voice and remembered the mission. "I was calling to invite you to Sergei's exhibit tomorrow. He said you should be there. That's all I'm calling for." I quickly hung up. My breath was ragged, my body shaking with adrenaline.

Sergei walked out. "Is she coming?"

"I don't know. She's acting weird."

He sighed. "Ah, okay. I call her. She needs to be there."

Of course she does, I thought bitterly.

Sergei brought two mimosas to the bed. We clinked glasses. He winked over his glass. "Cheers. Ready to turn this city red?"

I sipped the champagne, just enough for him to see me smile with pleasure. "Yes. Yes, I am definitely ready to paint the town red."

He leaned down as if to kiss but then slipped a pill from his mouth into mine. I used every ounce of energy not to show my repulsion. Then promptly turned my head and secretly spit out the pill, mentally preparing for the battle ahead.

The day of the exhibit was pandemonium. Sergei's phone rang nonstop, and he answered each call with an air of haughty boredom:

"No, you should have call me last week. No more interviews."

"Gigi, your kindness is much like your beauty. So big."

"I wearing what I wearing. I do not want your brand shirts."

A drug dealer named Clover popped over to the loft for drinks, followed by several popular graffiti artists.

"Dude"—Clover bumped fists with Sergei—"this is going to be fucking monumental." He handed over a black plastic bag. "What'dya say we start celebrating early?"

Champagne bottles were popped, cocktails were mixed, pills were passed, and lines were cut openly on the kitchen counter.

I fluttered around, dodging offers of coke and vodka. By the time we needed to get dressed, I was astonished that Sergei was still standing upright.

He had bought an ebony slip dress for me and asked me to paint my eyes charcoal black, heavy and gothic, to create the perfect outfit for his star of the evening. He dressed himself in a grungy black T-shirt, undoubtedly distressed by a high-end designer and sold for several hundred dollars, along with equally damaged jeans and black motorcycle boots. The perfect image of glamour and grunge, another piece of Sergei's artwork.

A sleek sedan delivered us to the event. As the driver opened my door, camera flashes blinded me. Not in any of my experiences with Bette had I seen so many paparazzi, reporters, and gawkers. Hands reached out to touch our arms, our clothes, to be able to say they had made physical contact with Sergei. He was a rock star.

The air was charged with palpable energy that bordered on dangerous. The throngs of people inside the velvet ropes were as strong as those outside, and steroid-addicted bouncers parted the crowd with monstrous arms.

The eyes of the beautiful art crowd fell on me with longing. I was again princess. Untouchable, regal, envied. But for the first time, I saw it all for what it truly was: A façade.

The mixture of conversation and shouting from the crowd, along with the music—the same techno music that had been playing nonstop at the loft—thundered through the venue. Sergei paused for a moment before entering the show. He squeezed my hand, then led us in.

A shocking show of strobe lights and wafts from a smoke machine hit me like a freight train. I nearly fell over as all my senses were assaulted at once. Fortunately, the crowd was moving en masse behind us and pressed me back to my feet and forward in space.

I scanned the room for Bette. My hand was wrenched from Sergei's as he began his rounds—hours of greetings and hugs and well-wishes from a hundred or more attendees were ahead. A waiter handed me a martini. I quickly sipped it—rationalizing that one drink wouldn't do me in—while laughing with Clover and some of Sergei's other friends who had followed in a second car.

They dispensed light blue pills, yellow pills, pale pink pills, throwing them back nonchalantly. I declined, but allowed myself a second martini to calm my nerves as I watched the doorway for Bette, who was nowhere to be seen. A few select reporters had been allowed entry, and they approached the group to speak with the artists. I stepped back to allow them in and turned, finally, to take in Sergei's great accomplishment.

I froze.

The fifteen-foot-tall pieces were mixed media. A collision of resin, pulp, and paint. But at their foundation were photographs.

Photographs of Bette.

Naked photographs of Bette.

Erotic photographs. Intimate photographs. Sexual. Personal. These were not pictures of a model. These were pictures of a lover.

My world exploded. Then imploded. I turned inside out.

Simon had been right. About everything.

I moved rapidly, pushing my way through groups of people, dashing from one photograph to the next, taking in every detail, trying to find something that would prove it was a hoax. But it was all there: The curve of Bette's hip, her tongue on the tip of her lip, her eyes. At one time, her eyes had looked at me with the same gaze. The shriek that formed in my throat came out as a whoosh of air, silent.

I whipped around in time to see lights flashing. Not lights from the strobe or lighting board, but from cameras. A cascade of flashing light falling onto one central figure.

She was there. Posing. A celestial angel in front of a wickedly erotic photo.

Then the cameras turned to me and, suddenly, I understood what was happening, why Sergei was so insistent Bette come to the event.

I had been set up.

He forced an element of performance art into the exhibit. I was his girlfriend. Bette was his muse. And we were on display as part of the show. We were another layer of his exhibit. I had naively assumed that I was playing the part of the chess master, strategically lining up all my pawns, knights, bishop, ready to win the battle. But I failed and fell right into Bette's trap.

Checkmate.

I looked hard at Bette. Bette smiled with soulless eyes. She had understood long before me. In the last phone call, there had been an opportunity for Bette to have a moment of guilt. A loyalty to drive her to tell the truth, to save me from the hell I'd be put through. But the moment had passed, and all bets were off. She was nothing more than Bette fighting for Bette, in all her glory. Deep down, I knew it wasn't personal. Bette did what Bette wanted to do. She had her own agenda. It was as simple as that.

Bette kept her callous eyes locked on me as she stepped down from the small pedestal on which she had been standing and slowly slithered toward her prey. People watched with fascination and moved quickly out of her way so as not to interrupt the show.

I stood my ground. Bette moved closer, finally near enough to smell her perfume. The heat coming off her body made me bristle. Without emotion, completely devoid of friendship or love, Bette parted her lips and kissed me. And I closed my eyes and allowed it to happen. Cameras flashed in quick succession. Our show was a hit.

"Fuck. You," I whispered in Bette's ear.

As slowly as she had approached, Bette took my hand and led me away from the crowd behind a large, paneled partition. Completely alone and out of view, Bette shed her sultry façade. She threw her arms around me, laughing.

"Oh, darling! Isn't it magnificent?" I could tell from her slur that she had already spent some alone time with Clover that evening. I was woozy, myself. The room spun with a mixture of the martinis and blood rushing to my head.

"Bette? What the hell—what are you doing?"

Bette cupped my face in her hands. "Don't you see how big this is?" She would not be deterred.

"Do you know what I've gone through? Don't say no, because I know you do. And this? He was my boyfriend."

"Was he?"

"And what you did—it's on display for the whole world to see. You both used me, screwed me over. But you, you screwed me over worse than anyone. I want to hear you say it. I want to know why."

I was babbling with shock and despair. And although my heart was breaking, no tears came. "Why?" I pleaded for an answer. "These pictures? That's you—that's what we've—why?"

Our relationship had meant nothing to her. The fact she wouldn't answer me told me everything. If Bette was capable of this, she was capable of so much more. She was capable of it all. I whispered, "Why?"

The real questions I wanted to ask would not find their way to my mouth. I had been rehearsing them over and over in my mind all week. Questions about the girl in the video. Questions about the night I was drugged and raped. I wanted to tell Bette, in detail, about the horrific event I'd endured and ask what part she'd played in it. But I was blindsided by Bette and Sergei and their disgusting performance. The crowd was deafening, and my thoughts were barely connecting.

Bette only shook her head with a sympathetic smile on her face. "Poor thing. You'll see. It'll all be worth it. It's the exhibit, nothing more. Isn't it beautiful? It's moving people and making them think. Trust me." She ducked around the curtains for a moment and returned with two cocktails.

Past the point of furious, I had hit a raging delirium. *Fuck it,* I thought, taking the drink without hesitation. The drink went down quickly, and Bette smiled innocently, sympathetically even. It enraged me further.

"See? Here, take mine. We'll get another when you're feeling yourself."

I wanted to disappear, wanted to forget this nightmare, wanted to wake up and laugh that it all had been a piece of fiction brought on by bad Thai takeout. My need to make sense of my assault had given me tunnel vision. I had been so preoccupied by a hunch, so sure that I would be able to bring to light an evil in Bette, that I blindly traipsed into the heart of the beast. I wasn't going to give Bette, or anyone present that evening the satisfaction of seeing me crumble—at least not on the outside. I needed to numb myself and let my brain float away from my body so the real pain wouldn't show.

I needed to feel nothing.

Instead, I swayed on my feet.

Bette kissed my cheek. Simultaneously, everything

around me became crisp, one sharp image after another. Then the strobe lights began to swirl out of control. As Bette lifted her glass to my lips, my body became numb.

Hooking her arm through mine, Bette led me back out into the spotlight. "Now, let's see what that devil Clover is up to."

In the far reaches of my mind, warning sirens were firing: *Clover. The pills. She drugged my drink again.* But drowning in Bette's poisonous concoction, I forgot my desperation, forgot to hate Sergei. I lost track of who I was or why I was there.

I hung onto Bette as she kissed my neck for the cameras. I kissed her back, pressed my breast against her shoulders, nibbled her ear, as the flashbulbs kept bursting. I played the part of her puppet until the early morning hours.

As five o'clock quickly approached, the mixture of toxins in my body pushed me past the point of fun and forgetfulness. I was a mess and so was everyone else left around me. Makeup was smeared, clothes were soiled with spilled drinks, and the smell of stale cigarettes hung in the air. The glamour had vanished, replaced by revulsion. The sun had begun its climb, casting an ugly glow in the showroom.

I staggered from the small crowd, not knowing where I was going, merely searching for some place of safety. Bette stumbled after. I stopped to vomit clear liquid in the corner. I wiped my mouth with the back of my hand while Bette cooed, "Poor thing. I should take you home and tuck you in bed."

I pushed her away with a limp arm. The hate for Bette, for everything that surrounded me, had found its way back in.

We were making our way to the door when I spotted Sergei. Behind him was an enormous photograph of Bette's head thrown back in ecstasy, and the emotions I had kept at bay, vicious dogs foaming at the mouth, ready to attack, were unleashed. He had taken my Bette. Blind rage took over and I charged him, scooping up a glass tumbler lying on the floor. With all my might, I smashed the glass into his forehead, slicing deep into his scalp and even deeper into my hand.

"Fucking *pizda!*" he screamed and pushed me out the door. "Take her home!" he yelled at Bette.

Clover followed, laughing. "Holy shit! You know how to finish off a party, pretty lady."

Bette wrapped my hand in her scarf, and Clover handed me another pill, but I shook my head.

"No, no more." I slurred and retched again on the sidewalk. Clover pushed the pill into my good hand. "Seriously, just take it for the pain. You're gonna hurt like a motherfucker when everything wears off."

I looked at Bette, who nodded in agreement. I sat on the edge of the street curb, swaying. "I can't."

Clover instructed everyone to stay put while he went to get a friend's car. Sitting on the curb, vomit at our feet, time lost all meaning. We could have been waiting five minutes or two hours as I drifted in and out of consciousness. My heart was beating hard. Too hard. I could tell something was wrong but couldn't form words or move my lips to speak, and I began to shake uncontrollably. My body had simply been through too much.

I looked at Bette, eyes wide and pleading. Bette stared

at me with shark-like eyes. She stood and walked away. Again, I vomited in the street and my skin became icy, covered in sweat. Bette returned with a drink from the gallery, watered down, a dead lime floating in it. She tossed a pill into it and stirred with her finger. Holding it to my lips, she said, "Drink."

I shook my head and mumbled, "I hate you."

Bette stood with a look of irritation.

"It's your fault. I know you . . ." I tried to finally say what I'd come to say, but my vision blurred to black again. When I came to, I was in the back seat of a car, being whipped back and forth as it turned sharp corners, hearing only snippets of conversation from the front seat.

"Party of the century."

"Miami."

"The bungalows. At the Delano."

"Pretty sexy. What did . . ."

"Don't be a pig, Clover. I don't kiss and tell."

"Come to some sort of arrangement."

"Dream on. I have money."

"Marin, why are you crying?"

We careened around another corner and my forehead hit the window hard. I yelped and raised my eyes just in time to see headlights. They were too close, and I felt the initial impact in slow motion. And then everything slowed to a frame-by-frame reel.

Complete silence.

Floating.

In air.

A sublime dream.

The cold, crisp night sky.

Weightless.
Bette's hair, a beautiful halo against the dark sky.
Icicles fell all around.
No.
Not icicles.
Shards of glass.
We weren't floating.
We were falling.
Tumbling.
Fast.
Crashing.
The noise rushed into my ears.
Screams.
Metal wrenched open.
Bette's hair hung limp from her head.
Her head tilted to one side.
Her head that wasn't moving.
I was pulled from the car.
A man screamed at her.
Clover.
"Get out of here!"
I didn't understand.
"Hurry up!"
He yelled again.
"Taxi! Taxi!"

His words made no sense, and I looked around, confused yet strangely calm. A horn was honking. Honking. Honking. Metal shards littered the street. Plastic. Glass. I blinked. Something was in my eye. I rubbed and rubbed but couldn't get it out, then looked down at my hand. Blood. Dripping into my eye. I looked back to the car. Bette. Unmoving.

Clover was shoving me, screaming, pushing me toward a taxi. "You have to get out of here. I'll take Bette. We have to go."

I looked at Clover, trying to make sense of what he was saying. He grabbed me by both shoulders and shook me hard. "I stole the car. We have to get out of here fast. Go!" He threw me into the taxi and handed the driver money, instructing him to take me back to school.

The driver sped off. Once a safe distance away, he looked at me in the rearview mirror. "Yo. What the fuck's up? This is 911, hospital shit."

I replied, "Okay," but didn't understand the conversation. I had gone into shock.

The driver shook his head sadly. "I ain't taking you. No way am I dealing with any police and shit. But you got friends that can take you, right?"

Friends?

He looked at my knees. Both resembled raw hamburger meat, splayed open to the bone. My eyes rolled back into my head.

When I opened them again, I was back in my own room, soaked in sweat. I shook violently, my jaw ached, and teeth chattered so hard I thought they might shatter. Trying to lift my head, my skull was crushed by a vise and black spots leapt from the angry pain. I was on top of my comforter, still in the slip dress.

I dared a glance down my body. I was caked with dirt and dried blood, while fresh blood oozed from my knees. Shaking, I lifted my hand and unwrapped the scarf from around it. The gash splayed open, and blood pooled in the crevice.

I reached out for my phone, but it had probably been

lost in the crash.

Rolling onto my side, I cried out in pain. Moving from the bed, let alone setting out to find my phone and purse, was futile. The door opened a crack. A pretty brunette popped her head in. "Cass, you here?" She looked around the room before her eyes fell on the corpse in the bed. "Oh my God."

My voice cracked. "Can I please use your phone?" The girl looked unsure. I was sure stories of Cassie's degenerate roommate had spread through the house. "Please. I need to call for help."

"Um, yeah." She handed me her phone, visibly uncomfortable. "I'm just going to step out. Take your time. I'll be back in a few."

First, a call to Sergei. I wasn't surprised he didn't answer.

Next, to Bette. No answer. I tried again. And again. On the fourth try, I left a message: "I'm hurt. I think I need to go to the hospital. I need help."

I was sorry as soon as I hung up. I didn't know anything about what had happened, except there was a stolen car and a horrible wreck. Was the other driver alive? Was Bette? I was suddenly petrified of being linked to the night's catastrophic events.

I began to shiver. I needed to reach someone before I passed out again. With shaking hands, I dialed the only other person I knew I could trust. He picked up after one ring.

"Simon, I'm in trouble."

16

"Kiddo, when are you going to call your parents?" Simon adjusted the pillow behind my head. I groaned and gently fingered the bandage covering the stitches in my scalp. A small beep began to sound, indicating the bag of fluids was empty. A nurse quickly came in and unlatched the IV tube to replace it.

My knees were stitched and bandaged, as were my forehead and hand. I was under observation for a concussion for the third day in a row, but the doctor indicated I'd be discharged soon. I had railed against Simon taking me to the hospital and ultimately won, arguing that if I had to file another report with the police, it would be me, not the driver, who would be in a world of trouble.

Simon had finally relented and called in a favor. "One of the perks of having friends in high places," he explained as we pulled into a private surgical center. The plastic surgeon's office looked like a movie set, sparkling and far more sanitary than an actual hospital would have been.

I sighed audibly. "I'm over eighteen. Legally, I don't have to call my parents. Besides, like you said, I'm an adult and I can make my own adult decisions."

"*Almost* adult—and this is your health. This is serious." He took my hand. "If you were my daughter, I'd want to know."

"Well, you do know. There's a reason you were the one I called." I squeezed his hand.

Simon had been wonderful. He had stayed the entire time, consulted with the doctor as my liaison, and even paid the medical bills after I began to sob and threatened to leave without treatment, saying I could never burden my parents with such expenses. He said the money didn't matter, but my life did.

In exchange for his kindness, I told him everything. The descent back into drugs. The exhibit. The betrayal. The accident. My broken heart. And I apologized to Simon for doubting him and unfairly lashing out at him. He hadn't been being cruel when he'd put the facts in front of me.

I had been blind; I'd fought hard to remain blind, and he simply tried to help me see. He had told me, quite bluntly and accurately, that it wasn't going to end well for me. The only thing I withheld from him was the nightmare in the motel. After finally seeing Bette's dark intentions, seeing through the façade of my two closest comrades, that piece of information had broken free of its locked confines. The rage, sober and pointed, had begun to bubble up and fester, and I wasn't ready to hand over that chunk of coal just yet. I was finding an odd strength in its presence.

"Here—I thought this might come in handy." Simon handed me a new phone. "Programmed and everything. Your contacts should all be in there. In case you need me for another emergency." He smiled kindly.

My eyes welled up. "I'm going to repay you for all of this. I don't know how, but I will. I promise."

"I don't want your money." He paused. "You can repay me by coming clean with your parents."

"I can't. Not yet." I saw the hurt in Simon's eyes; he was taking on the pain, as if it were his own. "I have to take care of something first."

While Simon stepped out to talk to the surgeon, I tried calling Bette and was sent straight to voicemail. Same with Oz and Harry. Sergei was silent, as well.

When the doctor finally released me, Simon offered to drive me back to my house. We stood outside the surgical center, me in a soft pair of sweats that Simon had picked up, Simon with car keys dangling from his fingers.

I shook my head. "Thank you, but I have to make a stop first." I pulled out the new phone and ordered a ride.

"No. You shouldn't be—"

"I promise I'm fine." I said with a steady voice.

"Okay, okay. But don't forget Sunday brunch."

I smiled softly. "I won't forget."

Simon gingerly pulled me in, taking care so as not to accidently brush against any of my wounds, and hugged me. I soaked in his fatherly love and gentle kindness and desperately hoped he knew the depth of all the appreciation and gratitude I held for him. He waited on the sidewalk until my ride pulled away, waving farewell.

As soon as we were out of sight, I instructed the driver to take me to the Fulton Market District. Both knees throbbed as the painkillers began to wear off, but I was determined to take nothing stronger than ibuprofen and promptly popped four. I had a clear head, and I wasn't about to screw it up again. The car pulled up at the corner of Green and Randolph. I asked the driver if he would wait; I wouldn't be long.

Mounting the steps leading up to the loft was grueling. But each spasm of pain fueled my commitment to the mess to the end. Out of habit, I knocked on the door with my right hand. A hot flash seared down my arm, and I doubled over. I took a moment to compose myself, unwilling to show any weakness, and knocked with my left knuckle. I knocked again. And again. Hard.

The metal door slid open, and Sergei stood with a sheet wrapped around his torso. I wasn't sure how I expected him to react, but he surprised me with a bored glance. He tilted his head. "Da?"

His eyes fell on my hand and the bandage, and he scoffed.

I glanced up at his head. An angry red gash traced a path from his hairline to his eyebrow. "I'm sorry."

He shrugged. "Scars are handsome." Then he added, without a smile, "On men. Not women."

My face reddened, but not from shame of what he thought of my appearance. It wasn't shame associated with the words from a cruel narcissist or because, somehow, he didn't find me worthy of his presence. The shame was in myself for ever trusting such a devious charlatan. *I should have hit him harder.*

About to ask Bette's whereabouts, I paused, able to see over his shoulder and into the loft.

A shape was in his bed.

Blonde curls topped the naked curves that languished in the sunlight. Her back was to the door, but it was obvious who it was. I knew she would be in hiding in Sergei's lair; that was why I had come.

I shoved past Sergei and stormed to the bed.

Bette turned slowly, smiling. "Hello, darling."

The room spun with my sudden movements, and I had to lower my head between my knees to breathe. Bette rose and walked toward me. Her body glistened in the sunlight while angry tears streamed down my face, a thunderstorm of emotions churning. Bette wiped the tears away, kissing my forehead.

"Come to bed." She took my hand and kissed my fingertips.

I looked at her head. "You were hurt. You were bleeding." I reached out to touch the injury I'd witnessed in the car.

Bette batted my hand away and tilted her head and I caught a fresh trickle of blood running down her neck. "I don't know what you're talking about."

I looked at Bette, supremely beautiful, the perfect seductive female. A deadly siren, promising forbidden fruit, luring a creature into her crosshairs. I looked at Sergei, leaning against the doorframe, waiting to see if I would lay with him again. He looked so calm in repose, but he watched intently. He was hunting. And I pictured myself as he must have seen me. Broken, fractured, fallen. Perfectly wounded prey.

I pulled myself together. "Bette, I've been calling you. Calling hospitals. I was worried about you." I reached out to brush the red droplets from her untended wound when she grabbed my hand with surprising force and thrust her thumb deep into my cut palm. I yelped, shrinking back.

Bette looked at me as she would an annoying child. "Don't tell me you were worried. Or care. It's a ridiculous cliché. That's what people do and say when they don't know how to really love."

I took a step backward as Bette went on. "Love is not kindness and sugar. Love is not goodness. They don't go together. True love is vicious. It's raw and dangerous and painful. We stab each other and bleed." Her bloodshot eyes flashed to Sergei, who simply threw back a shot of vodka and shrugged.

I scanned the room, searching for the prize I'd come for. I would find some truths in it, I was certain.

Bette lunged at me, grabbing my waist, bringing us cheek to cheek, her hot breath in my ear. "We're alive. We were then, and we are now. This is love. The pain. The heartache and longing. It's glorious. It makes us alive. It lifts us above all the small idiots who simply blow pathetic kisses to each other. We destroy each other and then come back together to heal. All of those broken pieces, fused together, make us stronger than the rest. You and I, we know how to love each other."

She was making no sense, but I pushed on, needing to hear her answer. "Was it love that made me a target at that party? Love that allowed me to be taken to the motel? You had a key stashed in your drawer. Your own key. Along with photos of Olivia."

Bette did not answer. She only looked at me, through me. Over Bette's shoulder, a hypodermic needle and rubber tubing sat among various pills and wine glasses on the bedside table. I winced in disgust. Suddenly, it was grotesque. Their whole world together. So ugly and meaningless.

I swiftly grabbed both of Bette's wrists and held her at arm's length.

I looked at Bette, her eyes wild and intoxicated, then looked to Sergei. A perverse smile spread across his face as he nodded to the bed.

I closed my eyes for a long moment. When they opened, they opened for good.

They saw Bette, spun out on opiates and heroin, a shell of the person I had once loved, and I understood—I wouldn't get the answer I was looking for. The flood of venom drained away. I had come to demolish a monster, had come to take down the beast that was Bette.

But I was wrong. There was no monster, no beast. She was a mentally ill young woman. Nothing more. Simon had been right when he'd said she lived in a hell of her own. I had thought at the time he meant living with the crushing grief of losing a loved one, but it was clear he meant the hell of her own mind. Still, I needed to say my peace.

I spoke slowly and lucidly. "This whole time, I believed you, Bette. I believed we had something special. We were sisters. We protected each other. We were there to help each other. That's what I believed. But I was wrong."

Bette laughed menacingly. "I did protect you. I protected you from your own miserable existence."

"You're sick."

"I helped you because no one else would. Out of pity, so you wouldn't be alone."

"You need help, Bette."

"I taught you. I taught you everything. You were so pathetic. A simpleton."

"You're so cruel, Bette. Is it a game for you? Is that all? Because I think it is. I think that's all it ever was to you. I loved you. Do you understand me? I know you're in there somewhere. You need to know I did love you. Maybe, for you, it meant nothing, but I don't want to believe I was just a butterfly pinned on display."

"Don't be stupid. You were never beautiful enough to be my butterfly." She sneered, gnashing her teeth, crazed and drug-addled.

I held her wrists tightly so she had to look me in the eye. "You're right, you know. You taught me a lot, Bette— just not what you thought you did." I released her with a slight shove. Bette teetered backward on unsteady legs and fell into bed, a skeleton of a useless body. I couldn't stand the sight of her for another moment.

Passing Sergei, I gave him one last head-to-toe once-over. "And you—" I paused. "You're just a dick."

My eyes fell on what I'd come hoping to find. Bette's phone sat on a table near the doorway, and I quickly palmed it, tucking it tight into my pants. Without another word, I walked out for good.

Gingerly, I slipped back into the waiting Uber. I was thankful for the quiet journey in the car. Pulling out Bette's phone, I took a deep breath. Even after all the ugly facts, there still was a part of me that didn't want to know. Still a part that loved Bette deeply, that wanted to eat cheese and croissants in the hazy morning light of her kitchen on Sundays, still wanted to giggle and conspire nose to nose under the sheets of her bed, still wanted to walk through our lives hand in hand, painted, ethereal, beautiful. But I knew this was not reality. The life we had shared was an illusion and the actual truth of our relationship rested in my hand.

I punched in Bette's security code that I'd seen used innumerable times before and began to search. Even though Bette eschewed the use of social media, all the apps were there, hidden in a back-screen page. I went to her Instagram account. Under the account name was "K. Hoover." The same for Facebook and Snapchat. I thought I would be elated in knowing the truth. Vindicated. Instead, my heart sank. There was no turning back.

Quickly scrolling direct messages, texts, and phone numbers, though, I found no further proof that Bette had been involved in anything more than her mentally ill fantasies and drug-fueled party girl lifestyle.

I fingered my mangled knees, the physical manifestation of my time with Bette. As the car drove north on Lake Shore Drive, I pulled out my own phone. I had two calls to make.

"I'm glad you're all right," Cassie said when she found me packing.

I hugged her, apologized again, and thanked her for putting up with such a louse of a roommate.

"I just wish I'd known what was going on."

"I wish I'd known, too."

Tears sprung to my eyes. Cassie. She was the type of girl I thought I'd wanted to be when I first came to school. But I never could have been. I hadn't known myself well enough to even know what I was starting with, let alone to build up layers. It requires more than a change of address, more than a new bedspread, a dress, a drink, or a drug to find yourself. Some have the fortune in finding tools of meditation, of therapy, or of faith while navigating their journeys. For me, it required a trip to hell and back to discover what I was made of.

Cassie laughed. "You were definitely not what I expected, but man, I've got some great college stories for when I'm old." She paused. "Good luck with everything. Really."

I smiled gratefully. Cassie wiggled her fingers goodbye with a smile, grabbed her notebooks, and shut the door behind her.

My mother was on her way from Kearney. I had opted to leave out the night at the motel, the wound still being too raw, but after hearing the tearful explanation of the drug use and car crash, she decided it would be best for me to come home immediately. I didn't protest.

I had expected a long lecture about responsibility or a valid fit of anger. But, to my dismay, Mother only cried and said it was her own fault. That if she had paid more attention, if she had come to visit or called more, then she could have caught on before my life spiraled out of control. I wished she had yelled; it would have been easier to take. In the end, I was relieved to be going home. I was ready to leave the rollercoaster behind once and for all.

However, I couldn't let down my guard quite yet and say goodbye to the whole nightmare. I longed to focus on cornfields and hometown football games, but I wasn't finished in Chicago. The anxiety surging through me wouldn't quiet until the afternoon was over. As I was closing my last suitcase, my phone buzzed, and I jumped, knowing the moment had come.

I'm downstairs.

I looked in the mirror one last time before going downstairs. Back to jeans and a T-shirt. Back to myself.

I breathed in through my nose and out through my mouth all the way down the hallway and stairs. Opening the front door, Bette stepped into the foyer.

The tip of her nose and cheeks were rosy from the wind's chill. She wore a heavy camel coat with a large ice-blue cashmere scarf that set off her eyes, which were now accompanied by dark, anemic-looking circles.

I remembered a time that I would have thrown my arms around Bette, breathing in her scent, feeling my heart expand. But Bette's cold and distant demeanor was a reminder of the mistake in trusting a person's façade. I had nothing to mourn.

Bette stood in front of me, her gaze daring me to say the wrong thing. "Well. I'm here. You said you had something for me?"

I smiled warmly, not wanting to set her off. "Thanks for coming. I really appreciate it. Want to sit down?" I led Bette to the living room a few feet away. The worn wool couches usually made the withering house seem more like a home, but compared to Bette, dressed in fine wool slacks and a silk top, they were shockingly tattered. I swallowed hard and sat.

She had shown up. She was sitting in front of me. We were halfway done.

"Thanks for coming over."

"You said that."

"Right. I mean, it's just that—I wanted to say goodbye. I'm going home. For good."

I thought Bette would have some reaction, but she didn't move, as if I hadn't said a word. I pulled out the orange Hermes box containing the scarf Bette had given me and handed it over. Bette set it on the couch next to me with disinterest.

"I just wanted to make sure we were parting on good terms. I mean, at least enough to say goodbye." Bette shifted in her seat as I went on. "And I want to tell you, no matter what happened in our past, no matter what happens in our future, I did love you. I do love you."

Out of the corner of my eye I caught movement, so I quickly added, "And I forgive you. I want you to know that."

Bette stood abruptly, indignant. "Forgive me? For what?" She had lifted a finger, mouth open to begin her tirade, when two men flanked her. They grabbed her firmly by the arms and elbows and began to steer her toward the door. Bette looked back and forth between the two men in confusion, trying to pull away.

"What are you doing? Who are you?"

I stood calmly and followed them to the door. Bette thrashed while the men gripped her tighter. She screamed to let her go; she screamed that she was being kidnapped. A girl coming out of the kitchen stopped and turned back. I had warned my housemates that morning of what was happening and what to expect.

Bette's eyes focused on the men's uniforms. They were embroidered in blue. *Anderson Psychiatric Center.* Bette's face transformed from ugly rage to pure terror. Her kicking and screaming intensified. "Marin! What's happening? No, no! What—why?"

As soon as they reached the door, I pulled it open, and the cold Chicago air blasted through the room. Two more men in uniform joined in and grabbed Bette by her legs, lifting her off the ground. She writhed in the air, her hair whipping back and forth, foam and spittle flying from her mouth.

She looked insane.

Her screams from inside the hospital van carried into the house, "Why, Marin? Why?"

Why?

I had left Sergei's loft with Bette's mother's words floating all around me: *If she becomes a danger . . . If she becomes a danger . . .*

Eleanor had listened intently when I called her during the cab ride back to school. I told her about Sergei, the drugs, the stolen car, and the car crash. And for the first time since the hospital, I spoke about the rape. I spared no detail. Rehashing the terror of the night in the motel initially felt as if I were reliving it. I'd cried, apologizing for all my stupid decisions.

Eleanor had sprung into action. She contacted the psychiatric hospital and a lawyer. Through her connections with a judge, she negotiated a plea bargain. She would give the judge Clover's name for the drug dealing and the stolen car in return for a court order mandating Bette's inpatient hospital care. Next, she called me with the plan to lure Bette from Sergei's home and place her in a neutral, open area where she could be subdued and taken.

When the hospital van pulled away, Eleanor got out of the Lexus parked across the street. She came to me, hugged me, and thanked me profusely, insisting I had saved Bette's life. She knew it had been hard to watch, but it had been in Bette's best interest, she explained. As the last part of the deal I made with Eleanor, I pulled out Bette's phone and put it in Eleanor's hands. She pulled me in again and held me as I cried. She assured me that the social media accounts and the Tor sites could be traced.

"Whoever did this will be caught, and they won't get off. I'll see to that myself. They're not going to hurt anyone again."

"I also think whoever it is must be connected to an art show Bette took me to. There were videos playing. It was the same situation. The same motel room."

When I mentioned Scott's name, Eleanor stiffened. I saw the same shadow pass over her face as I'd seen happen with Bette numerous times. A mask falling away, revealing another person altogether.

"Marin, was Bette with you at the club? The night you were out with Poppy?"

"No, not with me. Only the night that we went to Scott's showing."

Eleanor nodded slightly. I paused, then added, "But I think I saw her there. At the club."

"You *think* you saw her? But you're not sure?"

The change in Eleanor's demeanor threw me off. "I— uh—I honestly, don't know for sure."

"Well, you just said you drank a lot. And you were taking pills. Correct? And that you blacked out?"

Suddenly, I felt like I was the one who had committed a crime, that I had in some way brought on the attack myself and Eleanor was set on proving it. "I did. Yes, I did all those things. But I also remember seeing her in the crowd. It's hard to mistake her hair. I was so mad at her, though, I didn't try to find her."

Another wave passed over Eleanor's face, suddenly returning her to the concerned and sympathetic mother I had first met. "There are a lot of blondes in the world, Marin." She smiled with a pitying sadness.

I took a step backward. "You know him. You know Scott."

"I don't know him." Eleanor paused. But a fluttering in my gut, one I was learning to trust more and more, knew I was right. Eleanor might not be *exactly* lying. She might not know Scott personally, but Eleanor knew *of* him. I didn't know the extent, but I was certain there was a past between them.

"Tell me the truth," I whispered forcefully. "That's the least I deserve."

"Get in the car."

I slid onto the butter-soft seat of the Lexus and wrapped my arms around myself, no longer comfortable in Eleanor's presence. Eleanor sat in the driver's seat, staring straight ahead.

"It was Bette's freshman year here. She had been doing so well . . ." Eleanor's voice trailed off, apparently lost in thoughts of when life had been, for a moment, peaceful. "Then she disappeared. Things had been tumultuous in her past, so I didn't feel comfortable going to the police. It wouldn't have mattered, anyway. She was of age. I knew she was receiving our texts and calls." She turned to clarify. "The messages all showed *read*. So, she wasn't missing, exactly, just avoiding us."

She looked back out the window, frowning. "We hired

private investigators that found her. Two months later. She was with Scott."

Eleanor shook her head in disgust. "They had been living in squalor. A drug den in southside Chicago. She was strung out and completely incoherent when they brought her home. When the drugs were finally out of her system, she became enraged. She said they were in a *relationship*. He had been teaching an art class she took downtown."

She looked at me, pleading her own innocence. "She was taking so many classes outside of school. Everything from art history to writing classes to piano lessons. I just thought . . ." She trailed off again. "I should have known she was having a manic episode." Eleanor sat back in her seat, defeated. "Anyway, she said she loved him. That it was a love the world wouldn't understand. That they knew how to love each other."

I froze. It was the same sentiment Bette had conveyed to me in the loft during the peak of her mental meltdown.

Eleanor continued. "All I knew was that she was a child. A sick child, whose body Scott was violating on a daily basis, and it sickened me. So Thomas and I approached him. I threatened to call the police. I said, if nothing else, I'd find a way to get him on drug charges. We had enough evidence from the investigators. But he said that he had videos. Videos of Bette. Videos of her doing nauseating acts. Of them being done *to* her." A tear made its way down Eleanor's cheek. "Scott said that if we called the police, he would release the videos on the dark web. There would be no way to find them or erase them.

"So we made a poisonous truce. We wouldn't call the

police, and he wouldn't let those videos see the light of day. Our hands were tied." Eleanor sighed again. "I got Bette settled into a facility and spoke with the university. She finished her semester classes online. I thought that nightmare was over. I can't believe it's happening again."

I looked out my window as tears streamed down my face. I had not willingly slept with Scott, or whoever it was that had been sent to do his bidding. I had been raped. I didn't have the option of a second chance at school; I failed out. My entire future was dim with no light in sight. Scott had been left free to commit the same act over and over when he could have been stopped. I, and countless other girls, became sacrificial lambs, simply to protect Bette.

That's what happens when you're a Winston in the world, I thought bitterly.

As I opened the car door, Eleanor rushed to add, "You may be the bravest one out of all of us. Thank you."

A light sleet started as Eleanor drove away, but I stayed on the sidewalk, the tips of my hair frosting over.

Turning Bette in might have saved her life, but I didn't know if my intentions were as altruistic as Eleanor believed.

A part of me simply wanted revenge.

17

The arrival back home was a humiliating defeat, but overall uneventful. I welcomed the softness, the quiet and unassuming nature of small-town life. Mother, firmly and correctly, said it would only be right to pay back my own student loans, repay Eleanor for the clothes Bette bought her, and reimburse Simon for the hospital stay. She helped me find a job as a receptionist at a local orthodontist's office, and I resigned myself to days of filing, phone calls, and teenagers with braces.

Mother and I mended fences quickly. The first few days after I returned, we did little but talk. And talk. And talk. And cry. We cried over the loss of our family, over broken hopes and dreams. We cried over the shared heartache we'd endured. And when we thought all tears had been purged, we cried again.

I rested my head in Mother's lap, my tears soaking her jeans. "For a minute, I thought I was special, Mom. I really did. I thought I had broken out. Proven myself. Not like Ty. I know I'll never reach his level, but—"

My mother took me by the shoulders and sat me up, wiping away the tears. "You *are* special, Marin. Look what you faced."

"But it was my fault I got into trouble in the first place."

"Show me a perfect individual, and I'll show you a really boring person." Mother nudged me, trying to lighten the mood. "Let me tell you something: Ty has never faced adversity. He breezed through high school and entry exams. Med school has been a piece of cake for him so far. He has always been a golden child. Things just come easy for him."

She shook her head and sighed. "I don't know that it's a good thing, though. A person needs to fall down. When you fall, you learn how to get up. Ty has never had to get up. Sometimes that worries me. You? You fell. You tripped and fell down—really, really hard." She took my hand. "But you got up. You showed what you're made of. You had to make some very difficult choices, and your decisions, in the end, showed us all how strong you are."

"Maybe. All I know is that I'm back where I started."

"There will come a point when you'll realize that just to live a life, a true life, takes all the courage in the world, and that peace in your soul—I'm talking about genuine contentment—will overshadow the shallowness and folly of glitter and gold any day of the week."

I had been sincere when I'd told Bette that that she had taught me a lot. Bette had demystified a world that

I thought I desperately wanted. Though it had been out of survival, I found my voice because of Bette. She taught me that no money, fame, or popularity could fill up an empty sense of self—*that* would have to be of my own making.

I finally understood that embracing who I was at my core was the key, not an artificial wall of happiness. I had to learn to love who I was before meeting Bette, who I had become since, and who I would grow to be in the future. And I knew that if I were to find a truly fulfilled life, it meant being completely honest, not only with myself, but with anyone I allowed into my world.

I took a deep breath. "Mom, I have to tell you something, and it's really bad. And I need to just say it all at once and not have you say anything until I'm done."

Mother's brow creased, but she nodded an agreement.

I closed my eyes and began.

"I went out one night with a girl. We went to a club . . ."

The next day, my mother, after scouring the internet for the best therapists specializing in sexual assault, scheduled an appointment. Soon after, she found a therapist for herself as well, resolved to help me move forward.

The divide between Father and me, however, grew. He had no tolerance or empathy for any of my struggles that year. But I had made peace with the separation, going as far as visiting his new family and wishing them well, knowing our interactions would be rare. I couldn't continue a relationship in which I was invisible and carried no worth. In the end, I decided, as with Bette, I had to let my father go. For the first time, I fully understood what Simon had tried to tell me: You can't run away from where you come from, from the people who share your history, but you can make peace and move forward.

Time slipped by and, slowly, the heaviness lifted. Mother and I spent more time together as friends. Our weekly movie night resumed, and I had taken to giving Mother makeovers, complete with new hairstyles and wardrobe updates. She protested at first, arguing she could never pull off the trendy looks of *Vogue*, but when I had shown her a simplified version, she'd relented, thrilled with the final outcome. More and more often, she would pop into my bedroom in the mornings to ask which scarf or necklace would look best with her blouse. She even began testing the dating waters again. Even though no man lasted more than a few dates, I could see the twinkle of life returning to her eyes as she walked down the sidewalk with her head lifted a bit higher. And I almost cried with joy when, at last, I was allowed to donate her sequined holiday sweaters to a local charity.

By late autumn, gray clouds had moved in again and, though I had no specific complaints, there was a weight in my heart that matched the darkening sky. Ty said I had the winter blues early and suggested Mother and I go away for a quick vacation in the sun. Our therapists agreed.

Mother mapped out a week at an all-inclusive Caribbean resort and was already circling off-site excursions and umbrella drinks she wanted to try. I hadn't worked long enough at the orthodontist's office to have earned a full week's vacation time, but my mother only nodded and tenderly smoothed my hair.

"You need to get away."

I sighed. "You're right. And I'm going to. But you're not going to like it."

One week later, I stood in the center of my bedroom, an overnight bag zipped shut, and took a hard look around at the simple comforts of my life. The light green comforter, posters and stuffed animals, the flannel shirts and jeans. They anchored me as never before.

I'd sent my clothes, the ones Bette had gifted, to Eleanor. I'd needed to start over, to clear away the year before. My intent was to begin a new life with a clean slate, which meant in some ways, reverting back to the simplicity of my old self. But my old self no longer seemed so off-putting.

Still, I reached into the dresser and took out a photo I'd kept under a pile of sweaters. I was staring at it when my mother quietly slid into the room.

She set her hand on my shoulder, glancing at the picture. "You sure you want to take that?"

I nodded as the two pairs of eyes stared back at me. Eyes no longer familiar, strangers even, though it had been just over a year. Bette's piercing blue eyes and white lace. Me, with black leather hugging over my curves. A picture taken of us at an art opening, during the thick of our self-proclaimed reign. Two lost girls who believed they held the world in the palms of their hands.

"I kept this for a reason," I said, biting my lip. "It reminds me of who I can become." I dropped the photo into the suitcase. "And who I never want to be again."

The seven-hour drive from Kearney to the Chicago hospital gave me plenty of time to think. Bette had been in recovery and treatment for months and was finally allowed visitors. Mother was hesitant to let me go, but I explained it was a necessity to move on, that Bette was constrained and in no place to hurt me again. I reasoned that the visit could be an opportunity for us all to heal.

Secretly, I also saw it as an opportunity for truth. I knew what Bette felt for me—or better put, what she did *not* feel. As far as our friendship went, there was no closure needed, no healing to be done. It had ended, simple as that. What I wanted from her was the last piece of the whole puzzle.

I had made peace with the fact that I had been my own undoing. I had been correct when I'd told Harry that I made my own decisions. Bad as they may have been, it was nonetheless true. I chose to take on too much schoolwork. I chose to overdrink. I chose to take drugs. I chose to stop going to classes. I had no one to blame but myself. However, I was learning to give myself grace, knowing that, while I could make the decision to cause destruction, I could also make the decision to rebuild.

But there was one choice I had not made.

Pulling into the hospital parking lot, I gathered myself for whatever Bette's reaction might be.

The woman at the reception desk was stoic and firm, fit for the setting. She took my name and said to have a seat while she informed Bette she had a guest.

I sat, fidgeting in a hard chair, watching people pass by in the hallways, wondering who was crazy and who was not, who was a doctor and who was a patient. I couldn't tell.

A nurse appeared and led me in, quietly instructing me that a visitation slot constituted thirty minutes. The door closed behind me, and my pulse raced.

Bette stood looking out a large picture window. She wore a plush robe, and I could see she had added a few pounds to her lean frame. Her cheeks were a bit rounder, rosier, than before, and she wore no makeup. The whites of her eyes sparkled, and her skin was clear. She looked healthy, strong.

She regarded me for a moment without speaking, then moved to her bed, perching on the edge and looking out the window again. She spoke without prompting, as if she knew exactly why I had come.

"I had a sister. A twin. *My* twin. Did you know that?"

I didn't answer but took note that the artificial trademark lilt in her voice was gone. She sounded solid and sane.

"Of course you know. I'm sure my mother told you." She glanced at me and gave a quick nod. "And it's okay. I'm sorry I didn't tell you before."

Afraid to make a misstep, something that might cause Bette to stop talking, I sat on a chair near the bed and listened.

Bette spoke slowly, as if addressing no one in particular.

"Her name was Bette. Bettina. She was beautiful. We were physically identical, but she was *beautiful.*" She paused. "She was exquisite, ethereal and otherworldly. Perfect." Bette, the Bette in front of me, wrapped her robe tightly around her shoulders, hugging herself. "She was intuitive and funny and smart and popular. My parents loved her so much. And she could sing and act. She loved being on stage. Even offstage, she was onstage. She wasn't afraid of being laughed at or of failing. She just—was. And that was enough. She could walk into a room and immediately fill it with energy."

She swallowed hard. "But she's gone. And no matter what I do, I can never find anything that fills up space the way she did. Nothing has the same energy she had. Things are just empty."

Tears began to spill down her cheeks. "And I miss her." More tears came as she tried to catch her breath. "I just miss her so much sometimes." Slowly, she rested her head on her pillow. "It's my fault she's gone."

I could barely breathe.

Bette stared out the window and continued. "We were with the lake kids. It was always the same group, every summer. And every year, they got bolder. They'd drink, skinny-dip, make out. But never me. No one ever really wanted me there. Definitely no one was trying to get plain old Olivia's bikini off. They wanted Bette. Every time, it was Bette. Everyone loved her so much, and I envied her so much, and I hated her for that. I hated that we were formed together, grew in the same woman, came out together, but in life, she was always ahead." Bette pulled her knees into herself, wrapping her robe into a cocoon. She spoke to the ground, to no one, lost in her own memory.

"I don't know why I did it. I barely remember any of that night. She didn't want to swim. She'd had a lot of beer. But I persisted, wouldn't let up. So, we swam out and out and out. And she sparkled in the moonlight. That I do remember. How she sparkled in the moonlight. Then I was pulling her down. Pushing her down. Down, down. My head was above water but hers—"

Bette looked up, tears swimming in her eyes. "Physically, we were identical, in every way except one.

The summer before, she had gotten a tattoo. That's the kind of fun girl she was. Just a small butterfly, high up on one rear cheek. Our parents scolded her, and she wasn't allowed to ever wear anything that might show it. So no one else ever saw it."

Bette stopped for a moment and looked up at the ceiling, up toward heaven. "My parents never said anything when they had to identify the body, but I know they knew. They never told anyone the truth—that it was Bette that died that night, not Olivia. They knew I ate her. I swallowed her up. I wanted to be her, and so I ate her. I came out of the lake alive and left Olivia dead in the water. They let me become Bette. They let Olivia die."

Bette curled back into herself. "It's all my fault. And I can't make it better. And I can't make it up to her. To anyone. I want to trade places, but I can't. And it hurts. It hurts so much."

Bette cried silent tears alone in the bed. I didn't move. I didn't go to her and put my arms around her the way I once would have. The last string that tied me to Bette was cut, and I was free.

The truth. It was a secret that would stay between the two of us for the rest of our lives. There was no reason to bring the horrible pain back out into the light. Eleanor and Thomas had already lost one child. What good would come if Bette was sent to prison? Another child ripped from their arms; another mental patient put behind bars without the help she would always need. Here, in the ward, Bette was safe. At home, in Eleanor's care, Bette would be watched.

The pain Bette had caused would never wash away. It

would stay with me the rest of my life, always in some recess of my mind. I knew this without doubt. But I also knew Bette was extremely ill, and though it did not make the pain better, it helped to know that the gruesome journey we took together was the fallout of her mental state, not because I deserved it.

I left Bette in her hospital bed and quietly walked out the door without saying goodbye. I had almost made the entire drive back home when my phone rang.

"The nurses said you came to see Bette." Eleanor's voice was devoid of its usual warmth.

I treaded cautiously. "I did. A thirty-minute visitation." I paused. "Although I didn't stay the whole time."

"Why would you go see her?" she asked in a cold, accusatory tone.

"I just—" I chose my words carefully. "I just needed closure. I wanted to say goodbye."

"I don't think you should see her again."

A swelling rage surfaced. That Eleanor was aware of all that had occurred with her daughter, knew of all I had gone through, yet still spoke to me as if I were complicit, was abhorrent. I was finished using kid gloves with the Winston family. "Don't worry. I won't see her again. I got all of the answers I needed."

I ended the call before Eleanor could respond.

18

Hovering near the bathroom doors, I chewed on a hangnail until the last possible moment, then slipped into the courtroom. I had called in sick at work, citing possible strep throat, saying that I should probably stay away for a couple of days. I had told Mother that I was going to a friend's apartment after work for girls night and would be staying over. I knew she would have fought tooth and nail if she knew where I was truly going, and I wanted to save all my energy for the day. I had made the long drive to Chicago in silence, steeling myself in preparation.

Entering the courtroom, I slid into a chair as far back in the corner as possible. My hair, grown out several inches, was pulled up into a ball cap, and I wore large sunglasses, trying to shield every inch of my face.

The room itself was much smaller than I had imagined, my only prior idea of what a courtroom looked like coming from TV shows. It was also unbearably bright. I had imagined a large, two-story ballroom with dark-lacquered mahogany and enormous windows, shaded by blinds that would cast a soft glow over everything in the room.

Instead, the florescent bulbs magnified every sharp corner and turned the cream-painted walls into a garish yellow. There were no windows, giving the chamber a claustrophobic feel, and the two tables in front of the judge's bench, one with a lawyer already seated, one empty, reminded me of the folding tables used for grammar school art classes. Wood composite, glossy and impenetrable.

There had been very little in the news regarding the trial. I had scoured the internet during every break at work, certain that it would make headlines. But the only mention had come from a small op-ed questioning how state tax dollars were being spent:

Neighborhoods are left to fend for themselves as crime rises daily, and the Chicago Mayor's office is becoming the king (or queen, we should say) of Teflon. Money can't be directed towards police funding, yet in the small town of Kenilworth, we seem to find it of absolute necessity to protest artwork not deemed suitable for all.

Bile had risen in my throat, and I had thrown my phone into the break room sink as I screamed into my hands. The injustice of the outrageously incorrect news reporting had been enough to send me home for the day. While one part of me wanted to hide from the ugly truth of what had happened, to never have to tell another soul of the attack, I also couldn't bear the thought that the truth might stay buried. It had been buried once, only to rise again, even stronger and more brutal.

The prosecutors had contacted me as a witness. Shame crept in as I told them I wouldn't testify at the actual trial. The thought of looking Scott in the eye made me physically ill. I agreed, however, to give written testimony that would be read and reviewed by the judge. There would be no jury.

I was still grappling with the hell I had been put through. My body had been ripped into a new reality, and any innocence left in me had been stripped away. And still, the case did not make the cut.

There was also the issue of the other girls. After reliving the night of Scott's art show in my mind a thousand times, I was convinced the girl on the slab had been dead. Would there be a second trial? A murder trial? The prosecuting attorney would give me no information.

I scanned the small crowd in the courtroom. I had envisioned a mob of outraged people inside, demanding Scott's head on a stake. Instead, a few scattered couples sat together, a single woman, and a single man, some speaking in soft whispers but silent for the most part. I gathered these were parents, strangers united by trauma, hoping to find some peace after the atrocities committed.

I wondered what they thought of as they sat waiting. Had their daughters told them everything they had gone through? Were images now seared in their brains, playing on an endless loop? Or were they trying to remember their children as the beautiful toddlers they once were: Innocent, wide-eyed, and trusting? A pang of guilt swept through me as I thought of my own mother. She would be standing in front of her class at school, blissfully unaware that her own former toddler was sitting in another state, in disguise, waiting in hopes of seeing her rapist put behind bars.

The seated attorney turned and motioned to someone sitting behind him. A woman rose and approached, then gracefully knelt in front of the lawyer as he spoke to her. My breath caught, and I slid lower in my chair.

Eleanor.

Of course she would be here, I thought, and chastised myself for not thinking ahead. I watched Eleanor with new eyes. The calm composure and the air of authority. *Just another mask.* I knew that, under her cool demeanor, Eleanor had to be quaking in her heels, knowing that Bette's name—the Winston name—would soon be pulled into the spotlight and revealed to the world. This was part of why I had come.

A side door opened, and a sweaty gentleman in a suit—I assumed the defense attorney—made his way into the courtroom and straight to the empty table. He had a frazzled demeanor about him that I couldn't help but be grateful for.

A few more silent moments passed as the two lawyers shuffled papers and prepared their areas, then the door opened again. This time, a man in handcuffs, clothed in a gray jumpsuit, was led into the room by a police officer. Making his way to the table, I could see his face, his whole body, straight-on.

My entire body began to shake, my breaths coming in shallow gulps.

The man didn't make eye contact with anyone in the

room. His face was a blank canvas as he rounded the table and sat. Seeing the person who had violated me for the first time, starbursts of color began to dance in front of my eyes, and I quickly lowered my head between my knees. Crouched over, I began to tap my fingers together as the therapist had taught me. Thumb to the index finger, thumb to the middle finger, on and on, over and over, reminding myself that I could control my own body.

When I could finally take a full breath and slowly roll myself back up to a sitting position, I found the judge had entered the courtroom, with everyone standing at her entrance. I didn't even bother trying to get to my feet.

The judge began the trial with, "You may all be seated. Today's hearing is *The State of Illinois vs. Michael Flusser.* The defendant, Michael Flusser, has been charged with the following . . ."

The judge listed off the myriad offenses, repeating the same ones over and over. The same abuse doled out to eight young women, including me.

My ears were ringing so loudly that I missed most of what the judge said. I stopped tapping my fingers and, instead, dug nails deep into my palm as I angrily thought, *Get your act together. You're stronger than that. There he is. He has a name. Michael Flusser. He is not a demon hiding in the shadows.*

The prosecutor began to deliver his case first, stating again for the courtroom and judge that Michael was on trial for eight counts of aggravated criminal sexual assault. He asked permission to read a few of the written testimonies before calling his witnesses to the stands.

As the lawyer read the first two accounts, I lived them through their words. I felt the brutality, the shame, the guilt, the anger. The fear. Both testimonies stated that they feared Michael's return. That they feared him living outside a jail cell. That they live in constant fear of letting their guard down.

I knew this all too well. Before bed, I check the front and back door—twice—to make sure the deadlocks were bolted and the house alarm was on. Once inside my own bedroom, after checking the closet and under the bed, I lock that door. Finally, each window in the room is checked, unlocked then relocked to make sure they were secure. When out with friends, I click the lock on my car three times for good measure. My days of drinking more than two drinks were over, so intense was my fear of becoming incapacitated.

The prosecutor began reading the third testimony, and I began to shake all over again. They were my words, my account, and I went cold as I listened to them spoken by someone else. My mind left my body, floating above the room, and I heard the story from someone else's point of view, heard it as if for the first time, and was appalled all over again at the brutality. My knees, the cartilage still cracked, bounced up and down with adrenaline.

When the attorney finally set the testimony down on the table, I was flooded with a sense of gratitude for Cassie and Simon. They had helped save me when I didn't want to be saved. They forcibly pushed for help. If it wasn't for them, I would not be sitting in this courtroom, and Michael would be preying on his next victim.

After each testimony read, the judge asked the defense

if they wished to make a statement or had any questions. Each time, the defense declined.

The judge then asked the prosecutor to call his first witness. A slim brunette moved to the stand. When she turned to sit, I gasped audibly. It was the girl from Scott's show. Alexa. I couldn't hold back the tears. *Alexa was alive!* Although I had never met the girl before, we shared a tight bond of experience.

Alexa remained strong during the prosecutor's questions. A star witness. The story she told was chilling in its similarity to my own. There had been a method. A procedure. There were no coincidences or being "in the wrong place at the wrong time." Alexa explained how she'd pieced together the puzzle from social media posts, just as I had. The names, Kelly Hoover in particular, worked exactly as the police officer had explained. A trail of breadcrumbs for hungry monsters to follow. We had been picked out, groomed, and hunted. In hindsight, I found solace in the fact that I could never have seen it coming.

With every gentle question the attorney asked Alexa, I waited for Bette's name to be brought up. I waited to hear how Bette had groomed Alexa as she had groomed me, and undoubtedly all the other girls. But Bette's name was never spoken. There was not even mention of "another girl" in the mix of predators.

I thought hard. Had Bette's name come up in my own testimony that was read? My nerves were so on edge, seeing the man of my nightmares in the flesh, hearing other stories of his assaults, that my mind was blanking.

In a final blow from the prosecution, they announced that they would be showing video clips confiscated from

Michael's residence. The judge allowed the viewing to happen, and the courtroom was advised that the videos were graphic in nature. Many of the parents seated lowered their heads and covered their eyes. It would be one thing to hear about what their daughters had gone through, but something altogether different to witness it.

The video, short snippets of clips strung together, showed all the girls at various stages of their drugging and assault. I could not look away. My nightmare, what I knew was floating out in the world forever, downloaded and saved in secret by perverted individuals, was suddenly pushed in my face. A part of me needed to see it, to know what had happened. I needed to walk straight into the fire before I could begin to walk out of it. When the video ended, the silence in the room was deafening. It felt as if every molecule of air had been sucked out and all that was left was a huge, gaping void. A black hole of despondence.

I hadn't even realized I'd been crying until the lights came back on. I pulled up my T-shirt, swiping my dripping nose. In the end, the defense rested without ever asking a question or calling a witness. Low-voiced chatter began as soon as the judge asked for a short recess to review the case.

Bette had not been mentioned once. She was a ghost in the story, completely invisible. Scott's name had glaringly been left out as well. Fury burned in my heart. *Thomas and Eleanor.* They had made an agreement before, and it still stood. Scott was again spared to save Bette.

The prosecutor and the defense lawyer were easy to guess. It wouldn't take more than a quick threatening of their jobs to keep them quiet. The fact that Michael's lawyer did little more than pick at his teeth during the trial was evidence of that. The written testimonies had been doctored, inconvenient bits deleted. But the actual girls that took the stand—how had they been coerced? Their families were already on edge. Another threat would put them squarely in fight mode. The Winstons were too smart; they wouldn't have used fear. My only guess is that they used what they knew best: Money.

The judge returned. After the court had reseated themselves, she spoke. "These are the cases which, when we take our oaths and are sworn in to uphold the law, to try to help those who have no voice, we know we may encounter but pray to God we don't. To the victims of these crimes, I offer my condolences and my hope that you will be able to get help to cope with what you have endured. I doubt you will ever forget what happened, but I pray you find a way to forge on. To the families, I grieve for you. This is a nightmare that all parents fear. I hope today has brought you all one step closer to healing." The judge looked at Michael and opened her mouth to speak, then closed it again, shaking her head in disgust.

"I will now read the verdict for the court. Please let it be known that in the case of *The State of Illinois vs. Michael Flusser*, I hereby find you guilty on eight counts of Class 1 felony aggravated criminal sexual assault by penal code section 720 ILCS 5 / 11-1.20. For each of these counts, I am sentencing you to the maximum time of fifteen years in prison with no possibility of parole. Let me be clear"—the judge pulled down her reading glasses and glared at Michael—"that is fifteen years *per assault*. Good luck. You're going to need it. Court dismissed."

The gavel went down; court was adjourned. Michael, seemingly diminished from when he had first entered the room, was quickly ushered away.

The parents cried, clung to their spouses, and hugged strangers as the palpable energy of justice filled the room. I stood to leave and glanced up to see Eleanor staring at me. I planted both feet and returned the stare, refusing to flee in fear. I could go to Eleanor and thank her, hug her, and relish in the joy of victory.

However, I knew that Eleanor was there for one reason: To keep Bette safe. She had not come seeking justice for the other girls. She had come to make sure the Winston name was never uttered. And Eleanor knew I understood, as she continued to stare, unsmiling. I had broken our poisonous truce. I was not to be seen again, but there I stood, witness to Bette's escape.

Silently, taking off my sunglasses and with my back straight, I turned and walked out of the courthouse. I was ready to forge on.

19

he man is staring out the window into the distance. I finish telling him the story. The entire story. Every ugly detail.

We sit in silence while he digests it all. He looks like he's aged over the course of the last hour, and his shoulders roll in slightly as he slumps. The memories are like a contagious cancer, and I've just passed the illness on to him. When he turns back to me, his eyes are watery.

Mine, however, are astonishingly dry, and I square my shoulders, ready to take the brunt of whatever reaction might emerge from him. "I'm sorry, Mr. Winston. But you wanted every detail."

"I should say I'm sorry to you." He shakes his head. "But that sounds so trite. So empty."

We make eye contact, and for a brief moment, I see her in his face.

"Eleanor and I want to help you," he continues. "I needed to know what happened first, for my own sanity and understanding. Thank you for telling me. I can't fathom the pain you've endured."

I want to soften to Bette's father. I want to be his "partner" in moving forward, but I find myself running cold.

"Why didn't you watch her?" My breath comes in short spurts as anger rises in me. "Why didn't you make sure she was getting the help she needed? It was easier—is that it? To just let her traipse off to college, run amuck in the city, wreaking havoc at every turn? Out of sight, out of mind." I lean in closer as my emotional floodgates open wide.

"It could have been prevented. All of it. If you had just taken care of your own daughter, I would not have failed out of school, I would not have a dead-end future. I would not have been raped. You could have prevented it all. But you didn't. You took the easy way out. And you know who paid the price? Me."

I stand, ready to storm out. "You know, this is a gorgeous office. I bet it must have cost a fortune to build. Come to think of it, your house was probably super expensive, too. It reminded me of a castle when I was there. Probably amounts to a lot of hours billed. That's lots of hours away from home, with the excuse that you have to work to pay for everything, right? Well, just so you know, the tons of cash you earned and slipped to Bette did jack shit. She used it to fuel her craziness. She knew it was appeasement money, and it just made her reckless. But you didn't know that, did you? Because you were hiding."

I pause as images of Bette in Sergei's bed, a heroin needle lying next to her while she ground her teeth like a crazed animal, run through my head. "You say you want me to be your partner so you can protect me. You understand now why I find that hard to believe."

I turn to go.

"Wait." Thomas's eyes are red, his voice weak.

I turn back to him.

His voice is barely above a whisper. "Please don't leave yet."

I stay where I am. With defeat on his face, he gestures to the chair in front of him. I don't take my eyes off him as I move to sit.

"I understand why you're mad. I'm actually surprised you didn't explode at the time. You had every reason and right to." His eyes are scanning his desk, back and forth, as if he's waiting for an answer to pop up out of nowhere, some magic incantation he can chant to make the whole situation more bearable. I see him absentmindedly pick at his nail. He's genuinely uncomfortable. "I know this doesn't make it better. But I want you to know we did try."

Thomas stands and begins to slowly pace in front the large window. Back and forth, like a caged animal. I realize this is not his sanctuary. It's a cage. Everywhere is a cage for him, as long as Bette is out of his control.

"When Olivia died, I thought there was no greater pain I could ever feel. Nothing could hurt as bad as losing a child. A significant part of me died with her." He dares a glance at me. "I know that sounds dramatic, like I'm digging for sympathy, trying to tug at your heartstrings. But until you experience it, you will never understand that degree of heartbreak. I hope you never do." He continues pacing. "Bette began to slip immediately. Neither Eleanor nor I had the capacity to deal with it properly at the time. Eleanor was deeply depressed. And I was angry. I was so angry.

"I just wanted my little girl back." His voice cracks, but he

quickly recomposes. "We were devastated when Olivia died. And when we were finally functional enough to realize what was happening, it was too late. We were losing a second child before our eyes." Thomas stops pacing and looks out over the city. I picture him years before, staring at the same skyline, lost in bereavement, wondering why it had to be his daughter.

"On top of it all, horrible rumors began to surface." He turns toward me, but won't make eye contact. "I'm sure you've heard them."

I say nothing.

"Eleanor and I went into survival mode. Our hands were tied. She took over saving Bette, and I handled saving our family's name."

With this, he sits and looks right at me, daring me to protest or call him shallow. "It matters more than you think. We had already been through so much. Bette was hanging on by a thread. Can you imagine what would have happened if the media had gotten ahold of those rumors? Or worse, if there had been an actual trial? It would have destroyed Eleanor. Hell, I couldn't take anymore, myself." He leans back in his chair, looking exhausted, as if reliving the whole tragedy again for the first time.

"Eleanor found the best doctors, the best hospitals. She became an expert in mental illness. When she thought the medications were working, she let Bette go back to school. But it didn't last. We hadn't counted on the natural cruelty of teenagers. They were like a pack of hyenas, shunning one of their own. Vicious. It threw Bette back into the thick of it. So Eleanor decided to keep Bette home and hired a private tutor. She watched her like a hawk."

Tessa. A small pinpoint of light is blooming in my mind, as so many puzzle pieces start to fall into place. The hatred Bette had for Tessa now makes perfect sense. Bette hadn't been in "a bad place," as Ozzie had described. Bette had been in the abyss of mental illness, and Tessa had decided to finish her off. Thomas is right: They had acted like wild dogs, and it had been survival of the fittest.

"Meanwhile, I dealt with damage control. I met with each kid who was present that night at the lake, along with their parents. I convinced them that there was nothing to gain by spreading this rumor. I even hired a professional online team that scoured the internet and wiped clean any mention of Bette's involvement in Olivia's death."

They did a good job, I think, remembering how I couldn't find a single piece of information connecting Bette to the incident other than her being present. Thomas had succeeded in keeping up the appearance of a family in grief.

"We thought, together, that we had covered all our bases. We had four years of Bette under constant watch. That's why, when she left for her freshman year of college, we thought she was going to be okay. What we didn't know—not until you called Eleanor—was how good at deceiving us she'd become. We checked in on her regularly. Eleanor would go to our house in the city, where she stayed, to be sure everything was in order. It always seemed to be."

Bette's home, the one her "friend" let her stay in, belonged to her parents. The lavish opulence she lived in, that she called her own, had simply been another way for her parents to try to contain whatever damage might burst forth from her.

Thomas chokes on his words. "We didn't see this coming at all. It's like a bomb has gone off right under our noses."

My anger simmers. But I could walk away and expect to heal one day, while Thomas and Eleanor will never be free. Bette is their burden, one that they will carry until they die.

"I didn't see it, either," I say.

Thomas looks at me with a hint of relief in his eyes, the relief that comes from finally being heard and understood, remembering there is only one other person he can share this story with. But I'm raw and emotionally worn down from my own journey with Bette and have little desire to take on her parents' suffering, as well.

"I hope I was a help." I move to stand and he, again, raises his hand to halt me.

"I told you before . . . Eleanor and I want to thank you, to help you, for coming to us when you did."

"I don't want anything." I just want to leave.

Thomas's face changes again; he's wearing his lawyer mask now. "And, like I also told you, my job is to protect my family."

The hairs on my neck rise. He has an agenda, and his desperation scares me. I chastise myself. Why did I tell him everything? If I've learned anything, it's that information is power, and I just gave all my power away.

I gather up every last bit of courage I have and push back. "I don't want to hurt your family. You asked me to come here. I did. You asked me to tell you what happened. I told you. Now, I want to leave and go back to what is left of my life."

A shadow passes over Thomas. "I'm only going to say this out loud once: I am not my daughter. I am not going to harm you in any way. I'm not here for revenge."

He reaches under his desk, and I hear him open the safe. He closes the heavy metal door and reappears with four large envelopes—the same ones he gave to Bette. Thomas sets them on the desktop, very slowly, one at a time, then looks at me with powerful intensity.

"This is for you. Consider it our way of saying thank you for saving our last daughter."

Hush money. This was the only reason Thomas reached out. He and Eleanor know I know. This is not an act of reparation; they're simply removing yet another time bomb from their damaged lives. If I take the money, Bette remains unscathed once again.

I shake my head. "No."

Thomas's gaze turns menacing. "You have been through a lot. And unfortunately, Bette was involved. I've spent many years doing damage control, and I know the extent of injury this kind of news can cause. It would be a devastating blow to our family if this story came out."

My anger returns. "It wasn't a 'story,' and Bette wasn't 'involved.' It was rape, and your daughter was one of the masterminds behind it."

Suddenly, I am the wild animal, with rage clawing at my insides, demanding to be freed.

Thomas takes a deep breath and straightens his back. He reaches to his safe again and comes back with four more envelopes.

And there it is.

I have a choice to make.

The damage is already done. I am scarred, and that will never change. So, I can lick my wounds and retreat with a false sense of integrity. I can go back to my job at the orthodontist, maybe hope for a promotion to office manager, and if I'm lucky, one day I will buy a small run-down ranch home in Kearney to live out the rest of my gray-colored life.

But I realize that I'll never truly be free of Bette or of the trauma our time together inflicted. Even now, it's nothing new for me to find myself staring at a small smear on the wall, seeming to think of nothing really at all. Except I am. And when I finally pull myself back to reality, I find my thoughts are always focused on one person.

Memories.

Questions.

What is she doing right now? Where is she? I'll search the internet for any information. Social media, professional networks, chat boards. I'll continually scan Google Images, knowing she is still confined to the hospital walls while simultaneously sure that, one day, I'll see her sipping champagne on the back deck of a yacht in St. Barts or dangling from the elegantly clad arm of some international superstar in Cannes.

Obsession.

I try to remind myself that memories are liars. They rarely tell the truth. Never the whole truth, anyway. Only snippets. Those partial bits, though, are what keep my eyes softly gazing at the wall, transfixed on nothing.

I still carry the photograph with me, the only picture I saved. Two young girls, playing dress up as an angel and devil, pretending they have it all. The picture that moved with me from dorm to back home to wherever I end up next, on and on. It lies nestled safely between the pages of an old book on philosophy. When I start to feel overly sentimental, it reminds me of the deception inherent in memory. It asks me, "Nostalgic for what?"

Those days are just bits of color now, a jigsaw puzzle of glittering glass, each piece glorious on its own, mesmerizing when the light catches it and sets it aglow.

But when I pause and consider and exert myself to put it all together, just the way the pieces are meant to fit, a grotesque whole is revealed. The colors are ugly and garish and painful to my eye.

So, I can leave this tastefully decorated executive office with my head held high, what's left of my dignity intact, and hold on to the last shred of decency that I'm sure lies deep within me. I can remind Thomas that his daughter and his own choices, in one swoop, have robbed me of the last of my childhood innocence, and even with that, I am not for sale.

Or I can take the money. I can finally accomplish what I had set out to do in the first place. I can free myself. I will be able to pay back my parents and will no longer be indebted to my father. A fresh start. A new round of education, a place of my own in a city of my choosing, and an actual future. A future, not as an accountant, but as a psychologist, using the talent of kindness that Simon so graciously pointed out. I can help others. I can help myself. Turn all the negatives into something positive. I will no longer be mentally shackled to the confines placed upon me. And I can move on.

I consider the facts. Bette is being watched now. The girls Bette erased have been vindicated by Michael's arrest and sentencing. He will never see life outside of a prison as long as he is alive. The girls' families have closure, and I can begin to close that chapter now, too.

The one gift Bette did give me was belief in myself. No matter her insane methods, she helped me find my own strength. She showed me how to dream. Because of her, I gained the ability to look farther than my own backyard. There is a larger life waiting for me out there. I just have to take my own first step.

Freedom.

They are paying for my silence.

Who would I tell anyway? *I reason.*

Without a word, I reach in my back pocket, place the photo of happy and healthy Bette back on his desk, then scoop up the envelopes and walk out the door.

As I step out of the elevator on the ground floor, I stop to pull a thick winter scarf from my tote bag. Out of habit, my fingers search for and feel what has been my safety net, my last-ditch backup plan. There was no guarantee that Bette would stay away from me, and no initial promises were made to keep me safe, so I held on to the one item that would be as deadly to the Winston family name as a sharpened dagger.

I pull my cell phone from my bag, examine it, and hit Stop on the voice recorder. Before I'd handed Bette's phone over to Eleanor, I'd transferred all of the information onto my own phone. The one Simon had given me. At the time, I'd trusted no one, and with that act, the first brick in the walls of my personal protection was put in place. It hasn't left my side since, a constant security blanket with the power of an atomic bomb. It had captured Bette's confession in full and now implicated Thomas and Eleanor as well.

Checkmate.

I glance at the envelopes in my bag that contain a seemingly endless amount of cash. I may have made a deal to never bring Bette's transgressions to light again.

But there is someone else who can, if need be.

Someone who had been looking for evidence of the truth.

Quickly, I press a button and hold the phone to my ear as I walk out into the bitter, cold Chicago wind.

"Harry, it's Marin. Can we meet? I have something I want to give you."

BOOK CLUB QUESTIONS

1. Marin's journey is centered around transformation and self-discovery. In what ways does the butterfly metaphor reflect her personal struggles and growth throughout the novel?

2. Bette exerts a powerful influence over Marin. What aspects of Bette's personality make her so captivating, and why do you think Marin is so drawn to her despite the red flags?

3. How does the novel explore themes of power and privilege? In what ways does Bette's social standing affect the choices available to Marin?

4. Manipulation and control are key elements of the story. How does Bette's influence over Marin evolve over time, and at what point do you think Marin begins to recognize the toxic nature of their relationship?

5. The novel delves into Marin's internal conflict between seeking justice and protecting herself. What would you have done in her position, and do you think she made the right decision in the end?

6. Friendship plays a major role in *Butterfly Pinned*. How do Marin's relationships with Cassie and Bette differ, and what do they reveal about Marin's character and needs?

7. How does the setting—both the college environment and the luxurious social world Bette introduces—contribute to the novel's tension and suspense?

8. What role does social media and reputation play in the novel? How does it affect Marin's perception of herself and her fear of exposure?

9. This is partly a coming-of-age story. At what point does Marin become an adult?

10. Were there any moments in the novel where you felt Marin could have made different choices? What do these moments reveal about vulnerability and peer influence?

11. Guilt and trauma are recurring themes throughout the story. How does Marin cope with her experiences, and do you think she ultimately finds closure by the end?

12. Discuss the significance of the title, *Butterfly Pinned*. In what ways does it reflect Marin's experiences and the broader themes of the novel?

13. The novel ends with Marin taking a step toward reclaiming her life. Do you think she has truly broken free from Bette's influence, or do you believe the past will continue to haunt her?

ACKNOWLEDGEMENTS

Thank you to my editors, Michaeli and Amber, who kept my ramblings between the rails with grace and kid gloves. I'll happily kill my darlings for you any day of the week.

Thank you to the entire team at Blue Handle Publishing for believing in a manuscript that sat marinating for five years. To my team: Charles, Ricky, Amber, and Madison, your enthusiasm and unwavering support is unmatched and appreciated beyond words. It's an honor to call you all family.

Thank you to Danielle Egan-Miller for convincing me to write of darkness and the unthinkable with openness and without fear.

Thank you to Kasey, Hilary, Jenilee, Shari, Stephanie, and Christina for very early reads and very honest feedback. The good, the bad, and the ugly is invaluable.

As always, thank you to Jimmy, Spencer, Lucy, and Fred. You have continually cheered me on with a ferocious love that is unparalleled. It never goes unnoticed. You remain my whole heart.

ABOUT THE AUTHOR

Born in Kansas City, Missouri, Leslie Liautaud is the author of the immersive play *Southern Gothic*, which won three Joseph Jefferson Awards and ten Chicago Theatre Awards, including Best Play and Best New Work. She is also the author of *Black Bear Lake*, a first-place winner of the Chanticleer Reviews Somerset Literary & Contemporary Fiction award. Leslie resides in Nashville.